Glory

VLADIMIR NABOKOV

Glory

Translated from the Russian by
DMITRI NABOKOV
in collaboration with VLADIMIR NABOKOV

PENGUIN
CLASSICS

PENGUIN CLASSICS

Published by the Penguin Group
Penguin Books Ltd, 80 Strand, London WC2R ORL, England
Penguin Group (USA) Inc., 375 Hudson Street, New York, New York 10014, USA
Penguin Group (Canada), 90 Eglinton Avenue East, Suite 700, Toronto, Ontario,
Canada M4P 2Y3 (a division of Pearson Penguin Canada Inc.)
Penguin Ireland, 25 St Stephen's Green, Dublin 2, Ireland (a division of Penguin Books Ltd)
Penguin Group (Australia), 250 Camberwell Road, Camberwell, Victoria 3124, Australia
(a division of Pearson Australia Group Pty Ltd)
Penguin Books India Pvt Ltd, 11 Community Centre, Panchsheel Park,
New Delhi – 110 017, India
Penguin Group (NZ), 67 Apollo Drive, Rosedale, Auckland 0632, New Zealand
(a division of Pearson New Zealand Ltd)
Penguin Books (South Africa) (Pty) Ltd, 24 Sturdee Avenue,
Rosebank, Johannesburg 2196, South Africa

Penguin Books Ltd, Registered Offices: 80 Strand, London WC2R ORL, England

www.penguin.com

First published in the United States of America by McGraw-Hill 1971
First published in Great Britain by Weidenfeld & Nicolson 1972
Published in Penguin Books 1974
Reissued in Penguin Classics 2006
This edition published in Penguin Classics 2012
001

This edition published by arrangement with the Estate of Vladimir Nabokov

Set in 10.5/15pt Joanna MT Pro
Typeset by Jouve (UK), Milton Keynes
Text design by Claire Mason
Printed in Finland by Bookwell Ltd

A CIP catalogue record for this book is available from the British Library

ISBN: 978-0-141-19694-7

www.greenpenguin.co.uk

ALWAYS LEARNING **PEARSON**

To VÉRA

Foreword

The present work closes the series of definitive English versions in which my entire set of nine Russian novels (written in Western Europe between 1925 and 1937, and published by émigré houses between 1926 and 1952) is available to American and British readers. He who cares to scan the list given below should mark the dramatic gap between 1938 and 1959:

> *Mashenka*, 1926 (*Mary*, 1970)
> *Korol', Dama,Valet*, 1928 (*King, Queen, Knave*, 1968)
> *Zashchita Luzhina*, 1930 (*The Defense*, 1964)
> *Soglyadatay*, 1930 (*The Eye*, 1965)
> *Podvig*, 1932 (*Glory*, 1971)
> *Kamera obscura*, 1933 (*Laughter in the Dark*, 1938)
> *Otchayanie*, 1936 (*Despair*, 1966)
> *Priglashenie na Kazn'*, 1938 (*Invitation to a Beheading*, 1959)
> *Dar*, 1952 (*The Gift*, 1963).

The present translation is meticulously true to the text. My son took three years, on and off, to make a first draft, after which I spent three months preparing a fair copy. The very

vii

Russian preoccupations with physical movement and gesture, walking and sitting, smiling and glancing from-under-the-brows, seems especially strong in *Podvig*, and this made our task still tougher.

Podvig was begun in May 1930, immediately after my writing *Soglyadatay*, and completed by the end of that year. My wife and I, who were then still childless, rented a parlor and bedroom on Luitpoldstrasse, Berlin West, in the vast and gloomy apartment of the one-legged General von Bardeleben, an old gentleman solely occupied in working out his family tree; his large brow had a somewhat Nabokovian cast, and, indeed, he was related to the well-known chess player Bardeleben, whose manner of death resembled that of my Luzhin. One day in early summer Ilya Fondaminski, chief editor of the Sovremennye Zapiski, arrived there from Paris to buy the book *na kornyu*, 'in the rooted state' (said of grainfields before they are harvested). He was a Social-Revolutionist, a Jew, a fervent Christian, a learned historian, and an altogether delightful man (later murdered by the Germans in one of their extermination camps), and vividly do I remember the splendid zest with which he slapped his knees before rising from our grim green divan after the deal had been clinched!

The book's – certainly very attractive – working title (later discarded in favor of the pithier *Podvig*, 'gallant feat,' 'high deed') was *Romanticheskiy vek*, 'romantic times,' which I had chosen partly because I had had enough of hearing Western journalists call our era 'materialistic,' 'practical,' 'utilitarian,' etc., but mainly because the purpose of my novel, my only one with a purpose, lay in stressing the thrill and the glamour that my young expatriate finds in the most ordinary pleasures as well as in the seemingly meaningless adventures of a lonely life.

It would make things too easy for a certain type of reviewer (and particularly for those insular innocents whom my work affects so oddly that one might think I hypnotize them from the wings into making indecent gestures) were I to point out the faults in the novel. Suffice it to say that, after all but lapsing into false exoticism or commonplace comedy, it soars to heights of purity and melancholy that I have only attained in the much later *Ada*.

How do the main characters of *Glory* stand in relation to those of my other fourteen (Russian and American) novels? – the human interest seeker may ask.

Martin is the kindest, uprightest, and most touching of all my young men; and little Sonia, of the lusterless dark eyes and coarse-looking black hair (her father, judging by his name, had Cheremissian blood), should be acclaimed by experts in amorous lure and lore as being the most oddly attractive of all my young girls, although obviously a moody and ruthless flirt.

If Martin to some extent can be considered a distant cousin of mine (nicer than I, but also much more naive than

I ever was), with whom I share certain childhood memories, certain later likes and dislikes, his pallid parents, *per contra*, do not resemble mine in any rational sense. As to Martin's Cambridge friends, Darwin is totally invented, and so is Moon, but 'Vadim' and 'Teddy' existed in the reality of my own Cambridge past: they are mentioned under their initials, N. R. and R. C., respectively, in my *Speak, Memory*, 1966, Chapter Thirteen, penult. paragraph. The three staunch patriots, dedicated to counter-Bolshevist work, Zilanov, Iogolevich, and Gruzinov, belong to that group of people, politically situated just to the right of the old Terrorists and just to the left of the Constitutional Democrats, and as far from Monarchists on one side as from Marxists on the other, whom I was well acquainted with in the entourage of the very magazine which serialized *Podvig*, but none is an exact portrait of a specific individual. I feel obliged to give here the proper determination of this political type (recognized at once, with the unconscious precision of common knowledge, by the Russian *intelligent* who was the main reader of my books) because I still cannot reconcile myself to the fact – deserving to be commemorated by an annual pyrotechnical display of contempt and sarcasm – that in the meantime American intellectuals had been conditioned by Bolshevist propaganda into utterly disregarding the vigorous existence of liberal thought among Russian expatriates. ('You're a Trotskyite, then?' brightly suggested an especially limited left-wing writer, in New York, 1940, when I said I was neither for the Soviets nor for any Tsar.)

The hero of *Glory*, however, is not necessarily interested in politics – that is the first of two mastertricks on the part of the wizard who made Martin. Fulfillment is the fugal theme of his destiny; he is that rarity – a person whose 'dreams come true.' But the fulfillment itself is invariably permeated by poignant nostalgia. The memory of the childish reverie blends with the expectation of death. The perilous path that Martin finally follows into forbidden Zoorland (no connection with Nabokov's Zembla!) only continues to its illogical end the fairy-tale trail winding through the painted woods of a nursery-wall picture. 'Fulfillment' would have been, perhaps, an even better title for the novel: Nabokov cannot be unaware that the obvious translation of *podvig* is 'exploit,' and, indeed, it is under that title that his *Podvig* is listed by bibliographers; but if you once perceive in 'exploit' the verb 'utilize,' gone is the *podvig*, the inutile deed of renown. The author chose therefore the oblique 'glory,' which is a less literal but much richer rendering of the original title with all its natural associations branching in the bronze sun. It is the glory of high adventure and disinterested achievement; the glory of this earth and its patchy paradise; the glory of personal pluck; the glory of a radiant martyr.

Nowadays, when Freudism is discredited, the author recalls with a whistle of wonder that not so long ago – say before 1959 (i.e., before the publication of the first of the seven forewords to his Englished novels) – a child's personality was supposed to split automatically in sympathetic consequence of parental divorce. His parents' separation has no such effect on Martin's mind, and only a desperate saphead in the throes of a nightmare examination may be excused for connecting Martin's plunge into his fatherland with his having been deprived of his father. No less reckless would it be to point out, with womby wonder, that the girl Martin loves and his mother bear the same name.

My second wand-stroke is this: among the many gifts I showered on Martin, I was careful not to include talent. How easy it would have been to make him an artist, a writer; how hard not to let him be one, while bestowing on him the keen sensitivity that one generally associates with the creative creature; how cruel to prevent him from finding in art – not an 'escape' (which is only a cleaner cell on a quieter floor), but relief from the itch of being! The temptation to perform my own little exploit within the omnibus nimbus prevailed. The result reminds me of a chess problem I once composed. Its beauty lay in a paradoxical first move: the White Queen had four likely squares at its disposal but on any of these it would be in the way (such a powerful piece – and 'in the way'!) of one of White's Knights in four mating variants; in other words, being an absolutely useless spoilsport and burden on the board, with no part whatever in any of the subsequent play, it had to exile itself to a neutral corner behind an inert pawn and remain wedged there in idle obscurity. The problem was diabolically difficult to construct. So was *Podvig*.

The author trusts that wise readers will refrain from avidly flipping through his autobiography *Speak, Memory* in quest of duplicate items or kindred scenery. The fun of *Glory* is elsewhere. It is to be sought in the echoing and linking of minor events, in back-and-forth switches, which produce an illusion of impetus: in an old daydream directly becoming the blessing of the ball hugged to one's chest, or in the casual vision of Martin's mother grieving beyond the time-frame of the novel in an abstraction of the future that the reader can only guess at, even after he has raced through the last seven chapters where a regular madness of structural twists and a masquerade of all characters culminate in a furious finale, although nothing much happens at the very end — just a bird perching on a wicket in the grayness of a wet day.

Vladimir Nabokov

8 December 1970

Montreux

GLORY

One

Funny as it may seem, Martin's grandfather Edelweiss was a Swiss – a robust Swiss with a fluffy mustache, who in the 1860s had been tutor to the children of a St Petersburg landowner named Indrikov, and had married his youngest daughter. Martin assumed at first that the velvety white Alpine flower, that pet of herbariums, had been named in honor of his grandfather. Even later he could not fully relinquish this notion. He remembered his grandfather distinctly, but only in one form and position: a corpulent old man, dressed completely in white, fair-whiskered, wearing a Panama hat and a piqué waistcoat rich in breloques (the most amusing of which was a dagger the size of a fingernail), sitting on a bench in front of the house in a linden's mobile shade. It was on this very bench that his grandfather had died, holding in the palm of his hand his beloved gold watch, whose lid was like a little golden mirror. Apoplexy overtook him during this timely gesture and, according to family legend, the hands stopped at the same moment as his heart.

For many years after, Grandfather Edelweiss was preserved in a massive leather album; in his day photographs were made tastefully, with elaborate deliberation. The operation was no joking matter; the patient had to be immobilized for a long time, and permission to smile had yet to come – with the advent of the snapshot. The complexity of heliography acc-ounted for the weightiness and solidity of Grandfather's manly poses in those somewhat pale but very good-quality pictures: grandfather as a youth with a freshly killed woodcock at his feet; Grandfather astride the mare Daisy; Grandfather on a striped veranda seat, with a black dachshund that had refused to sit still, and had come out with three tails in the photograph. Only in 1918 did Grandfather Edelweiss disappear altogether, for the album went up in flames, as did the table where the album lay, and, in fact, the whole country house, which the peasant chaps from the nearby village foolishly burned to the ground as it stood, instead of realizing a profit from the furnishings.

Martin's father was a dermatologist, and a famous one. Like Grandfather, he too was very white-skinned and stout, enjoyed fishing for gobies in his spare time, and possessed a magnificent collection of daggers and sabers, as well as long, strange pistols, on account of which the users of more modern weapons nearly sent him before the firing squad. In the beginning of 1918 he grew bloated and short of breath, and died around March 10 in unclear circumstances. His wife Sofia and their son were living at the time near Yalta: the town kept trying on now one regime, now another, and could not make up its finicky mind.

She was a rosy, freckled, youthful woman, with pale hair in a big bun, high eyebrows that were thickish toward the bridge of her nose and nearly imperceptible toward her temples, and little slits (once made for now absent earrings) in the elongated lobes of her delicate ears. Only recently, in their Northern country place, she still used to play a powerful, agile game of tennis on the garden court, which had been in existence since the eighties. In the autumn she would spend a lot of time riding a black Enfield bicycle along the avenues of their park, across noisily rustling carpets of dry leaves. Or else she would set out on foot along the resilient shoulder of the highway and cover the long way, dear to her since childhood, from Olkhovo to Voskresensk, raising and lowering the end of her expensive coral-knobbed cane like a seasoned walker. In St Petersburg she was known as an Anglo-maniac, and relished this fame – she would discuss eloquently such topics as Boy Scouts or Kipling, and found a quite special delight in frequent visits to Drew's English Shop where, still on the stairs, before a large poster (a woman thickly lathering a boy's head) you were greeted by a wonderful smell of soap and lavender, with something more mixed in, something that suggested collapsible rubber tubs, soccer balls, and round, heavy, tightly swaddled Christmas puddings. It follows that Martin's first books were in English: his mother loathed the Russian magazine for children *Zadushevnoe Slovo* (The Heartfelt Word), and inspired in him such aversion for Madame Charski's young heroines with dusky complexions and titles that even later Martin was wary of any book written by a woman, sensing even in the best of such books an unconscious urge on the part of a middle-aged and perhaps chubby lady to dress up in a pretty name and curl up on the sofa like a pussy cat. Sofia detested diminutives, kept a strict check on herself so as not to use them, and was annoyed if her husband said 'Sonny's got the coughikins again – let's check his *temperaturka*': Russian children's literature swarmed with cute lisping words, when not committing the sin of moralizing.

If Martin's grandfather's family name bloomed in the mountains, the magical origin of his grandmother's maiden name was a far cry from the various Volkovs (Wolfs), Kunitsyns (Martens) or Belkins (Squirrelsons), and belonged to the fauna of Russian fable. Once upon a time there prowled marvelous beasts in our country. But Sofia found Russian fairy tales clumsy, cruel, and squalid, Russian folksongs inane, and Russian riddles idiotic. She had little faith in Pushkin's famous nanny, and said that the poet himself had invented her, together with her fairy tales, knitting needles, and heartache. Thus in early childhood Martin failed to become familiar with something that subsequently, through the prismatic wave of memory, might have added an extra enchantment to his life. However, he had no lack of enchantments, and no cause to regret that it was not the Russian knight-errant Ruslan but Ruslan's occidental brother that had awakened his imagination in childhood. But then what does it matter whence comes the gentle nudge that jars the soul into motion and sets it rolling, doomed never again to stop?

Two

On the bright wall above the narrow crib, with its lateral meshes of white cord and the small icon at its head (lac-quered saint's brown face framed in foil, crimson underside plush somewhat eaten by moths or by Martin himself), hung a watercolor depicting a dense forest with a winding path disappearing into its depths. Now in one of the English books that his mother used to read to him (how slowly and mysteriously she would pronounce the words and how wide she would open her eyes when she reached the end of a page, covering it with her small, lightly freckled hand as she asked, 'And what do you think happened next?') there was a story about just such a picture with a path in the woods, right above the bed of a little boy, who, one fine night, just as he was, nightshirt and all, went from his bed into the picture, onto the path that disappeared into the woods. His mother, thought Martin anxiously, might notice the resemblance between the watercolor on the wall and the illustration in the book; she would then become alarmed and, according to his calculations, avert the nocturnal journey by removing the picture. Therefore every time he prayed in bed before going to sleep (first came a short prayer in English: 'Gentle Jesus meek and mild, listen to a little child,' and then 'Our Father' in the sibilant, and sibylline, Slavonic version) pattering rapidly and trying to get his knees up on the pillow – which his mother considered inadmissible on ascetic grounds – Martin prayed God that she would not notice that tempting path right over his head. When, as a youth, he recalled the past, he would wonder if one night he had not actually hopped from bed to picture, and if this had not been the beginning of the journey, full of joy and anguish, into which his whole life had turned. He seemed to remember the chilly touch of the ground, the green twilight of the forest, the bends of the trail (which the hump of a great root crossed here and there), the tree trunks flashing by as he ran past them barefoot, and the strange dark air, teeming with fabulous possibilities.

Grandmother Edelweiss, née Indrikov, worked diligently at watercolors in her youth, and, as she mixed the blue paint with the yellow on her porcelain palette, she could hardly foresee that in this nascent greenery her grandson would one day wander. The thrill which Martin discovered and which, in various manifestations and blendings, accompanied him throughout his life from that moment on, proved to be precisely the feeling that his mother hoped to develop in him, even though she herself would have been hard put to find a name for it; she just knew that every evening she must feed Martin what she had once been fed by her late governess, old, wise Mrs Brook, whose son had collected orchids in Borneo, had flown over the Sahara in a balloon, and had died in a Turkish bath when the boiler burst. She would read, and Martin would listen, kneeling on a chair with his elbows propped on the lamplit round table, and it was very hard to stop and lead him to bed, since he would always beg her to read some more. Sometimes she would carry him upstairs to the nursery on her back – this was called 'logging.' At bedtime he would be given an English biscuit from a blue-papered tin box. The top ones were of wonderful kinds, coated with sugar; next came ginger and coconut cookies; and on the sad night when he reached the bottom layer he would have to reconcile himself to a third-rate variety, plain and insipid.

Nothing was wasted on Martin – neither the crunchy English cookies, nor the adventures of King Arthur's knights. What a rapturous moment that was when a youth – perchance a nephew of Sir Tristram's? – donned for the first time piece by piece his shiny, convex plate armor and rode off to his first single combat! There were also those distant, circular islands at which a damsel gazed from the shore, her garments streaming in the wind and a hooded falcon perched on her wrist. And Sinbad with his red kerchief and the gold ring in his ear; and the sea serpent, its green tire-shaped segments jutting out of the water all the way to the horizon. And the child finding the spot where the end of the rainbow met the ground. And, like an echo of all this, an image somehow related to it, there was the magnificent model of a brown-paneled sleeping car in the window of the *Société des Wagons-Lits et des Grands Express Européens* on the Nevsky Avenue, where one was walked on a dull frosty day with slight spinners of snow, and had to wear black knit snow pants over one's stockings and shorts.

Three

His mother's love for Martin was so jealous, so violent, and so intense that it seemed to make the heart hoarse. When her marriage broke up and she began living separately with Martin, he would go on Sundays to visit his father at their former apartment, where he would potter for a long time with pistols and daggers, while his father read the paper impassively, and answered every now and then, without looking up, 'Yes, loaded,' or 'Yes, poisoned.' On these occasions

Sofia could hardly bear to stay at home, tormented by the ridiculous thought that her indolent husband might try something after all, and keep his son with him. Martin, on the other hand, was very affectionate and polite with his father, so as to mitigate the punishment as much as possible; since he believed that his father had been banished for a misdemeanor committed one summer evening, at their country house, when he had done something to the piano that made it emit an absolutely staggering sound, as if someone had stepped on its tail, and the day after had left for St Petersburg and never returned. This happened in the very same year when the grand duke of Austria was assassinated in a seraglio. Martin imagined that seraglio and its divan very distinctly, with the grand duke, in a plumed hat, defending himself with his sword against half-a-dozen black-cloaked conspirators, and was disappointed when his error became evident. The blow on the piano keys occurred in his absence: he was in the adjoining room, brushing his teeth with thick, foamy, sweet-tasting toothpaste, rendered especially attractive by the inscription in English: 'We could not improve the paste, so we improved the tube.' Indeed, the aperture formed a transverse slit, so that the paste, as it was squeezed out, slid onto the brush not like a worm but like a ribbon.

That last discussion with her husband Sofia recalled in its entirety, complete in every detail and shading, on the day the news of his death reached her in Yalta. Her husband had been sitting near a little wicker table, examining the tips of his short, outspread fingers, and she had been telling him that they could not go on like that any longer, that they had long since become strangers, that she was willing to take her son and leave, even tomorrow. Her husband smiled lazily and answered in a quiet, slightly husky voice that she was right, alas, and said he would leave himself, and find a separate apartment in town. His quiet voice, his placid obesity, and, most of all, the file with which he continually mangled his soft nails drove her out of her wits, and the calm with which they both discussed their separation seemed to her monstrous, even though violent language and tears would of course have been more awful still. Presently he got up, and, still fiddling with the nail file, began pacing back and forth across the room, speaking with a gentle smile about the minor household details of their forthcoming separate existence (and here a town carriage played an absurd role). Then, suddenly and without any reason, as he passed the open piano, he brought his closed fist down on the keyboard with all his might, and it was as if a discordant howl had burst in through a momentarily closed door. After this he resumed the interrupted sentence in the same quiet voice, and the next time he passed the piano he carefully closed the lid.

The death of his father, whom he did not love much, shocked Martin for the very reason that he did not love him as he should; and besides, he could not rid himself of the thought that his father had died in disgrace. It was then that Martin understood for the first time that human life flowed in zigzags, that now the first bend had been passed, and that his life had turned at the instant his mother summoned him from the cypress avenue to the terrace and said in a strange voice, 'I have received a letter from Zilanov,' then continuing in English, 'I want you to be brave, very brave – it is about your father – he is no more.' Martin turned pale and smiled a bewildered smile. Then he roamed for a long time in Vorontsov Park, repeating now and then an infantine nickname he had once bestowed on his father, and trying to imagine – and imagining with a certain warm, dreamy cogency – that his father was beside him, in front, behind, under that cedar over there, there on that sloping lawn, nearby, far off, everywhere.

It was hot, even though a rainstorm had raged a short time before. Blowflies buzzed around the glossy medlar shrubs. An ill-tempered black swan floated in the pool, moving from side to side its bill which was so crimson that it seemed painted. Petals had fallen from the almond trees, and stood out pale on the dark earth of the damp path, like almonds in gingerbread. Not far from some enormous cedars of Lebanon grew a lone birch tree, with that particular slant to its foliage that only a birch has (as if a girl had let her hair down on one side to be combed, and stood still). A zebra-striped swallowtail glided past, its tails extended and joined. The sparkling air, the shadows of the cypresses (old trees, with a rusty cast, their small cones half-hidden under their cloaks); the black glass of the pool, where concentric circles spread around the swan; the radiant blue into which serrated Mount Petri rose wearing a broad belt of karakul-like pine – everything was permeated with agonizing bliss, and it seemed to Martin that somehow his father played a part in the distribution of shadow and shine.

'If you were twenty instead of fifteen,' said his mother that evening, 'if you had already finished high school, and if I were no longer alive, then, of course, you could . . . I suppose it would be your duty to –' She paused in mid-sentence, thinking of the White Army and seeing with her mind's eye the South Russian prairie and Cossack-capped horsemen, among whom she tried to recognize Martin from afar. But, thank God, he stood next to her, in an open-necked shirt, his hair close-cropped, his skin sun-browned, with untanned little lines radiating from the corners of his eyes. 'While, on the other hand, if we return to St Petersburg –' she went on in a questioning tone, and at some anonymous station a shell exploded, and the locomotive reared up. 'All this will probably end one day,' she added after a pause. 'In the meantime we must think up something.'

'I'm going for a swim,' put in Martin, with a conciliatory intonation. 'The whole gang is there – Nicky, Lida.'

'Yes, go, by all means,' said Sofia. 'After all, the revolution will end some day, and it will be strange remembering it. Our stay in the Crimea has done wonders for your health. And you will somehow finish your schooling at the Yalta Gymnasium. Look, isn't that cliff beautifully lit up over there?'

That night neither mother nor son could sleep, and both thought about death. Sofia tried to think in an undertone, that is, without sobbing or sighing (the door to her son's room was ajar). She recalled again, punctiliously and in detail, everything that had led up to her separation from Edelweiss. Going over every instant, she saw clearly that in this circum-stance and in that she could not have acted otherwise. But still a mistake lurked hidden somewhere; still, if they had not parted, he would not have died like that, alone in an empty room, suffocating, helpless, perhaps recalling their last year of happiness (and very comparative happiness at that), and their last trip abroad, to Biarritz, the excursion to Croix-de-Mouguère, and the little galleries of Bayonne. She firmly believed in a certain power that bore the same resemblance to God as the house of a man one has never seen, his belong-ings, his greenhouse and beehives, his distant voice, heard by chance in an open field, bear to their owner. It would have embarrassed her to call that power 'God,' just as there are Peters and Ivans who cannot pronounce 'Pete' or 'Vanya' without a sensation of falsity, while there are others who, in reporting a long conversation to you, will pronounce their own names or, still worse, nicknames, with gusto twenty times or so. This power had no connection with the Church, and neither absolved nor chastised any sins. It was just that she sometimes felt ashamed in the presence of a tree, of a cloud, of a dog, or of the air itself that bore an ill word just as religiously as a kind one. And now Sofia, as she thought about her unpleasant, unloved husband and about his death, even though she repeated the words of prayers natural to her ever since childhood, actually strained her whole being so that – fortified by two or three happy memories, through the mist, through great extensions of space, through all that would always remain incomprehensible – she might give her husband a kiss on the forehead.

She never discussed things of that kind openly with Martin, but she always had the feeling that everything else they talked about created for Martin, through her voice and her love, the same sense of divinity as lived within her. Lying in the next room and feigning to snore so his mother would not think he was awake, Martin also recalled harrowing things, also tried to comprehend his father's death and to catch a wisp of posthumous tenderness in the dark of the room. He thought about his father with the full force of his soul, and even made certain experiments: if, right now, a board in the floor creaks or there is a knock of some kind, that means he hears me and responds. Martin felt afraid, waiting for the knock. The closeness of the night air oppressed him; he could hear the surf boom; mosquitoes emitted their high-pitched whine. Or else, with absolute clarity, he would suddenly see his father's round face, his pince-nez, the fair crop of his brush cut, the fleshy button of a wart near his nostril, and the shiny ring formed of two little gold serpents around the knot of his tie. Then, when at last he fell asleep, he found himself sitting in a classroom with his homework not done, while Lida kept idly scratching her shin as she told him that Georgians did not eat ice cream: 'Gruziny ne edyat morozhenogo.'

Four

He did not inform either Lida or her brother of his father's death since he doubted that he could utter the news naturally, while it would have been indecorous to tell it with feeling. From early childhood his mother had taught him that to discuss in public a profound emotional experience – which, in the open air, immediately evanesces and fades, and, oddly, becomes similar to an analogous experience of one's interlocutor – was not only vulgar, but also a sin against sentiment. She detested the ribbons of funeral wreaths with silver inscriptions such as 'To a Young Hero,' or 'To Our Unforgettable Darling Daughter,' and disapproved of sedate but mawkish people who, when they lose a dear one, find it possible to shed tears in public while, in another moment, on a day of good luck, even though bursting with joy, they would never allow themselves to break out laughing in a passing stranger's face. Once, when Martin was about eight, he had attempted to shear the hair off a shaggy little dog, and had inadvertently cut its ear. Embarrassed for some reason to explain that he simply had intended to snip off the excess tufts, before painting it to look like a tiger, Martin met his mother's indignation with stoic silence. She ordered him to lower his pants and lie down prone. He did so in complete silence, and in complete silence she whipped him with a riding switch of tawny bullgut. Then he pulled up his pants, and she helped him button them to his little undervest, as he had begun doing it askew. He then went out, and only there, in the park, let himself go, wailing his heart out, the tears mixed with bilberries. Meanwhile his mother was weeping in her bedroom, and in the evening she was barely able to hold back new tears as a very cheerful and plump Martin sat in the tub, nudging along a celluloid swan, and presently stood up to let his back be lathered, and she saw the vivid pink stripes on his tender buttocks. Such chastisement took place only once, nor did Sofia ever lift her

hand threatening to slap him for this or that petty misdemeanor as French and German mothers do.

Martin, who had learned early to control his tears and
conceal his emotions, astonished his schoolteachers with his
insensitivity. Meanwhile, he soon discovered in himself a
trait that he felt compelled to conceal with particular ten-
acity, and at sixteen, in the Crimea, this was the cause of a
certain amount of torment. Martin noticed that on occasion
he was so afraid of seeming unmanly, to become known as
a coward, that he involuntarily reacted in just the way a coward would – the blood left his face, his legs trembled, and
his heart pounded tightly in his chest. Admitting to himself
that he was not possessed of genuine, innate *sang-froid*, he
nevertheless firmly resolved to behave always as a fearless
man would in his place. At the same time vanity and self-
esteem were highly developed in him. Lida's brother Kolya,
though of the same age as Martin, was skinny and short.
Martin felt that he could pin him without much trouble. And
yet the possibility of a chance defeat made him so nervous,
and he imagined it with such hideous clarity, that never once
did he try to start a wrestling match with that coeval; however, he would willingly accept a challenge from Ivanov, a
twenty-year-old cavalry officer, with muscles like round
rocks (killed six months later in the battle of Melitopol),
who would rough him up mercilessly and, after an exhausting tussle, at last press him, red and grinning, to the grass.

There also was that night, that warm Crimean night, with the blue-black of cypresses, brought out by the chalky white of ghostly Tartar walls in the moonlight, when, on his way home from Adreiz, where Lida's family lived, a human shape abruptly appeared at a turn of the flinty path that led to the highway, and a deep voice asked, 'Who goes there?' Martin noted with chagrin that his heart missed a beat. 'Aha, must be Dedman the Tartar,' added the voice, and a man's face advanced menacingly through the torn black web of shadows.

'No,' said Martin. 'Please let me pass.'

'And I say you are Dedman-Akhmet,' insisted the other, quietly but even more grimly, and, in a gleam of moonlight, Martin noticed that he was holding a large revolver in his hand. 'All right – stand against the wall,' said the man, his tone no longer threatening, but conciliatory and matter-of-fact. Shadow again engulfed the pale hand and dark weapon, but a glistening speck remained where it had been. Martin was faced with two alternatives. The first was to insist on an explanation; the second, to dodge into the darkness and run. 'I think you've mistaken me for someone else,' he said awkwardly and gave his name.

'Against the wall, against the wall,' shouted the man in a treble.

'There isn't any wall right here,' said Martin.

'I'll wait until there is,' enigmatically observed the man and, with a crunch of pebbles, either squatted or sat down – it was impossible to tell in the dark. Martin remained standing where he was, feeling a kind of faint itch in the whole left part of his chest, where the now invisible barrel must be pointing.

'One move and I'll kill you,' murmured the man, and added something unintelligible. Martin stood for a while, and then for a while longer, trying painfully to think what a daredevil, unarmed, would do in his place; he could think of nothing, and suddenly asked:

'Would you like a cigarette? I have some.'

He did not know how this had escaped, and immediately felt ashamed, especially since the offer remained without reply. Then Martin decided that the only means of redeeming his shameful words was to go straight at the man, to knock him down if necessary, but to pass. He thought of the picnic planned for tomorrow, of Lida's legs, evenly coated with a lacquer-smooth reddish-gold tan, and imagined that perhaps his father was expecting him that night, that perhaps he was making preparations of some kind for their meeting – and here Martin caught himself feeling a strange hostility toward his father, for which he reproached himself for a long time. The sea's woosh could be heard, with regularly spaced booms; loud crickets engaged in clockwork competitive chirring; and here was this imbecile in the dark. Martin, as he now realized, was protecting his heart with his hand; calling himself a coward one last time, he moved forward abruptly. Nothing happened. He stumbled over the man's leg, but the latter did not remove it: he was sitting hunched over, head bowed, snoring softly, and giving off a thick, rich reek of wine.

After getting home safely, and enjoying a good night's sleep, Martin, as he stood next morning on the wisteria-entwined balcony, regretted that he had not disarmed the inert reveler: it would have been nice enigmatically display-ing the confiscated revolver. He remained cross with himself because, in his opinion, he had not quite risen to the occa-sion upon encountering long-awaited danger. How many times, on the highroad of his dreams, wearing a half-mask and jack boots, he had stopped either a stagecoach, or a bulky berlin, or a horseman and then distributed the mer-chants' ducats to the poor! During his term as captain of a pirate corvette he had stood with his back to the mainmast, singlehandedly fighting off the on-rush of the mutinous crew. He had been sent into the depths of Africa to search for a lost explorer, and when at last he found him – in the wildwood of a nameless region – he went up to him with a polite bow, flaunting his self-control. He would escape from hard-labor camps across tropical swamplands; walk toward the pole past astonished, erect penguins; astride a lathery steed, with bared saber, he would be the first to burst into insurgent Moscow. And now Martin would catch him-self embellishing in retrospect the inept and rather insipid nocturnal incident, which bore no more resemblance to the real life he lived in his fantasies than an incoherent dream does to full, authentic reality. And as sometimes, when recounting a dream, we smooth over, round off, embellish here and there, so as to raise it at least to the level of plausible, realistic absurdity, in exactly the same way Martin, when rehearsing the account of his night-time encounter (which he did not, however, intend to make public), made the stranger more sober, his revolver more functional, and his own words wittier.

Five

The next day, while passing a soccer ball back and forth with Kolya or searching with Lida, on the shingly beach, for sea-side curios (a round pebble with a colored belt, a little horseshoe, grainy and red-brown with rust; pale-green sea-polished fragments of bottle glass that reminded him of his early childhood and Biarritz), Martin wondered at the night's adventure, doubted that it had really happened, and promoted it more and more decisively into that realm where all that he selected from the world for the use of his soul would take root and begin living a marvelous, independent existence. A wave would swell, boil with foam, and topple rotundly, spreading and running up on the shingle. Then, unable to hold fast, it would slip back to the grumbling of awakened pebbles; and hardly had it receded when a new one, with the same round, joyful splash, would come toppling and stretching out in a transparent stratum to the limit set for it. Kolya was throwing a piece of board he had found for Lady, the fox terrier, to retrieve and she would lift both front paws together and bounce across the water before tensely proceeding to swim. The next wave that came would catch her up and sweep her powerfully back to deposit her in perfect safety on the shore. Then she would drop on the shingle before her the stick wrested from the sea and shake herself violently. While the two boys were bathing in the buff, Lida, who took her dip with her mother and Sofia much earlier in the morning, would retire toward some rocks which she called Ayvazovskian in honor of that painter's seascapes. Kolya swam with a tumbling motion, Tartar-style, while Martin prided himself on his swift and correct crawl, which he had learned from an English house-tutor during his last summer in the North. However, neither of the boys would swim very far out, and in this connection one of Martin's sweetest and creepiest daydreams was of a desolate, stormy sea, after a shipwreck, and himself alone in the dark, holding above water a Creole girl with whom he had danced the tango on deck the evening before. After a swim, it was wonderfully pleasant to stretch out naked on the hot stones and, with head tipped back, look at the cypresses, thrust like black daggers deep into the sky. Kolya, a Yalta doctor's son who had lived all his life in the Crimea, accepted these cypresses, and the ecstatic sky, and the marvelous blue sea with its dazzling metallic scales, as something normal and routine, and it was difficult to draw him into Martin's favorite games, and transform him into the Creole's husband, by chance cast up onto the same uninhabited island.

In the evening they would climb along narrow corridors of cypresses to Adreiz. The large, ridiculous villa, with its many stairways, passages, and galleries (so amusingly constructed that sometimes you simply could not tell on what level you were, or having gone up a few steep steps you suddenly found yourself not on the expected mezzanine floor but on the garden terrace), was already shining through with yellow kerosene light, and the sound of voices and the clink of crockery came from the main veranda. Lida would go over to the adult camp. Kolya would gorge himself and immediately go off to bed. Martin sat in the dark on the bottom steps and, consuming cherries out of his hand, hearkened to the gay, brightly lit voices, to Ivanov's guffaws, Lida's cozy patter, and an argument between her father and the painter Danilevski, a garrulous stutterer. In general the guests were numerous: giggly girls in bright kerchiefs, officers from Yalta, and panicky elderly neighbors, who had taken en masse to the hills during an incursion of the Reds the previous winter. It was never clear who had brought whom and who was friends with whom, but the hospitality of Lida's mother, an inconspicuous woman who wore a gorget and spectacles, knew no bounds. Thus one day appeared Arkady Zaryanski, a lanky, deathly pale man who had some connection or other with the theater – one of those absurd people who tour battle-fronts giving poetry recitals with musical accompaniment, arrange performances on the eve of a town's devastation, run off to buy epaulets and never manage to run far enough, returning instead, puffing happily, with a miraculously obtained top hat for the last act of *A Dream of Love*. He was balding and had a fine, dynamic profile, but *en face* he turned out to be less handsome: bags swelled beneath the mud-colored eyes, and one incisor was missing. As for his personality, he was a gentle, kind, sensitive man, and, when they all would go out for a walk at night, he would sing in a velvety baritone the *romance* beginning:

> Do you recall our sitting on the seashore,
> The sunset's glow with scarlet striped the sky,

or tell an Armenian joke in the darkness, and in the darkness someone would laugh. On meeting him for the first time, Martin, with amazement and even with a certain horror, recognized in him the drunk who had invited him to stand against the wall and be shot, but apparently Zaryanski remembered nothing, so that Dedman's identity remained unclear. Zaryanski was an outstanding drinker, and got violent when in his cups, but the revolver, which reappeared one day – during a picnic on the mountain plateau above Yalta, on a night steeped in moonlight, cricket-chirr, and muscatel wine – turned out to have an empty cylinder: for a long time Zaryanski went on shouting, threatening, and mumbling, talking of some fatal love of his; they covered him with a military greatcoat, and he went to sleep. Lida sat close to the campfire with her chin propped on her hands, and with shiny, dancing eyes, reddish brown from the flames, watched the escaping sparks. Presently Martin stood up, stretched his legs, ascended a dark turfy slope, and walked to the edge of the precipice. Right under his feet he saw a broad black abyss, and beyond it the sea, which seemed to be raised and brought closer, with a full moon's wake, the 'Turkish Trail' spreading in the middle and narrowing as it approached the horizon. To the left, in the murky, mysterious distance, shimmered the diamond lights of Yalta. And when Martin would turn, he saw the flaming, restless nest of the fire a short distance away, and the silhouettes of people around it, and someone's hand adding a branch. The crickets kept crepitating; from time to time there came a sweet whiff of burning juniper; and above the black alpestrine steppe, above the silken sea, the enormous, all engulfing sky, dove-gray with stars, made one's head spin, and suddenly Martin again experienced a feeling he had known on more than one occasion as a child: an unbearable intensification of all his senses, a magical and demanding impulse, the presence of something for which alone it was worth living.

Six

That moon's scintillating wake enticed one in the same ways as had the forest path in the nursery picture, and the clustered lights of Yalta amid the extensive blackness of unknown composition and properties reminded him too of a childhood impression: aged nine, wearing only his nightshirt, with chilled heels, he knelt at a sleeping-car window; the Sud Express hurtled across the French countryside. Sofia, having put her son to bed, had joined her husband in the dining car; the maid was sound asleep in the upper berth. It was dark in the narrow compartment; only the blue fabric of the night lamp's flexible shade let some light through; its tassel swayed, and panels creaked softly. Having wriggled out from under the sheet, he had crawled along the blanket to the window and raised the leathern curtain – for this he had to undo a button, after which the curtain slid smoothly up. He shivered with cold, and his knees ached, but he could not tear himself away from the window, beyond which the oblique hillsides of night rushed past. It was then that he suddenly saw what he now remembered on the Crimean plateau – a handful of lights in the distance, in a fold of darkness between two black hills: the lights would hide and reappear, and then they came twinkling from a completely different direction, and abruptly vanished, as if somebody had covered them with a black kerchief. Soon the train braked and stopped in darkness. Strangely disembodied noises became audible within the car: monotonous speech, coughing; then his mother's voice passed down the corridor; and, deducing that his parents were returning from the dining car and might look in on the way to the adjacent compartment, Martin slipped quickly back into bed. A little later the train began to move, but then stopped for good, emitting a long, softly sibilant sigh of relief, and simultaneously pale stripes of light passed slowly across the dark compartment, Martin once again crawled over to the window: he saw a lighted station platform; a man passed trundling an iron baggage cart with a muffled clatter, and on the cart was a crate with the mysterious inscription 'FRAGILE.' Several midges and one large moth circled around a gas lantern; shadowy people shuffled along the platform conversing about unknown things as they went; then there was a jangle of buffers and the train glided off. Lamps passed and disappeared; a small structure, brightly lit inside and housing a row of levers, appeared and also passed. The train rocked gently as it switched tracks, everything grew dark beyond the window, and once again there was only the rushing night. And again, out of nowhere, no longer between two hills but somehow much closer and more tangible, the familiar lights spilled forth, and the engine emitted a long, plaintive whistle as if it, too, was sorry to leave them behind. Then came a sharp bang, and an oncoming train shot past – and vanished as if it had never existed. The undulating black night resumed its smooth course and the elusive lights gradually thinned into nothingness.

When they had finally disappeared Martin fastened the window shade and lay down. He awoke very early. The train's motion seemed smoother and more relaxed, as if it had become accustomed to the rapid pace. When he unfastened the shade he felt a momentary dizziness, for the ground was running past in the opposite direction, and the early ash-pale light of the clear sky was unexpected too, and absolutely new to him were the terraced, olive-covered slopes.

From the station they went to Biarritz in a hired landau along a dusty road bordered by dusty brambles, and since Martin saw blackberries for the first time in his life, and the station was for some reason called 'The Negress,' he was full of questions. Today, at the age of sixteen, he kept comparing the Crimean sea with the ocean in Biarritz: yes, the Biscay waves were higher, and the breakers more violent, and the

fat Basque *baigneur* in his perennially wet bathing suit ('That's
a killing profession,' his father used to say) would take Martin by the hand and lead him into shallow water; then they
would both turn their backs to the surf and a huge, roaring
wave would rush upon them from behind, drowning and
overturning the entire world. On the first, mirrorlike strip
of beach a swarthy-faced woman with gray wisps of hair on
her chin would meet those who had finished bathing and
throw a fluffy beach towel over one's shoulders. Further on,
in a cabin that smelled of tar, an attendant would help you
yank off the clammy and clingy bathing suit and would bring
a tub of hot, almost boiling water, where you had to immerse
your feet. Then, when Martin and his parents had dressed,
they would sit on the beach – Mother, with her big white
hat, under a frilly white umbrella; Father also under an
umbrella, but a cream-colored masculine one; and Martin,
in striped jersey and sun-browned straw hat with 'H.M.S.
Indomitable' on the ribbon around its crown. His pants rolled
all the way up, he would build a sand castle surrounded by
moats. A waffle man, wearing a beret, would come by and
turn with a grinding noise the handle of the red tin cask that
contained his wares, and those large, curved chunks of
waffle, mixed with flying sand and sea salt, remained among
the most vivid memories of that period. Behind the beach,
on the stone promenade, inundated by the waves on stormy
days, a pert, well-rouged, far from young flower woman

would insert a carnation in the buttonhole of Father's white jacket, while Father kindly and comically observed the procedure of insertion, thrusting out his lower lip and pressing the folds of his chin against the lapel.

It was a shame, at the end of September, to leave the happy seaside and the white villa with its gnarled fig tree that refused to yield even one ripe fruit. On the way home they stopped in Berlin, where boys on roller skates, and even an occasional adult with a briefcase under his arm, would clatter by along the asphalt of streets. And then there were marvelous toy shops (locomotives, tunnels, viaducts), and tennis courts in the outskirts of the city, on the Kurfürstendamm, and the starry-night ceiling of the Wintergarten, and a trip to the pine woods of Charlottenburg on a cool, clear day, in a white electric cab.

At the frontier where one had to change trains Martin realized that he had forgotten in his compartment the penholder with the tiny glass lens, in which, when held up to your eye, a mother-of-pearl and blue landscape would flash into being; but during supper at the station (hazel hen with lingonberry sauce) the sleeping-car attendant brought it, and Father gave him a ruble. Snow and frost met one on the Russian side of the border, a whole mountain of logs swelled up on the tender, the crimson Russian locomotive was equipped with a fan-shaped snowplow, and abundant white steam flowed, curling, from the huge smokestack. The

Nord-Express, russified at Verzhbolovo, retained the brown facings of its cars, but now became more sedate, wide-flanked, thoroughly heated, and, instead of gathering full speed right away, took a long time to gain momentum after a stop. It was pleasant to perch on one of the flap seats in the blue-carpeted corridor, and the fat lantern-jawed attendant, in his chocolate-colored uniform, stroked Martin on the head in passing. White fields stretched outside; here and there leafless sallows stuck up out of the snow. By a crossing gate stood a woman in felt boots, holding a green flag; a peasant, who had jumped down from his sledge, shielded with his mittens the eyes of his backing nag. And at night he saw something wonderful: past the black, mirrory window flew thousands of sparks – arrowlike flourishes of a fire-tipped pen.

Seven

From that year on Martin developed a passion for trains, travels, distant lights, the heartrending wails of locomotives in the dark of night, and the waxworks vividness of local stations flashing by, with people never to be seen again. The slow heaving off, the grating of the rudder chain, the internal tremor of the Canadian freighter on which he and his mother left Crimea in April 1919, the stormy sea and the driving rain were not as conducive to viatic excitement as an express train, and only very gradually did Martin get penetrated with this new enchantment. A disheveled raincoated young woman with a black and white scarf around her neck strolled about the deck, blowing at the hair that tickled her face, accompanied by her pale husband until the sea got the better of him, and in her figure, in her flying scarf, Martin fully recognized the travel thrill that captivated him at the sight of the checkered cap and suede gloves his father would put on in a railroad compartment, or the crocodile satchel worn with its strap over her shoulder by that little French girl with whom it was such fun to roam along a fast train's long corridor, inserted into the fleeting landscape. This young woman was the only one that looked an exemplary sailor, very much unlike the rest of the passengers whom the captain of this rashly chartered vessel, finding no cargo in crazed Crimea, had agreed to take on board so as not to make the return journey empty. Despite the abundant luggage – lumpy, hastily gathered, fastened with rope instead of straps – all these people somehow gave the impression of traveling light, of sailing as if by chance; the formula of distant journeys could not accommodate their bewilderment and melancholy. They were fleeing before a mortal danger but for some reason Martin was little disturbed by the fact that this was so, that the ashen-faced profiteer over there with a load of precious stones in a belt next to his skin, had he stayed ashore, would have been killed on the spot by the first Red Army fellow to be tempted by his diamond innards. And Martin followed the Russian shore with an almost indifferent gaze as it receded in the rainy mist, so restrainedly, so simply, without a single sign that might have hinted at the supernatural length of the separation. Only when everything had vanished in the fog did he avidly recall, in a flash, Adreiz, and the cypresses, and the cheerful house, whose denizens would reply to the astonished questions of restless neighbors, 'Flee? But where would we live if not in the Crimea?' And his recollection of Lida was colored differently than their former, actual relationship: he remembered how once, when she was complaining about a mosquito bite and was scratching the place, grown red through the tan, on her calf, he wanted to show her how you were supposed to cut a cross on the swelling with your fingernail, and she had slapped him on the hand for no reason at all. He also remembered the farewell visit, when neither of them knew what to talk about, and kept mentioning Kolya, who had gone shopping in Yalta, and what a relief it was when he finally arrived. Lida's elongated, delicate face, about which there was something doelike, now haunted Martin quite obsessively. As he lay on a couch beneath a ticking clock in the cabin of the captain, with whom he had become great friends, or shared, in reverent silence, the watch of the first mate, a pockmarked

Canadian who spoke rarely – and when he did, pronounced English as if masticating it – but who had sent a mysterious chill through Martin's heart once when he informed him that old salts never sit down even when they go into retirement, that grandchildren sit while their grandfathers walk ('the sea remains in one's legs'); as he grew accustomed to all this nautical novelty, to the tang of oil and the ship's rolling, to the diverse and strange varieties of bread, one of which tasted like the Russian Eucharistic *prosfora*, Martin kept trying to convince himself that he had gone voyaging out of grief, that he was mourning an ill-starred love, but that no one, seeing his tranquil, already windburned face, could have suspected his anguish. Mysterious, wonderful people cropped up: there was the person who had chartered the ship, a sullen puritan from Nova Scotia, whose raincoat hung in the captain's toilet (which was in a state of hopeless disrepair), pendulating right over the seat. There was the second mate, by the name of Patkin, a Jew originally from Odessa, who, despite his American speech, could still perceive the blurry outlines of Russian words. And among the seamen there was a certain Silvio, a Spanish-American, who always walked barefoot and carried a dagger. One day the captain appeared with an injured hand, saying at first that the cat had scratched him, but later out of friendship confiding to Martin that he had gashed it on Silvio's teeth when he hit him for drunkenness on board. Thus was Martin initiated into seamen's life. The complex architectural structure of the ship, all those steps, mazy passages, swinging doors, soon yielded their secrets to him, and it became difficult to find a still unfamiliar corner. Meanwhile the lady with the striped scarf seemed to share Martin's curiosity, flitting past in the most unexpected places, always with wind-blown hair, always gazing into the distance; already by the second day her husband was laid up, moping, collarless, on the oilcloth'd bench in the saloon, while on another bench lay Sofia, with a slice of lemon between her lips. Now and then Martin, too, felt a sucking void in the pit of his stomach and a kind of general unsteadiness, while the lady was indefatigable, and Martin had already picked her as the one to save in case of disaster. But in spite of the turbulent sea the ship safely reached the harbor of Constantinople one cold, milkily gloomy dawn, and suddenly a wet Turk appeared on deck, and Patkin, who felt the quarantine should be reciprocal, yelled 'I'll "sunk" you!' at him (*ya tebya utonu*), and even threatened him with a pistol. Next day they moved on into the Sea of Marmara, and the Bosporus left no impression at all in Martin's memory except for three or four minarets that looked like factory chimneys in the mist, and the voice of the lady in the raincoat, who talked to herself out loud as she gazed at the gloomy coast; Martin, straining to overhear, seemed to distinguish the adjective 'amethyst' (*ametistovïy*), but decided he was mistaken.

Eight

After Constantinople the sky cleared, though the sea remained 'ochen (very) choppy,' as Patkin expressed it. Sofia ventured on deck, but promptly returned to the saloon, saying that there was nothing more hateful in the world than this servile sinking and rising of all one's insides in rhythm with the rising and sinking of the ship's prow. The lady's husband moaned, inquired of God when this would end, and hurriedly, with trembling hands, grabbed for the basin. Martin, whom his reclining mother was holding by the hand, felt that unless he left at once, he would throw up too. At that moment the lady came in with a flick of her scarf, and addressed a compassionate question to her husband. Her husband, without speaking or opening his eyes, made a Russian slicing gesture with his hand across his Adam's apple (meaning: I'm being slaughtered), whereupon she asked the same question of Sofia, who responded with a martyred smile. 'You don't look too happy either,' said the lady, with a severe glance at Martin. Then she staggered, tossed the end of her scarf over her shoulder, and went out. Martin followed her, and the fresh wind in his face and the sight of the bright-blue, whitecapped sea made him feel better. She was sitting on some coiled ropes, writing in a small morocco notebook. The other day one of the passengers had said about her 'not bad, that broad,' and Martin turned angrily but could not identify the rascal among several despondent, middle-aged men with turned-up collars. Now, as he looked at her red lips, which she kept licking as her pencil whipped across the page, he was embarrassed, did not know what to talk about, and felt a salty taste on his lips. She wrote on and seemed not to notice him. And yet Martin's nice round face, his seventeen years, a certain trim solidity of build and movement, often present in Russians, but for some reason classified as 'something British' – the whole appearance of Martin in his belted blue overcoat had made a certain impression on the lady.

She was twenty-five, her name was Alla, and she wrote poetry: three things, one would think, that were bound to make a woman fascinating. Her favorite poets were two fashionable mediocrities, Paul Géraldy and Victor Gofman; and her own poems, so sonorous, so spicy, always addressed the man in the polite form ('you,' not 'thou') and were asparkle with rubies as red as blood. One of them had recently enjoyed great success in St Petersburg society. It began thus:

On purple silks, beneath an Empire pall,
You vampirized me and caressed me all,

And we tomorrow die, burned to the end;
Our lovely bodies with the sand will blend.

The ladies would copy it from each other, learn it by heart and recite it, and one naval cadet even set it to music. Married at eighteen, she remained faithful to her husband for more than two years, but the world all around was saturated with the rubineous fumes of sin; clean-shaven, persistent males would schedule their own suicides at seven Thursday evening, midnight Christmas Eve, or three in the morning under her windows; the dates got jumbled, and it was hard to keep all of those assignations. A Grand Duc languished because of her; Rasputin pestered her for a month with telephone calls. And sometimes she said that her life was but the light smoke of an amber-perfumed Régie cigarette.

Martin did not understand any of this at all. Her poetry left him somewhat perplexed. When he said that Constantinople was anything but amethyst-colored, Alla objected that he was devoid of poetic imagination, and, on their arrival in Athens, gave him Pierre Louys's *Chansons de Bilitis* in the cheap edition illustrated with the naked forms of adolescents, from which she would read to him, meaningfully pronouncing the French, in the early evening on the Acropolis, the most appropriate place, one might say. What he found particularly appealing about her speech was the ripply way she pronounced the letter 'r,' as if there were not just one letter, but a whole gallery, accompanied, as if that were not enough, by its reflection in water. And instead of those French corybantics, guitar-filled Petersburgan white nights, or libertine sonnets of five dactylic stanzas, he managed to find in this girl with the hard-to-assimilate name something quite, quite different. The acquaintance that had imperceptibly begun on shipboard continued in Greece, at the seaside, in one of the white hotels of Phaleron. Sofia and her son ended up in a nasty, tiny room; its only window gave on a dusty courtyard where, at dawn with various agonizing preparatives, with a preliminary flapping of wings and other sounds, a young cock commenced his series of hoarse, cheerful cries. Martin slept on a hard blue couch; Sofia's bed was narrow and unsteady with a lumpy mattress. The only representative of the insect kingdom in the room was a solitary flea, which, in recompense, was very crafty, voracious, and absolutely uncatchable. Alla, who had had the good fortune to get an excellent room with twin beds, offered to have Sofia sleep with her, sending her husband over to Martin in exchange. After saying, several times in a row, 'I wouldn't think of it, I wouldn't think of it,' Sofia willingly accepted, and the transfer took place that very same day. Chernosvitov was big, lanky, and sullen, and filled the little room with his presence. Apparently his blood immediately poisoned the flea, as it did not reappear. His toilet implements – a small mirror bisected by a crack, eau-de-cologne, a shaving brush that he always forgot to rinse and that would stand the whole day, all stuck together by gelid lather, on windowledge, table, or chair — depressed Martin, and the encroachment was especially hard to bear at bedtime, when he was obliged to clear his couch of the man's various neckties and mesh undershirts. While undressing, Chernosvitov would scratch himself listlessly between gaping yawns; then he would place an enormous, naked foot on the edge of the chair and, thrusting his hand into his hair, freeze in this uncomfortable attitude, until he slowly came once more into motion, wound his watch, got into bed, and then, for a long time and with many grunts and groans, kneaded the mattress with his body. Some time later, in the dark, his voice would always pronounce the same sentence: 'One special request, my boy: don't foul the air.' While shaving in the morning, he would invariably say, 'Pimplekill face cream. Indispensable at your age.' As he dressed, choosing, whenever possible, socks that guaranteed decorum by having holes at the big toe rather than above the heel, he would exclaim (quoting a popular bard), 'Ah, yes, in our day we were young coursers too,' and whistle softly through his teeth. This was all very monotonous and unfunny. Martin would smile politely.

Yet his awareness of a certain risk afforded some consolation. Any night, in a treacherous dream, he might distinctly pronounce a full-voweled name, and any night the exasperated husband might steal up with a sharpened razor.

Chernosvitov, of course, used only a safety razor; he treated this little instrument just as sloppily as his brush, and the ashtray always contained a rusty blade with a fringe of petrified foam dotted with black hairs. His sullenness and his insipid sayings seemed to Martin proof of a deep-seated but restrained jealousy. Going as he did to Athens on business for the whole day, he could not help suspecting that his wife was passing the time alone with the good-humored, calm, yet worldly-wise young fellow that Martin fancied himself.

Nine

It was very hot and very dusty. The cafés served one a tiny cup of sweet black goo to accompany a huge glass of ice-cold water. On the beach fences, posters with the name of a Russian soprano were growing tattered. The electric train that ran to Athens filled the idle blue day with a soft rumble, whereupon everything grew quiet again. The sleepy little houses of Athens reminded one of a Bavarian townlet. The tawny mountains in the distance were wonderful. Pale poppies quivered in the wind among bits of broken marble on the Acropolis. Right in the middle of the street, haphazardly, began the tracks on which stood the cars of resort-bound trains. Oranges were ripening in the gardens. There might be a vacant lot with a superb growth of columns – one of them fallen and fractured in three places. All of this crumbling, yellow marble was gradually being turned over to nature's curatorship. Martin's hotel, destined to remain new for its allotted span, would share the same fate.

As he stood on the seashore with Alla, he told himself with an ecstatic chill that he was in a lovely remote land; and what a condiment that was to being in love, what bliss to stand in the wind next to a laughing woman with wind-blown hair, whose bright skirt would now be worried, now pressed against her knees by the same breeze that had once filled Ulysses' sails. One day, while they strolled across the uneven sand, she stumbled, Martin caught her, she glanced over her shoulder at the sole of her shoe, raised high, heel-upward, then stumbled again; that settled it, and he pressed his mouth against her half-open lips. During this lengthy, rather clumsy embrace they both nearly lost their balance. She freed herself and, laughing, declared he kissed too wetly and ought to take some lessons. Martin was aware of a humiliating trembling in his legs, and of the pounding of his heart. He was furious with himself for this agitation, which reminded him of the moment after a fight at school when his classmates exclaimed: 'Look how pale he is!' However, this first kiss of his life – shut-eyed and deep, with a kind of quivering point inside whose exact origin he did

44

not immediately understand – was so wonderful, so generously fulfilled his forefeeling, that his dissatisfaction with
himself was soon dispelled. The windy wild day passed in
passionate repetitions and improvements, and that evening
Martin felt as tired as if he had been toting logs. And when Alla,
accompanied by her husband, entered the dining room, where
he and his mother were already peeling their oranges, and sat
down at the next table (nimbly undoing the miter of her napkin, dropping it in her lap with a slight upward flight of her
hands, then moving closer to the table together with her chair)
a slow flush invaded Martin's face, and for a long time he
lacked the courage to meet her gaze, but when at last he did,
he failed to find an answering embarrassment in her look.

Martin's avid, unbridled imagination would have been
incompatible with chastity. Fantasies known as 'impure' had
plagued him for the last two or three years, and he made no
particular effort to resist them. At first they existed separately
from the actual infatuations of his early boyhood. One mem-
orable winter night in St Petersburg, after he had taken part
in some home theatricals and was still made up, with char-
coaled eyebrows, and dressed in a white Russian blouse, he
shut himself in a closet with a coeval girl cousin, also made
up and with a kerchief at eyebrow level, and as he squeezed
her moist little hands, Martin had keenly sensed the romantic nature of his behavior, but had not been excited by it.
Mayne Reid's hero Maurice Gerald, having stopped his

steed side-by-side with that of Louise Pointdexter, put his arm around the blond Creole's limber waist, and here the author exclaimed in a personal aside: 'What can compare with such a kiss?' Things like that provided a far greater erotic thrill. What fired him as a rule was the remote, the forbidden, the vague – anything sufficiently indistinct to make his fantasy work at establishing details – whether a portrait of Lady Hamilton or a popeyed schoolmate's whisperings about 'houses of evil repute.' Now the mist had thinned, visibility had improved. He was too engrossed in those sensations to give due attention to Alla's actual pronouncements: 'I shall remain for you a glamorous dream,' 'I am insanely voluptuous,' 'You will never forget me, as one forgets "an old novel read long ago" (know that song?).' 'And you must never, never talk about me to your future mistresses.'

As for Sofia she was pleased and displeased at the same time. When some acquaintance would coyly report, 'We were out strolling today and we saw him, yes, we did – with the poetess on his arm – lost his head completely, that boy of yours,' Sofia replied that this was all quite natural at his age. Martin's early revelation of manly passions made her proud, yet she could not ignore the fact that even though Alla was a sweet, affable young lady, she was perhaps a little too 'fast,' as the English say, and, while excusing her son's folly, Sofia did not excuse Alla's attractive vulgarity. Fortunately their stay in Greece was coming to an end: within a few days Sofia expected from Henry Edelweiss (her husband's cousin) in Switzerland a reply to a very frank letter, written with great difficulty, about her husband's death and the exhaustion of their means. Henry used to visit them in Russia, was good friends with her and her husband, was fond of his nephew, and always enjoyed the reputation of an honest and generous man. 'Do you remember, Martin, when was the last time that Uncle Henry came to see us? In any case it was *before*, wasn't it?' That '*before*,' always lacking on object, meant before the quarrel, before the separation from her husband, and Martin also would say 'before' or 'after' without further qualification. 'I think it was after,' he answered, recalling how Uncle Henry had arrived at their dacha, had had a long private interview with his mother, and emerged red-eyed, as he was particularly lachrymose, and even cried at the movies. 'Yes, of course – how stupid of me,' Sofia said quickly, suddenly reconstructing his visit, the discussion they had about her husband, Henry's exhortations that they make up. 'And you remember him well, don't you? Every time he came he brought you something.'

'The last time it was a room-to-room telephone,' said Martin, making a face: installing the telephone was boring, and when somebody finally did install it, running it from the nursery to his mother's room, it never worked well, then broke down altogether, and was abandoned, along with other previous gifts from Uncle, such as *The Swiss Family Robinson*, for instance, which was extremely dull after the real *Robinson*

Crusoe, or the little tin freight cars which had provoked secret tears of disappointment, for Martin liked only passenger trains.

'Why are you grimacing?' asked Sofia.

He explained, and she said with a laugh, 'That's true, that's true,' and stopped to think for a moment about Martin's child-hood, about irretrievable, ineffable things, and there was a heartrending charm about this reverie: how quickly everything passes! . . . Just think – has begun to shave, has clean nails, that smart lilac necktie, that woman. 'That woman is very sweet, of course,' said Sofia, 'but don't you think she's just a little too lively? You shouldn't get carried away like this. Tell me – no, I prefer not to ask you anything. Only they say she was a terrible flirt in St Petersburg. And don't tell me you really like her poetry? That female demonism? She has such an affected way of reciting verse. Is it true you've reached the point of – I don't know, of holding hands, or something like that?'

Martin smiled enigmatically.

'I'm sure there's nothing between you,' Sofia said slyly, considering with love the twinkling, equally sly eyes of her son. 'I'm certain there is nothing. You aren't old enough yet.'

Martin laughed, she pulled him close, and planted a juicy, greedy kiss on his cheek. All this was taking place at a garden table on the terrace before the hotel, early in the morning. The day promised to be lovely; the cloudless sky still had a hazy cast, as a sheet of gauze paper sometimes covers an exceptionally vivid frontispiece in an expensive edition of fairy tales. Martin carefully removed this translucent sheet, and there, down the white steps, swinging her low hips ever so slightly, wearing a bright-blue skirt across which an orderly ripple ran back and forth as, stepping down with calculated unhurriedness, first one foot and then the other extended the tip of its polished shoe, rhythmically balancing her brocaded handbag and already smiling, her hair parted on one side, came a limpid-eyed, slender-necked woman with large black earrings that also swung in rhythm with her descent. Martin went to meet her, kissed her hand, stepped back, and she, laughing and trilling her 'r's,' greeted Sofia, who sat in a wicker armchair smoking a thick English cigarette, her first after morning coffee.

'You were sleeping so prettily, Alla, that I didn't want to wake you,' said Sofia, her long, enameled cigarette holder held at a distance and glancing out of the corner of her eye at Martin, who now sat on the balustrade, swinging his legs. Bubbling over with excitement Alla began recounting the dreams she had seen last night, marvelous marble dreams with priests of ancient Greece, whose capacity to appear in dreams Sofia strongly doubted. And the freshly watered gravel glistened moistly.

Martin's curiosity grew. The rambles on the beach, and the kisses that anyone could spy on began to seem too lengthy a foreword; at the same time his desire for the main text was mixed with anxiety: Martin failed to imagine certain details, and his inexperience alarmed him. The unforgettable day on which Alla said that she was not made of wood, that he must not caress her like that, and that after lunch, when her husband was safely away in the city, and Sofia was enjoying her siesta, she would slip into Martin's room to show him somebody's poems – that day was the very same one that opened with the conversation about Uncle Henry and the room-to-room telephone. When, later in Switzerland, Uncle Henry gave Martin a black statuette (a soccer player dribbling the ball) for his birthday, Martin could not understand why, at the very instant his uncle placed that useless object on the table, he pictured with astounding clarity a distant, tender morning in Greece with Alla descending the white stairs. Right after dinner he had gone to his room and begun to wait. Chernosvitov's shaving brush he hid behind the mirror: somehow its presence encumbered him. From the courtyard came the clang of water pails, the splashing of water, and the sound of guttural speech. The yellow window curtain swelled mellowly, and a spot of sunlight changed its shape on the floor. Instead of circles the flies described parallelograms and trapezoids around the shaft of the ceiling lamp, settling every now and then on the brass. He took off his jacket and collar, lay down supine on the couch, and communed with the thump of his heart. When he heard her light footfalls and the knock on his door, something seemed to snap in the pit of his stomach. 'Look, I've brought a whole batch,' said Alla in a conniving whisper, but at the moment Martin could not care less about verse. 'What a wild boy, goodness, what a wild boy,' she kept whispering as she helped him discreetly. Martin hurried, pursued rapture, overtook it, and she covered his mouth with her hand, saying under her breath 'Sh, sh – the people next door …'

'This, at least, is a little object that will stay with you always,' said Uncle Henry in a clear voice, and leaned back, openly admiring the statuette. 'At eighteen a person must already think about decorating his future study and, since you're fond of English games –'

'It's beautiful,' said Martin, not wishing to hurt his uncle, and ran his fingers over the motionless ball at the tip of the player's boot.

Around the wooden chalet grew dense firs; fog hid the mountains. Hot, tawny Greece was indeed left far behind. But how vibrant the emotion of that proud, festive day: I have a mistress! What a conspiratorial air the blue couch had had later that evening! At bedtime Chernosvitov as usual scratched his shoulder blades, assumed weary attitudes, then creaked in the dark, requested that winds should not go free, and at last snored, whistling through his nose, while Martin thought, ah, if only he knew . . . And then, one day, when by all rights her husband ought to have been in the city, and in his and Martin's room Alla was rearranging her dress (having already 'taken a peek into paradise,' as she put it), while

Martin, sweaty and disheveled, was searching for a cufflink dropped in that same paradise, suddenly, with a powerful nudge at the door, Chernosvitov came in and said, 'So that's where you are, my dear. I forgot, of course, to take Spiridonov's letter with me. Fine muddle that would have been.'

Alla ran her hand over her wrinkled skirt and asked with a frown, 'Has he signed yet?'

'That old bastard Bernstein keeps dawdling,' said Chernosvitov, digging in a suitcase. 'If they want to delay payment, they can damn well get out of the mess by themselves, the swine.'

'Don't forget the postponement, that's the main thing,' said Alla. 'Well, have you found it?'

'Damn his mother to mucking hell,' muttered Chernosvitov, rummaging through some envelopes. 'It's got to be here. It can't have got lost, after all.'

'If it is lost, then the whole thing has fallen through,' she said with displeasure.

'Dawdling, dawdling,' muttered Chernosvitov. 'That's no way to do business. It's enough to drive you nuts. I'll be very glad if Spiridonov refuses.'

'Now, don't you get upset like that, it'll turn up,' said Alla, but she, too, was visibly disturbed.

'Here it is, thank heavens!' cried Chernosvitov, and scanned the paper he had found, while his jaw hung loose with concentration.

'Don't forget to mention the postponement,' Alla reminded him.

'Righto,' said Chernosvitov and hurried out of the room.

This business conversation left Martin somewhat perplexed. Neither husband nor wife had pretended: they had really quite forgotten that he was present, absorbed as they were by their problems. Alla, however, immediately resumed her previous mood, joked about the inefficiency of Greek door locks that opened all by themselves, and shrugged off Martin's alarmed question, 'Oh, don't worry, he didn't notice anything.' That night Martin could not get to sleep for a long time, and, with the same perplexity, kept listening to the complacent snoring. When, three days later, he sailed with his mother for Marseille, the Chernosvitovs came to see them off at Piraeus; they stood on the pier, arm in arm, and Alla was smiling and waving a mimosa branch. The day before, though, she had shed a tear or two.

Ten

Upon her, upon that frontispiece, which, after the removal of the gauze paper, had proved to be a little coarse, a little too gaudy, Martin replaced the haze and through it the colors reassumed their mysterious charm.

Then, on the big transatlantic liner, where everything was clean, polished, and spacious, which had a store selling toilet articles, a picture gallery, and a barber shop, and whose passengers danced the two-step and the fox-trot at night on the deck, he thought with rapt nostalgia about that amiable woman, with the touchingly hollow chest and the clear eyes, and about the way her fragile frame crunched in his embrace, causing her to say softly, 'Ouch, you'll break me.' Meanwhile Africa drew close, the purple strip of Sicily passed by on the northern horizon, then the ship glided between Corsica and Sardinia, and all these patterns of torrid land that existed somewhere around, somewhere near, but passed by unseen, captivated Martin with their disembodied presence. During the night journey from Marseille to Switzerland he thought he recognized his beloved lights among the hills, and, even though it was no longer a *train de luxe* but a plain express, jolty, dark, grimy with coal dust, the magic was strong as ever: those lights, those wails in the night. From Lausanne they drove by car to the chalet situated about a thousand meters higher in the mountains and Martin, who was sitting beside the chauffeur, every now and then would look back smiling at his mother and uncle, who both wore large motoring goggles and both held their hands in their laps clasped the same way. Henry Edelweiss had remained a bachelor, wore a bushy mustache, and certain intonations of his, and his way of fiddling with a toothpick or a nail file, reminded Martin of his father. On greeting Sofia at the Lausanne station Uncle Henry broke into tears, covering his face with his hands, but later, in the restaurant, he calmed down and, in his somewhat pompous French, began talking about Russia and his trips there in the past. 'How fortunate,' he said to Sofia, 'how very fortunate that your parents did not live to see that terrible revolution. I remember perfectly the old princess, with her white hair. How fond she was of poor, poor Serge,' and, at the recollection of his cousin, azure tears again welled in Henry's eyes.

'Yes, my mother was fond of him, it's true,' said Sofia, 'but then she was fond of everybody and everything. But tell me, how do you find Martin,' she hastily continued, trying to take Henry's mind off melancholy subjects, which, in his soft-mustached mouth, took on a shade of unbearable sentimentality.

'Yes, yes, he looks like him,' nodded Henry. 'The same forehead, the same fine –'

'But hasn't he grown up?' quickly interrupted Sofia. 'And, you know, he has already been in love, passionately –'

Uncle Henry passed on to political matters. 'That revolution,' he asked rhetorically, 'how long can it last? Yes, nobody knows. Poor, beautiful Russia is perishing. Perhaps the firm hand of a dictator will put an end to the excesses. But many beautiful things – your lands, your devastated lands, your country mansion, burned down by the rascally mob – to all that you can bid adieu.'

'How much does a pair of skis cost here?' asked Martin.

'I don't know,' replied Uncle Henry with a sigh. 'I have never indulged in that English sport. By the way, you speak French with a British accent. That is bad. We'll have to change all that.'

'He's forgotten a lot,' Sofia interceded for her son. 'The last few years Mlle Planche no longer gave him lessons.'

'Dead,' said Uncle Henry with feeling. 'One more death.'

'No, no,' smiled Sofia. 'Whatever gave you that idea? She married a Finn and is living peacefully in Vyborg.'

'In any case this is all very sad,' said Uncle Henry. 'I wanted so much for Serge to come here with you one day. But one never obtains what one longs for, and God alone knows what is to come. If you have assuaged your hunger and are sure you don't want anything more, we can start.'

The road was brightly sunlit and had many turns; a wall of rock with thorny bushes blooming in its cracks rose on the right, while on the left there was a precipice and a valley where water in crescents of foam ran down over ledges; then came dark conifers clustering in close ranks now on one side, now on the other; mountains loomed all around, imperceptibly changing position; they were greenish with streaks of snow; grayer ones looked out from behind their shoulders, and far beyond there were giants of an opaque violet whiteness, and these never moved, and the sky above them seemed faded in comparison with the bright-blue patches between the tops of the black firs under which the car passed. Suddenly, with a sensation still new to him, Martin remembered the dense fir fringe of their park in Russia as seen through a lozenge of blue glass on the veranda. And when, stretching his slightly vibrating legs and feeling a transparent humming in his head, he got out of the car, he was struck by the fresh rough smell of earth and melting snow, and by the rustic beauty of his uncle's house. It stood by itself half a kilometer from the nearest hamlet, and the top balcony offered one of those marvelous views that are even frightening in their airy perfection. The same Russian vernal blue sky looked into the window of the neat little wc, with its odor of wood and resin. All around, in the garden with its bare, black platbands and white apple bloom, and in the fir forest right behind the orchard, and on the dirt road leading to the village, there was a cool, happy silence, a silence that knew something, and Martin felt a little dizzy, perhaps from this silence, perhaps from the smells, or perhaps from the newfound blissful immobility after the three-hour drive.

In this chalet Martin lived until late fall. It was presumed that he would enter the University of Geneva that very winter; however, after a lively exchange of letters with friends in England, Sofia sent him to Cambridge. Uncle Henry did not immediately reconcile himself to this: he disliked the English, whom he considered a cold, perfidious nation. On the other hand the thought of the expenses the famous university required not only did not sadden him, but, on the contrary, was tempting. Fond as he was of economizing on trifles, clenching a penny in his left hand, he willingly wrote large checks with the right, especially when the expense was an honorable one. Sometimes, rather touchingly, he would feign eccentric pig-headedness, slapping the table with his palm, puffing out his mustache, and shouting, 'If I do it, I do it because it gives me pleasure!' With a sigh Sofia would slip the bracelet watch from Geneva on her wrist, while moist-eyed Henry would dig in his pocket for a voluminous handkerchief, trumpet once, twice, and then smooth his mustache to the right and to the left.

With the onset of summer the cross-marked sheep were herded higher into the mountains. A babbling metallic tinkling, of unknown origin and from an unknown direction, would gradually become audible. Floating nearer, it enveloped the listener, giving him an odd tickling sensation in the mouth. Then, in a cloud of dust, came flowing a gray, curly, tightly packed mass of sheep rubbing against each other, and the moist, hollow tinkle of the bells, which delighted all of one's senses, mounted, swelled so mysteriously that the dust itself seemed to be ringing as it billowed above the moving backs of the sheep. From time to time one of them would get separated from the rest and trot past, whereupon a shaggy dog would drive it back into the flock; and behind, gently treading, walked the shepherd. Then the tintinnabulation would change timbre, and once more grow hollower and softer, but for a long time it would hang in the air together with the dust. 'Nice, nice!' murmured Martin to himself, hearing the tinkle out to the end, and continued on his favorite walk, which began with a country lane and forest trails. The fir grove abruptly thinned out, lush green meadows appeared, and the stony path sloped down between hawthorn hedges. Occasionally a cow with wet pink nose would stop on its way in front of him, twitch its tail and with a lurch of the head move on. Behind the cow came a spry little old woman with a stick, who glanced malevolently at Martin. Further down, surrounded by poplars and maples, stood a large white hotel, whose owner was a distant relative of Henry Edelweiss.

In the course of that summer Martin grew still sturdier, his shoulders broadened, and his voice acquired an even, deep tone. At the same time he was in a state of inner confusion, and feelings he did not quite understand were evoked by such things as the country coolness of the rooms, so keenly perceptible after the outdoor heat; a fat bumblebee knocking against the ceiling with a chagrined droning; the paws of the fir trees against the blue of the sky; or the firm brown bolete found at the edge of the forest. The imminent journey to England excited and gladdened him. His memory of Alla Chernosvitov had reached its ultimate perfection, and he would say to himself that he had not sufficiently appreciated the happy days in Greece. The thirst she had quenched, only to intensify it, so tormented him during that alpine summer that at night he could not go to sleep for a long time, imagining, among numerous adventures, all the girls awaiting him in the dawning cities, and occasionally he would repeat aloud some feminine name – Isabella, Nina, Margarita – a name still cold and untenanted, a vacant, echoing house, whose mistress was slow to take up residence; and he would try to guess which of these names would suddenly come alive, becoming so alive and familiar that he would never again be able to pronounce it as mysteriously as now.

In the mornings, Marie, the niece of the old chambermaid, would come to help with the household chores. She was seventeen, very quiet and comely with cheeks of a dark-pink hue and yellow pigtails tightly wound about her head. Sometimes, while Martin would be in the garden, she would throw open an upstairs window, shake out her dustcloth, and remain motionless, gazing, perhaps, at the bright clouds, at their oval shadows gliding along the mountain slopes, then pass the back of her hand across her temple, and slowly turn away. Martin would go up to the bedrooms, determine from the drafts where the cleaning was going on, and would find Marie kneeling in meditation amidst the gloss of wet floorboards; he would see her from behind, with her black wool stockings and her green polka-dot dress. She never looked at Martin, except once – and what an event that was! – when, passing by with an empty pail, she smiled uncertainly, tenderly – not at him, though, but at the chicks. He resolutely vowed to start a conversation with her, and to give her a furtive hug. Once, however, after she had left, Sofia sniffed the air, made a face, and hurriedly opened all the windows, and Martin was filled with dismay and aversion toward Marie, and only very gradually, in the course of her subsequent appearances in the distance – framed in a casement, or glimpsed through the foliage near the well – he began again to succumb to that enchantment; only now he was afraid to come closer. Thus something happy and languorous lured him from afar, but was not addressed to him. Once, when he had scrambled far up the mountainside he squatted on a big round-browed rock, and below a herd passed along the winding trail, with a melodious, melancholy jingling and, behind it, a gay, ragged shepherd and a smiling girl who was knitting a stocking as she walked. They went by without a glance at Martin, as if he were incorporeal, and he watched them for a long time. Without breaking step, the man put his arm around his companion's shoulders, and from her nape you could tell that she kept knitting on and on as they walked into another valley. Or

else, bare-armed young ladies in white frocks, yelling and
chasing off the horseflies with their rackets, would appear by
the tennis court in front of the hotel, but, as soon as they
started playing, how clumsy and helpless they became, particularly since Martin himself was an excellent player, beating
to shreds any young Argentine from the hotel: at an early age
he had assimilated the concord essential for the enjoyment of
all the properties of the sphere, a coordination of all the elements participating in the stroke dealt to the white ball, so
that the momentum begun with an arching swing still continues after the loud twang of taut strings, passing as it does
through the muscles of the arm all the way to the shoulder, as
if closing the smooth circle out of which, just as smoothly, the
next one is born. One hot August day Bob Kitson, a professional from Nice, turned up at the court, and invited Martin
to play. Martin felt that familiar, stupid tremor, the vengeance
of too vivid an imagination. Nevertheless he started well, now
volleying at the net, now driving powerfully from the baseline
to the furthest corner. Spectators gathered around the court,
and this pleased him. His face was aflame, he felt a maddening
thirst. Serving, crashing down on the ball, and transforming
at once the incline of his body into a dash netward, Martin
was about to win the set. But the professional, a lanky, cool-
headed youth with glasses, whose game until then had
resembled a lazy stroll, suddenly came awake and with five
lightning shots evened the score. Martin began to feel weary

and worried. He had the sun in his eyes. His shirt kept coming out from under his belt. If his opponent took this point that *was* the end of it. Kitson hit a lob from an uncomfortable corner position, and Martin, retreating in a kind of cakewalk, got ready to smash the ball. As he brought down his racket he had a fleeting vision of defeat and the malicious rejoicing of his habitual partners. Alas, the ball plumped limply into the net. 'Bad luck,' said Kitson jauntily, and Martin grinned back, heroically controlling his disappointment.

Eleven

On the way home he mentally replayed every shot, transforming defeat into victory, and then shaking his head: how very, very hard it was to capture happiness! Brooks burbled, concealed among the foliage; blue butterflies fluttered up from damp spots on the road; birds bustled in the bushes: everything was depressingly sunny and carefree. That evening after dinner they sat as usual in the drawing room; the door to the piazza was wide open, and, since there had been a power failure, candles burned in the chandeliers. From time to time their flame would slant, and black shadows reach out from under the armchairs. Martin picked his nose

63

as he read a small volume of Maupassant with old-fashioned illustrations: mustachioed Bel Ami, in a stand-up collar, was shown undressing with a lady's maid's skill a coy, broad-hipped woman. Uncle Henry had laid down his newspaper and, arms akimbo, considered the cards that Sofia was laying out on a green-baize table. The warm, black night pressed in through window and door. Suddenly Martin raised his head and hearkened as if there were a vague beckoning in this harmony of night and candle flame. 'The last time this patience came out was in Russia,' said Sofia. 'In general it comes out very seldom.' Spreading her fingers she collected the cards scattered about the table and began shuffling them anew. Uncle Henry sighed.

Tired of reading. Martin stretched and went out on the terrace. It was very dark out, and the air smelled of dampness and night-blooming flowers. A star fell: as so often annoy-ingly happens, it fell not quite in his field of vision, but off to the side, so that his eye caught only the twinge of a sound-less change in the sky. The outlines of the mountains were indistinct, and here and there, in the folds of the darkness, dots of light scintillated in twos and threes. 'Travel,' said Martin softly, and he repeated this word for a long time, until he had squeezed all meaning out of it, upon which he set aside the long, silky skin it had shed – and next moment the word had returned to life. 'Star. Mist. Velvet. Travelvet,' he would articulate carefully and marvel every time how tenuously the sense endures in the sound. In what a remote spot this young man had arrived, what far lands he had already seen, and what was he doing here, at night, in the mountains, and why was everything in the world so strange, so thrillful? 'Thrillful,' Martin repeated aloud, and liked the word. Another star went tumbling. He fixed his eyes on the sky as, once upon a time, when they were driving home in the victoria from a neighbor's estate along a dark forest road, a very small Martin, rocking on the brink of slumber, would throw back his head and watch the heavenly river, between the amassments of trees, along which he was floating. Where again in his life, he wondered, would he gaze – as then, as now – at the night sky? on what pier, at what station, in what town square? A feeling of opulent solitude, which he often had experienced amid crowds – the delight he took in saying to himself: not one of these people, going about their business, knows who I am, where I am from, what I am thinking about right now – this feeling was indispensable to complete happiness, and Martin, in a breathless trance, imagined how, completely alone, in a strange city – say, London – he would roam at night along familiar streets. He saw the black hansom cabs splashing through the fog. A policeman in a shiny black cape, lights on the Thames, and other images out of English novels. He had left his luggage at the station and was walking past innumerable illuminated English shops, excitedly looking for Isabel,

Nina, Margaret – someone whose name he could give to that night. And she – who would she think *he* was? An artist, a sailor, a gentleman burglar? She would not accept his money, she would be tender, and in the morning she would not want to let him go. How foggy the streets were, though, and how crowded, and how difficult the search! And although there was much that looked different, and the hansoms were mostly extinct, he nevertheless recognized certain things when, one autumn evening, he walked baggageless out of Victoria station; he recognized the dark, greasy air, the bobby's wet oilskin cape, the reflections, the swashy sounds. At the station he had taken an excellent shower in a cheerful, clean cubicle, dried himself with a warm, fluffy towel brought by a ruddy-cheeked attendant, put on clean linen and his best suit, and checked both his bags, and now he was proud that he had managed so sensibly. He hardly felt fatigued by his journey; there was only buoyant excitement. Huge buses fiercely, heavily splattered the pools on the asphalt. Lighted advertisements went running up dark-red façades and dissipating again. He would pass girls; he would turn to look; but the prettier the face, the harder it was to take the plunge. Inviting cafés such as in Athens or Lausanne did not exist here, and in the pub where he drank a glass of beer he found only men, inflamed, morose, with red veins on the whites of their prominent eyes. Little by little a vague sense of irritation overcame him: surely, the Russian family with which, by epistolary agreement, he was to stay for a week, was right then waiting for him, worrying. Should he quietly take a taxi and forget about that imaginary night? But his lack of faith in it struck him as shameful – how intensely he had longed for it that morning at dawn, looking out of the train window at the plains, the cold pink sky, the black silhouette of a windmill. 'Cowardliness and betrayal,' Martin said softly. He noticed that he was walking along the same street for the second time, recognizing it by a shop window filled with pearl necklaces. He stopped and made a cursory check of his long-standing aversion for pearls: oysters' hemorrhoids with a sickly sheen. A girl under an umbrella stopped beside him. Martin glanced out of the corner of his eye: slender figure, black suit, glittering hat pin. She turned her face toward him, smiled, and, pursing her lips, made a small 'oo' sound. In her eyes Martin saw the sparkling lights, the play of reflected colors, the shimmer of rain, and hoarsely muttered, 'Good evening.'

As soon as they were in the dark of the taxicab he embraced her, frenzied by the feel of her supple slenderness. She covered her face with her hands, giggling. Later, in the hotel room, when he awkwardly extracted his billfold, she said, 'No, no. If you want, take me tomorrow to a fancy restaurant.' She asked where he came from, whether he was French, and at his behest started guessing: Belgian? Danish? Dutch? She did not believe him when he said he was Russian. Later he hinted that he lived by gambling on ocean liners, told her of his travels, embellishing a bit here, adding something there, and, as he described a Naples he had never seen, he gazed lovingly at her bare, childish shoulders and blond bob, and felt completely happy. Early next morning, as he slept, she dressed quickly and left, stealing ten pounds from his billfold. 'Morning after the orgy,' thought Martin with a smile, slapping shut the billfold, which he had picked up from the floor. He doused himself from the pitcher, splashing water all over the place, and kept smiling as he thought of the blissful night. It was something of a pity that she had left so foolishly, that he would never meet her again. Her name was Bess. When he went out of the hotel and started walking the spacious morning streets, he felt like jumping and singing with joy and, to give release to his spirits, climbed a ladder leaning against a lamppost, and as a result had a long and comical argument with an elderly passer-by, who from below gestured threateningly with his cane.

Twelve

A second scolding came from Olga Zilanov. The day before that lady had waited for him late into the night and, since she assumed for some reason that he was younger and more helpless than he actually turned out to be, she grew increasingly worried. He explained that on the previous day he had misplaced the address, had found it too late in a seldom-visited pocket, and had spent the night at a hotel near the station. Mrs Zilanov wanted to know why he had not telephoned, and which hotel. Martin invented a good, uncommon name, Good-Night Hotel, explaining that he had looked for her number in the book but had not found it. 'Shame on you,' said Mrs Zilanov crossly, and suddenly smiled a marvelous, beautiful smile that completely transfigured her flabby, melancholy face. Martin remembered that smile from St Petersburg days, and, as he had been a child then, and as women usually smile when addressing strange children, his memory had retained a radiant-faced image of Mrs Zilanov, and he had at first been perplexed to find her so old and gloomy.

Her husband, who had been a well-known public figure in Russia, happened to be out of town, and Martin was lodged in his study. The study and the dining room were on the first floor, the parlor on the second, and the bedrooms on the third. The whole quiet, residential street consisted of such narrow houses, indistinguishable from each other, with an identical, vertical configuration of rooms inside. A dash of color was contributed by a plump red letter-pillar at the corner. Behind the right row of houses were gardens where rhododendrons bloomed in the summer, and behind the left row a small park containing tall elms and a grass tennis court was growing yellow and bare of leaves.

Zilanov's elder daughter Nelly had recently married a Russian army officer who had arrived in England after captivity in Germany. Sonia, the younger daughter, was about to finish a London preparatory school to which she had transferred from the Stoyunin Gymnasium in St Petersburg. There was also Mrs Zilanov's sister Elena and her daughter Irina, a poor hideous half-witted creature.

The week he spent in that house, while getting used to England, seemed rather tiresome to him. The whole livelong day he was among strangers, and could not take one step alone. Sonia needled him, making fun of his wardrobe — shirts with starched cuffs and stiffish fronts, his favorite bright-purple socks, his orange-yellow knobby-capped shoes, bought in Athens. 'These are American,' said Martin with a studied calm.

'The Americans make them specially to sell to Negroes and Russians,' glibly replied Sonia. Furthermore, it turned out that Martin had not brought a dressing gown with him, and when in the mornings, he would go to the bathroom proudly wrapped in his bedclothes, Sonia would say that this reminded her of her cousins and their chums at the Lyceum school who, when visiting the Zilanovs' country house, slept naked, walked around in the morning draped in bedsheets, and relieved themselves in the garden. In the end Martin made so many purchases in London that ten pounds was not enough, and he had to write to his uncle, which was particularly unpleasant because of the hazy explanations necessitated by the disappearance of the other ten pounds. Yes, it was a hard, unfortunate week. Even his English accent, on which Martin quietly prided himself, proved to be an occasion for derisive corrections on Sonia's part. Thus Martin quite unexpectedly found himself classified as ignorant, adolescent, and a mamma's boy. He felt this was unfair, that he had had infinitely more experiences and adventures than a sixteen-year-old maiden. It was therefore with a certain malicious glee that he drubbed some young man of hers at tennis, and on his last night had a chance to show he could dance an impeccable two-step (which he had learned back in Mediterranean days) to Hawaiian wails from the phonograph.

At Cambridge he felt still more foreign. Upon talking to his English fellow students he noted with wonder his unmistakably Russian essence. From his semi-English childhood he retained only such things as had been relegated by native Englishmen of his age, who had read the same books as children, into the dimness of the past properly allotted to nursery things, while Martin's life at a certain point had made an abrupt turn and taken a different course, and for this very reason his childhood surroundings and habits had assumed a certain fairy-tale flavor, and a book he had been fond of in those days was now more enchanting and vivid in his memory than the same book in the memory of his English coevals. He remembered various expressions that ten years ago had been current among English schoolboys, but now were considered either vulgar or ridiculously old-fashioned. Plum pudding, blazing with a blue flame, was served in St Petersburg not only at Christmas, as in England, but any day of the year, and, in the opinion of many people, the Edelweiss chef made a better one than could be bought in a store. Petersburgers played soccer on hard ground, not on turf, and the penalty kick was called 'pendel,' a term unknown in England. No longer would Martin dare wear the colors of the striped jersey bought once, long ago, at Drew's, the English shop on the Nevski, for they corresponded to the athletic uniform of a public school he had never attended. In truth, all this Englishness, really of a rather haphazard nature, was filtered through his motherland's quiddity and suffused with peculiar Russian tints.

Thirteen

The splendid autumn he had just seen in Switzerland some-how kept lingering in the background of his first Cambridge impressions. In the mornings a delicate haze would enshroud the Alps. A broken cluster of rowan berries lay in the middle of the road, whose ruts were filmed with micalike ice. Despite the absence of wind the bright-yellow birch leafage thinned out with every passing day, and the turquoise sky gazed through it with pensive gaiety. The luxuriant ferns grew reddish; iridescent shreds of spiderweb, which Uncle Henry called 'the Virgin's hair,' floated about. Martin would look up, thinking that he heard the remote blare of migrating cranes, but no cranes were to be seen. He used to wander around a great deal, as if searching for something; he rode the dilapidated bicycle belonging to one of the menials along the rustling paths, while his mother, seated on a bench beneath a maple, pensively pierced the damp crimson leaves on the brown ground with the point of her walking stick. Such wild, varied beauty did not exist in England, where nature had a tame greenhouse quality, and an unimaginative autumn faded away in geometrical gardens under a drizzly sky. But the pinkish-gray walls, the rectangular lawns, frosted with pale silver on the rare sunny mornings, the narrow river, the stone bridge whose arch formed a full circle with its perfect reflection, all had a beauty of their own.

Neither the foul weather nor the icy chill of the bedroom, where tradition forbade heating, could alter the meditative *joie de vivre* characteristic of Martin. He grew sincerely fond of his little living room, with its comfortable fireplace, its dusty pianola, innocuous lithographs on the walls, low wicker armchairs, and the cheap china bric-a-brac on the shelves. When, late at night, the sacred flame of the fireplace threatened to die, he would scrape the embers together, pile some wood chips on them, heap on a mountain of coal, fan the fire with the asthmatic bellows, and make the chimney draw by spreading an ample sheet of the *Times* across the mouth of the hearth. The taut sheet would grow warm and transparent, and the lines of print, mingling with the lines showing through from the reverse side, looked like the bizarre lettering of some mumbo-jumbo language. Then, as the hum and tumult of the fire increased, a fox-red, darkening spot would appear on the paper and suddenly burst through. The whole sheet, now aflame, would be instantly sucked in and sent flying up. And a belated passer-by, a gowned don, could observe, through the gloom of the gothic night, a fiery-haired witch emerge from the chimney into the starry night. Next day Martin would pay a fine.

Being of lively and sociable temperament Martin did not remain alone for long. Fairly soon he made friends with his downstairs neighbor Darwin, as well as with various men at the soccer field, the club, and the dining hall. He noticed that everyone felt it his duty to discuss Russia with him and to learn what he thought about the Revolution, intervention, Lenin and Trotsky; while some, who had visited Russia, praised Russian hospitality and asked if he happened to know a Mr Ivanov in Moscow. Such talk nauseated Martin; casually taking a volume of Pushkin from his desk he would read aloud 'Autumn' in Archibald Moon's translation:

> O dismal period, visual enchantment!
> Sweet is to me thy farewell loveliness!
> I love the sumptuous withering of nature,
> The woods arrayed in gold and purple dress.

This caused some astonishment, and only Darwin, a large, sleepy-looking Englishman in a canary-yellow jumper, who sprawled in an armchair, making wheezing sounds with his pipe and gazing up at the ceiling, would nod approvingly.

This Darwin, who often dropped in after dinner, elucidated certain strict, primordial rules in full detail for Martin's edification: a student must not walk outdoors in hat and overcoat, no matter how cold it was; one did not shake hands or wish a good morning, but greeted an acquaintance one happened to meet, even if it were Atom Thompson himself, with a grin and a breezy interjection. It was bad form to go out on the river in an ordinary rowboat: for this purpose there were punts and canoes. One should never repeat the old college witticisms, of which freshmen become immediately enamored. 'Remember, though,' Darwin added wisely, 'that even in observing these traditions you mustn't overdo, for sometimes, to shock the snobs, it's a good thing to go out in a bowler hat and with an umbrella under your arm.' Martin got the impression that Darwin had already been at the university a long time, several years, and he felt sorry for him as he did for any homebody. Darwin amazed him by his sleepiness, the sluggishness of his movements, a certain comfortableness about his whole being. Trying to stir his envy, Martin impetuously told him about his wanderings, unconsciously throwing in some of what he had invented for Bess's benefit, and barely noticing how the fiction had consolidated. True, these exaggerations were innocent enough: the two or three picnics on the Crimean plateau turned into a habitual roaming of the steppes with a stick and knapsack; Alla Chernosvitov became a mysterious companion on yacht cruises, his walks with her a prolonged sojourn on one of the Greek islands, and the purplish outline of Sicily actual gardens and villas. Darwin would nod approvingly as he gazed at the ceiling. His eyes were pale bluish, vacant, and expressionless; the soles that he always exhibited, fond as he was of semireclining poses with his feet lodged in some high, comfortable position, were equipped with a complicated system of rubber strips. Everything about him, from those solidly shod feet to his bony nose, was high-quality, large, and imperturbable.

Fourteen

About three times a month Martin was summoned by his 'tutor,' that is the professor in charge of keeping an eye on lecture attendance, visiting the sick student, giving permission for trips to London, and making reprimands when one was fined (for getting home after midnight or not wearing the academic gown in the evening). He was a wizened, pigeon-toed, keen-eyed little old man, a Latinist, a translator of Horace, and a great oyster fancier. 'Your English is improving,' he once said to Martin. 'That's good. Have you got to know many people?'

'Oh, yes,' answered Martin.

'Are you friends with Darwin, for instance?'

'Oh, yes,' Martin repeated.

'I'm glad. He's a splendid specimen. Three years in the trenches, France and Mesopotamia, the Victoria Cross, and not a scratch, either morally or physically. Literary success might have gone to his head, but that didn't happen either.'

Besides the facts that Darwin had interrupted his college studies at eighteen to enlist and had recently published a collection of short stories which connoisseurs were raving about, Martin learned that he was a boxing Blue, that he had spent his childhood in Madeira and Hawaii, and that his father was a famous admiral. Martin's own meager experience seemed insignificant, pathetic, and he felt ashamed about certain yarns he had spun. When Darwin slouched into his room that evening, the situation seemed both humorous and embarrassing to Martin. Little by little he began to fish for information about Mesopotamia and the short stories, and Darwin kept giving facetious answers, saying that the best book he had ever written was a little manual for students entitled 'A Complete Description of Sixty-seven Ways of Getting inside Trinity College after Closing of the Gates, with a Detailed Plan of its Walls and Railings, First and Last Edition, Verified many Times by the Author, who has never been Caught.' But Martin insisted on what was interesting and important to him: the collection of short stories connoisseurs were raving about. At last Darwin said, 'All right, I'll give you a copy. Let's go to my digs.'

He had furnished his digs himself according to his taste. There were supernaturally comfortable leather armchairs, in which the body would melt as it sank into a yielding abyss, and on the mantelpiece stood a large photograph depicting a bitch lying in complete mollitude on her side and the plump behinds of her six sucklings in a row. Martin had already seen numerous students' rooms: there were those like his, pleasant, but not pampered by the lodger, containing extraneous objects belonging to the landlord; there was the athlete's room with silver trophies on a shelf and a broken oar on the wall; there was the den littered with books and dusted with cigarette ash; finally, there was one of the nastiest abodes you could discover – nearly bare, with bright-yellow wallpaper, a room where there was only one picture, but that one a Cézanne (charcoal doodle vaguely resembling the female form), and where a fourteenth-century bishop of colored wood stood proffering the stump of his forearm. The most cordial digs of all were Darwin's, especially if you looked carefully and browsed a bit: what a gem, for example, that set of newspaper issues Darwin had edited in the trenches! The paper was cheerful, jaunty, full of funny jingles; heaven only knows how and where the type was set; and it used chance clichés to beautify blanks – corset advertisements found in the ruins of some printing plant.

'Here,' said Darwin, producing a book, 'take it.'

The book proved to be remarkable. The pieces were not really short stories – no, they were rather more like tractates, twenty tractates of equal length. The first was called 'Corkscrews,' and contained a thousand interesting things about corkscrews, their history, beauty, and virtues. Another was on parrots, a third on playing cards, a fourth on infernal machines, a fifth on reflections in water. And there was one on trains, and in it Martin found everything he loved: the telegraph poles, cutting short the wires' upward sweep, the dining car with those bottles of Vichy or Evian that seemed to scan through the window the trees flying past; and those crazy-eyed waiters, and that minuscule kitchen, where swaying and sweating a white-capped man cook could be seen crumbing a fish.

If Martin had ever thought of becoming a writer and been tormented by a writer's covetousness (so akin to the fear of death), by that constant state of anxiety compelling one to fix indelibly this or that evanescent trifle, perhaps these dissertations on minutiae that were deeply familiar to him might have aroused in him a pang of envy and the desire to write of the same things still better. Instead, such warm good will toward Darwin overwhelmed him that his eyes even began to tickle. And next morning when, on the way to his lecture, he overtook his friend at the corner, he said with perfect decorum and not looking him in the face that he had liked the book, and silently walked beside him, falling in with Darwin's indolent but swingy step.

The lecture halls were scattered about the whole town. If one lecture immediately followed another but was given in a different hall, you had to hop on your bicycle, or else scuttle along back alleys and across the echoing stone of courts. Limpid chimes called back and forth from tower to tower; the din of motors, the crepitation of wheels, and the tinkle of bicycle bells filled the narrow streets. During the lecture the glittering swarm of bicycles clustered at the gates, awaiting their owners. The black-gowned lecturer would mount the platform and with a thump put his tasseled square cap on the lectern.

Fifteen

When he entered the university it took Martin a long time to decide on a field of study. There were so many, and all were fascinating. He procrastinated on their outskirts, finding everywhere the same magical spring of vital elixir. He was excited by the viaduct suspended over an alpine precipice, by steel come to life, by the divine exactitude of calculation. He understood that impressionable archeologist who, after having cleared the path to as yet unknown tombs and treasures, knocked on the door before entering, and, once inside, fainted with emotion. Beauty dwells in the light and stillness of laboratories: like an expert diver gliding through the water with open eyes, the biologist gazes with relaxed eyelids into the microscope's depths, and his neck and forehead slowly begin to flush, and, tearing himself away from the eyepiece, he says, 'That settles everything.' Human thought, flying on the trapezes of the star-filled universe, with mathematics stretched beneath, was like an acrobat working with a net but suddenly noticing that in reality there is no net, and Martin envied those who attained that vertigo and, with a new calculation, overcame their fear. Predicting an element or creating a theory, discovering a mountain chain or naming a new animal, were all equally enticing. In the study of history Martin liked what he could imagine clearly, and therefore he was fond of Carlyle. With his poor memory for dates and scorn for generalizations, he avidly sought out what was live and human, what belonged to that class of astonishing details which well may satiate coming generations as they watch old, drizzly films of our day. He vividly visualized the shivering white day, the simplicity of the black guillotine, and the clumsy tussle on the scaffold, where the executioners roughly handle a bare-shouldered fat man while, in the crowd, a good-natured *citoyen* raises by the elbows a *citoyenne* whose curiosity exceeds her stature.

There were other vaguer fields, such as the mists of law, government, economics. What scared him away from them was that the scintilla he sought in everything was too deeply buried there. Undecided what to undertake, what to select, Martin gradually rejected all that might take a too exclusive hold over him. Still to be considered was literature. Here, too, Martin found intimations of bliss; how thrilling was that humdrum exchange about weather and sport between Horace and Maecenas, or the grief of old Lear, uttering the mannered names of his daughters' whippets that barked at him! Just as, in the Russian version of the New Testament, Martin enjoyed coming across 'green grass' or 'indigo chiton,' in literature he sought not the general sense, but the unexpected, sunlit clearings, where you can stretch until your joints crunch, and remain entranced. He read a very great deal, but it was mostly rereading; and he did have occasional accidents in the course of literary conversation. For example, he once confused Plutarch with Petrarch, and once called Calderón a Scottish poet.

Not every writer was able to stir him. He remained unmoved when, on his uncle's advice, he read Lamartine, or when his uncle himself declaimed '*Le Lac*' with a sob in his voice, shaking his head and adding with helpless emotion, '*Comme c'est beau.*' The prospect of studying wordy, watery works and their influence on other wordy, watery works did not attract him. At this rate he probably never would have made a choice if some mysterious voice had not kept whispering that he was not free to choose, that there was one thing he must study. During the sumptuous Swiss autumn he felt for the first time that he was, after all, an exile, doomed to live far from home. That word 'exile' had a delicious sound: Martin considered the blackness of the coniferous night, sensed a Byronic pallor on his cheeks, and saw himself in a cloak. This cloak he donned at Cambridge, albeit it was only a lightweight academic gown, of a bluish fabric, semitransparent when held up to the light, with many pleats on the shoulders and with winglike half-sleeves that were worn thrown back. The bliss of spiritual solitude and the excitement of travel took on a new significance. It was as if Martin had found the right key to all the vague, tender, and fierce feelings that besieged him.

At that time the chair of Russian literature and history was occupied by the distinguished scholar Archibald Moon. He had lived fairly long in Russia, and had been everywhere, met everyone, seen everything there. Now, pale and dark-haired, with a pince-nez on his thin nose, he could be observed riding by, sitting perfectly upright, on a bicycle with high handlebars; or, at dinner in the renowned hall with oaken tables and huge stained-glass windows, he would jerk his head from side to side like a bird, and crumble bread extremely fast between his long fingers. They said the only thing this Englishman loved in the world was Russia. Many people could not understand why he had not remained there. Moon's reply to questions of that kind would invariably be: 'Ask Robertson' (the orientalist) 'why he did not stay in Babylon.' The perfectly reasonable objection would be raised that Babylon no longer existed. Moon would nod with a sly, silent smile. He saw in the Bolshevist insurrection a certain clear-cut finality. While he willingly allowed that, by-and-by, after the primitive phases, some civilization might develop in the 'Soviet Union,' he nevertheless maintained that

Russia was concluded and unrepeatable, that you could embrace it like a splendid amphora and put it behind glass. The clay kitchen pot now being baked there had nothing in common with it. The civil war seemed absurd to him: one side fighting for the ghost of the past, the other for the ghost of the future, and meanwhile Archibald Moon quietly had stolen Russia and locked it up in his study. He admired this finality. It was colored by the blue of waters and the transparent porphyry of Pushkin's poetry. For nearly two years now he had been working on an English-language history of Russia, and he hoped to squeeze it all into one plump volume. An obvious motto ('A thing of beauty is a joy forever'), ultra-thin paper, a soft Morocco binding. The task was a difficult one: to find a harmony between erudition and tight picturesque prose, to give a perfect image of one orbicular millennium.

Sixteen

Archibald Moon amazed and captivated Martin. His slow Russian speech, from which it had taken him years of patience to weed out the last vestige of English velarity, was smooth, simple, and expressive. His knowledge was distinguished by freshness, precision, and depth. He would read aloud from Russian poets whose very names Martin did not know. Holding down the page with long, slightly trembling fingers, Archibald Moon poured out iambic tetrameters. The room was in penumbra, and the lamplight picked out only the page and Moon's face, with a pale gloss on the cheekbones, fine creases on the forehead, and translucent pink ears. When he had finished he would compress his thin lips, take off his pince-nez as carefully as if it were a dragonfly, and clean the lenses with chamois cloth. Martin sat on the edge of his armchair with his square black cap on his knees.

'For Heaven's sake take off your gown and put that cap away somewhere,' Moon would say with a pained frown. 'Don't tell me you enjoy fussing with that tassel. Away, away with it.'

He would push a glass cigarette box with the college blazon on its silver lid toward Martin, or, from a cabinet in the wall, produce a bottle of whisky, a soda siphon and two glasses.

'By the way, do you know what a grape-transporting cart is called there?' he asked with a toss of his head, and, having ascertained that Martin did not, went on with gusto: '*Mozhara, mozhara*, sir,' and it was not clear which gave him greater pleasure: that he knew the Crimea better than did Martin, or that he could pronounce the word 'sir' according to its

Russian pronunciation which rhymes it with 'air.' He joyfully informed Martin that the Russian 'huligan' came from the name of a gang of Irish robbers, and that Golodai Island was named not after 'golod' (hunger) but for an Englishman named Holliday who built a factory there. Once, when, speaking of some ignorant journalist (whom Moon had wrathfully taken to task in the Times), Martin said that the journalist had not replied because he probably sdreyfil (had funked), Moon raised his eyebrows, consulted a dictionary, and asked Martin if by chance he had ever lived in the Volga region. On another occasion, when Martin used the colloquialism ugrobil ('bumped off'), Moon grew angry and shouted that such a word did not and could not exist in Russian. 'I've heard it, everybody knows it,' Martin said meekly, and was sustained by Sonia, who was sitting on the couch next to Mrs Zilanov and watching not without curiosity Martin playing the host.

'Russian wordbuilding, the birth of neologisms,' said Moon, suddenly turning to the smiling Darwin, 'ended together with Russia, that is, two years ago. Everything subsequent is blatnaya muzïka (thieves' lingo).'

'I don't understand Russian, please translate,' replied Darwin.

'Yes, we keep drifting into it,' said Mrs Zilanov. 'That's not nice. English, please, everybody.' Meanwhile Martin lifted a metal dome from above the muffins and crumpets (which a waiter had brought from the college canteen), checked whether they had sent the right thing, and moved the platter closer to the flaming hearth. In addition to Darwin and Moon he had invited a Russian student whom everyone called simply by his first name, Vadim, and now Martin did not know whether to wait for him or go ahead with tea. This was the first time that mother and daughter Zilanov had come to visit him, and he was in constant fear of derision from Sonia. She wore a navy-blue suit and sturdy little brown shoes, with long tongues that passed beneath the laces and then folded back on top, covering them and ending in leathern lappets. Her bobbed black, somewhat coarse-looking hair fell in an even fringe over her forehead. The dimples of her pale cheeks went singularly well with her dull-dark, slightly slanting eyes. That morning, when Martin had met her and Mrs Zilanov at the station, and afterward, when he was showing them the ancient courts, the fountains, the avenues of gigantic, bare trees, out of which flew cawing the heavy and awkward crows, Sonia had looked moody and cross, and said she was cold. As she gazed over a stone parapet at the ripply Cam, at its matgreen banks and at the gray towers beyond, she suddenly narrowed her eyes and inquired of Martin if he were planning to join General Yudenich's anti-Bolshevist forces in the North. Martin answered with surprise that he was not.

'And what's that pinkish house over there?'

'That's the library building,' Martin explained. A few minutes later, as he walked under an arcade beside Sonia and her mother, he said enigmatically, 'One side is fighting for the ghost of the past and the other for the ghost of the future.'

'Yes, exactly,' Mrs Zilanov chimed in. 'This contrast keeps me from really appreciating Cambridge. I'm bothered by the fact that alongside all these marvelous old buildings there are so many cars, bicycles, sporting-goods stores, footballs –'

'They used to play football in Shakespeare's time too,' said Sonia. 'What bothers *me*,' she added, 'is the platitudes some people spout.'

'Sonia, behave yourself, please,' said her mother.

'Oh, I didn't mean you,' said Sonia with a sigh. They walked on in silence.

'I think it's beginning to drizzle-drozzle,' said Martin, stretching out his palm.

'Why not say "Jupiter Pluvius" or "Lord Rainsford"?' observed Sonia sarcastically, and changed step to match her mother's. Later, at lunch in the town's best restaurant, she cheered up. The 'simian name' of Martin's friend amused her, and she liked Darwin's dialogue with the unbelievably cozy old waiter.

'What are you studying?' her mother asked politely.

'I? Nothing,' replied Darwin, raising his head. 'I just thought this fish had one more bone than it was supposed to.'

'No, no, I meant your studies, the lectures you attend.'

'Sorry, I misunderstood you,' said Darwin, 'but your question catches me unawares all the same. Somehow my memory does not stretch from one lecture to the next. Only this morning I asked myself what the deuce was I reading. Mnemonics? Hardly.'

After lunch they had another walk, but a much pleasanter one, for, in the first place, the sun came out, and, in the second, Darwin took them all to a gallery where, according to him, there was an ancient, remarkably alert echo: stamp your foot, and it would bounce off a distant wall like a rubber ball. Darwin stamped, but no echo turned up, and he said some American must have bought it for his house in Massachusetts. Then they strolled over to Martin's room, and soon Archibald Moon arrived, and Sonia asked Darwin softly why the professor's nose was powdered. Moon started to speak in his mellow Russian, flaunting rare and rich proverbs. The girl's conduct, thought Martin, was decidedly reprehensible. She would sit with stonelike countenance, or laugh for no reason at all as her eyes met Darwin's. The latter sat with crossed legs, tamping the tobacco in his pipe.

'I wonder why Vadim hasn't shown up yet,' said Martin uneasily, and touched the teapot's full cheek.

'Oh, go ahead and pour,' said Sonia, whereupon Martin busied himself with the teacups. They all grew silent, watching him. Moon smoked a tan-tinted cigarette belonging to the kind referred to as Russian in England.

'Does your mother write to you often?' asked Mrs Zilanov.

'Every week,' answered Martin.

'She must miss you,' said Mrs Zilanov, and blew on her tea.

'Well, I don't see the national lemon,' Moon subtly observed, in Russian again. Darwin, lowering his voice, asked Sonia to translate. Moon gave him a sidelong glance and switched to English; deliberately and maliciously imitating the average Cambridge manner, he said that there had been some rain, but that now it had cleared, and most likely would not rain any more; he mentioned boat races; he gave a detailed version of the well-known joke about the student, the closet, and the girl cousin. Darwin kept smoking and murmuring, 'Very good sir, very good. That's your authentic, sober Briton at moments of leisure.'

Seventeen

A pounding of feet came from the stairs, the door flew open, and Vadim appeared. Simultaneously his bicycle, which he had left in the lane with one pedal lowered and propped against the edge of the sidewalk, tumbled with a jingling noise, which easily reached the low second story. Vadim's small hands had bitten nails, and were red from holding the handlebars in the cold. His face, suffused with an extraordinarily delicate and uniform rosiness, bore an expression of dazed confusion, which he tried to conceal by panting as if he were out of breath and making sniffling sounds with his nose which was habitually humid inside. He had on wrinkled pale-gray flannel trousers, an excellently tailored brown jacket, and an old pair of pumps that he wore at all times and in all kinds of weather. Still sniffling and smiling a bewildered smile, he said hello to everybody and sat down beside Darwin, whom he liked very much and for some reason called 'Mamka' (wet-nurse). Vadim had one inevitable jingle, with a limerick arrangement of Russian rhymes: *priyátno zret', kogdá bol'shóy medvéd' vedyót pod rúchku málen'kuyu súchku, chtob eyó poét'* (What fun to stare when a great big bear walks home arm in arm with a tiny bitch to lay her there). His rapid, staccato manner of speaking was accompanied by all kinds of hissing, trumpeting and squeaking sounds like the speech of a child short both of ideas and words but incapable of keeping still. When embarrassed he would grow even more disjointed and absurd, and would seem like a cross between a shy, tongue-tied adult and a whimsical infant. Otherwise, he was a nice, chummy, attractive fellow, always ready for a laugh and capable of subtle perception (once, at a much later date, out for a row on the river with Martin one spring evening, when a chance breath of air brought a vague odor of myrtle from Heaven knows where, Vadim said, 'Smells like the Crimea,' which was perfectly true). He was a great hit with English people. His college tutor, a fat, asthmatic old man, specialist in mollusks, pronounced his name with guttural tenderness and treated his perfect idleness with perfect indulgence. One dark night Martin and Darwin helped Vadim take the sign off a tobacco shop, and that sign had graced his room ever since. Vadim also procured a police helmet, by means of a simple but ingenious trick: for half-a-crown that he flashed in the moonlight he asked a good-natured bobby to help him climb over a wall, and, once on top, he leaned down and snatched the helmet off the man's head. He was also the instigator in the episode of the fiery chariot: it happened during the Guy Fawkes Day celebration; the entire city was spewing fireworks, a bonfire burned in the square, and Vadim and his pals harnessed themselves to an old landau acquired for a couple of pounds, filled it with straw and set it on fire. Dragging this landau they sped through the streets, nearly burning down the town hall. On top of everything he was a master of foul language – one of those who become attached to a ditty and repeat it endlessly and are fond of comfortable mother-oriented oaths, caressive physiological terms, and fragments of obscene poetry attributed to Lermontov. His education was undistinguished, his English very droll and endearing but barely intelligible. He had a passion for the navy, for mine-layers, for the beauty of dreadnoughts in battle array. He could play for hours with toy soldiers, firing peas from a silver cannon. His quips, his pumps, his shyness and mischievous-ness, his delicate profile, with its outline of golden bloom – all this, combined with the splendor of his princely title, had an irresistible, heady effect on Archibald Moon, some-what like the champagne and salted almonds which he relished formerly, a lone, pale Englishman in a bemisted pince-nez, listening to Moscow gypsies. At present, however, Moon sat by the fire with a cup in his hand, munching a muffin and listening to Mrs Zilanov, who was telling him about the Russian newspaper her husband planned to start in Paris. Martin, meanwhile, reflected with alarm that it had been a mistake to invite Vadim, who sat silent, embarrassed by Sonia, and furtively kept shooting raisins, borrowed from the cake, at Darwin. Sonia had grown silent too, and sat gaz-ing pensively at the pianola. With an easy swing Darwin walked over to the fireplace, knocked the ashes out of his pipe, and, turning his back to the flames, began warming himself. 'Mamka,' Vadim mouthed softly and chuckled. Mrs Zilanov kept speaking excitedly of matters that did not inter-est Moon in the slightest. It grew dark outside, and somewhere far off newsboys were shouting 'pie-pa, pie-pa!'

Eighteen

It was time for the Zilanovs to catch the train back to London. Archibald Moon said good-bye at the very first corner and, with a tender smile for Vadim (who behind his back usually referred to him by an indecent noun supplemented by 'on rollers'), glided away, holding himself very erect. For a while Vadim rode slowly right next to the sidewalk, with one hand on the shoulder of Darwin, who walked alongside; then he said a quick but fussy good-bye and sped off, making a sound with his lips like a broken klaxon. They reached the station, and Darwin bought platform tickets for himself and Martin. Sonia was tired, irritated, and kept slitting her eyes.

'Well, thank you for the hospitality, for the nice party,' said Mrs Zilanov. 'Give my regards to your mother when you write to her.'

But Martin did not transmit the regards: such things are seldom transmitted. As a rule, he had trouble writing letters: how to tell, for example, about that rather muddled, somehow unsuccessful and unpleasant day? He scribbled ten lines or so, recounted the anecdote about the student, the closet, and the cousin, assured his mother that he was in perfect health, ate regularly, and wore an undershirt (which was not true). Suddenly, in his mind, he saw the mailman walking across the snow; the snow crunched slightly, and blue footprints remained on it. He described it thus: 'My letter will be brought by the mailman. It is raining here.' He thought it over and crossed out the mailman, leaving only the rain. He wrote out the address in a large and careful hand, remembering for the tenth time as he did so what a fellow student had once said to him: 'Judging by your last name I thought you were American.' He regretted that he always remembered about working this into his letter only after it had been sealed; and he was too lazy to reopen it. He inadvertently made a blot in a corner of the envelope. He squinted at it for a long time, and finally made it into a black cat seen from the back. Mrs Edelweiss preserved this envelope along with his letters. She would gather them into a batch at the end of each semester and tie them crosswise with a ribbon. Several years later she had occasion to reread them. The first-semester letters were relatively abundant. Here was Martin's arrival in Cambridge; here was the first mention of Darwin, of Vadim, of Archibald Moon; here was a letter dated November ninth, his nameday: 'This is the day,' wrote Martin, 'when the goose sets foot on the ice, and the fox changes his lair'; and here was a letter with the crossed-out but distinctly legible line 'My letter will be brought by the mailman.' Mrs Edelweiss recalled with piercing clarity how she used to walk with Henry along the scintillating road between fir trees weighted down by lumps of snow, and suddenly there was the rich tinkling of multiple bells, the postal sleigh, the letter, and she hastened to take off her gloves in order to open the envelope. She recalled how, during that period, and for almost a year after, she was terribly afraid that without telling her anything, Martin might join the Northern White Army. She found some consolation in the knowledge that there, at Cambridge, a veritable angel exerted a pacifying influence on her son – excellent, sensible Archibald Moon. Yet Martin might still slip away. Her mind was completely at ease only when Martin was with her in Switzerland, on vacation. Years later, when she reread those letters with such anguish, they seemed, despite their tangibility, of a more ghostly nature than the intervals between them. Her memory packed the intervals with Martin's living presence – Christmas, Easter, summer. Thus, for a period of three years, until Martin finished college, her life was like a series of windows. She remembered them well, those windows. There was the first winter holiday, and the skis Henry had bought him on her advice, and Martin putting them on. 'I must be brave,' Mrs Edelweiss softly said to herself. 'After all, miracles do happen. One must only have faith and wait. If Henry appears once more with that black armband, I shall simply leave him.' And she smiled through the tears that streamed down her face, as with trembling hands she continued unwrapping the letters.

That first Christmas homecoming, which remained so vividly impressed in his mother's memory, was also a festive occasion for Martin. He had a queer sensation of having returned to Russia, so white was everything, but, being ashamed of his own sensitivity, he did not share it with his mother, thus depriving her in the future of yet another poignant recollection. His uncle's gift pleased him; for an instant there materialized a snow-covered slope in a St Petersburg suburb – although, of course, in those distant days the toes of Russian felt boots used to be inserted in the plain loops of light children's skis, which, moreover, had a string (for the skier to hold on) attached to their upturned tips. Not so the new ones – real, substantial skis of flexible ash, and the boots, too, were real ski boots. Bending one knee, Martin adjusted the heel cable and bent back the stiff lever of the side throw. Its ice-cold metal stung his fingers. When he had put on the other ski as well, he picked up his mittens from the snow, straightened up, stamped his feet once or twice to see if everything was secure, and swung forward.

Yes, he found himself back in Russia. Here were the splendid 'rugs' of snow spreading in the Pushkin poem which Archibald Moon recited so sonorously, reveling in the scuds of its iambic tetrameter. Above the burdened firs the blue sky shone clear and bright. The cluster of snow dislodged by a jay, flying from perch to perch, would dissipate in midair. Martin passed through the woods into the clearing from which, the previous summer, he used to descend to the local Majestic. He could see it far below, with a straight column of rose-colored smoke coming out of a chimney. What was it about that hotel that lured him so strongly, why must he again hasten there, when in the summer all he had found there had been a bevy of raucous, angular English flappers? But there was no doubt that it beckoned to him: the reflected sunlight in its windows flashed a silent sign of invitation. Martin was even frightened by such enigmatic intrusion, such abstruse insistence. He had seen that signal before, displayed by some detail of the landscape. There he must go down: it would be wrong to ignore such blandishments. The firm surface began whistling delightfully under his skis as Martin sped down the slope faster and faster. And how many times afterwards, sleeping in his chilly Cambridge room, he dream-sped like that and suddenly, in a stunning explosion of snow, fell and awakened. Everything was as usual. He could hear the clock ticking in the adjacent parlor. A mouse was rolling a lump of sugar on the floor. Footfalls passed on the sidewalk and faded away. He would turn over in bed and instantly fall asleep again; in the morning, still drowsy, he heard other sounds from the parlor: Mrs Newman fussing about, moving things, putting coals on the fire, tearing paper, scratching a match – and presently she departed, and the silence was gradually and delectably filled with the morning hum of the ignited hearth.

'Nothing special there after all,' reflected Martin, and reached toward the night table for cigarettes. 'Mostly middle-aged blokes in sweaters. Good example of how metaphysics can fool you. Ah, it's Saturday today – off to London. How come Darwin keeps getting letters from Sonia? I'll have to worm it out of him. Good idea to cut Grzhezinsky's lecture. Here comes the hag to wake me.'

Mrs Newman brought his tea. She was elderly, red-haired, and had foxy little eyes. 'Last night, sir, you went out without your gown,' she remarked phlegmatically. 'I'll have to inform your tutor.' She drew open the curtains, gave a brief but exact report on the weather, and was gone.

Martin put on his bathrobe, descended the creaky stair-case, and knocked on Darwin's door. Darwin, already shaven and washed, was eating scrambled eggs and bacon; Marshall, a fat textbook on political economy, lay open near his plate.

'Got another letter today?' sternly inquired Martin.

'From my tailor,' said Darwin chewing juicily.

'Sonia's handwriting isn't too good,' remarked Martin.

'It's rotten,' agreed Darwin, gulping some coffee. Martin walked around behind him, placed both hands around Darwin's neck, and started squeezing.

'The bacon went down anyway,' said Darwin in a smugly strained voice.

Nineteen

That evening they were both off for London. Darwin spent
the night in one of those charming two-room flats provided
by clubs for bachelors – and Darwin's club was one of the
smartest and staidest in London, with overstuffed armchairs,
glossy magazines, and thick silent rugs. Martin ended up this
time in one of the upstairs bedrooms at the Zilanovs', Nelly
being in Reval, and her husband marching on St Petersburg.
When Martin arrived, nobody was at home but Mihail Platonovich Zilanov himself, busy writing in his study. A sturdy,
thickset man, with Tartar features and the same dark lusterless eyes as Sonia, he invariably wore cylindrical detachable
cuffs and a starched shirt; the shirt front bulged, imparting
a dovelike quality to his chest. He was one of those Russians
who, upon awaking, first of all pull on trousers with dangling
suspenders; who wash only face, nape, and hands in the
morning, but wash them most thoroughly, and who regard
their weekly bath as an event not devoid of a certain risk. He
had done a goodly amount of traveling around in his time,
was intensely active in liberal politics, conceived life as a
succession of congresses in various cities, had miraculously

escaped a Soviet death, and always carried a bulging brief-case. And when someone said meditatively, 'What shall I do with these books – it's raining,' he would wordlessly, instantly, and extremely skillfully swaddle the books in a sheet of newspaper, rummage in his briefcase, produce some string and, in a flash, tie it crosswise around the neat pack-age, a process which the luckless acquaintance, shifting from foot to foot, watched with apprehensive *attendrissement*. 'There you are, sir,' Zilanov would say and, after a hasty good-bye, was off to Riga, Belgrade, or Paris. He always traveled light, with three clean handkerchiefs in his briefcase, and would sit in the railway carriage completely blind to picturesque spots (which the fast train traversed in its trusting efforts to please), immersed in a brochure and making occasional notes in the margin. While marveling at his inattention to landscapes, comforts, and cleanliness, Martin nevertheless admired Zilanov for that plodding dryish courage of his, and every time he saw him could not help recalling that this seemingly unathletic and unfashionable man, who probably played only billiards and perhaps bowls, had escaped from the Bolshevists by crawling through a drainpipe, and had once fought a duel with the Octobrist Tuchkov.

'Welcome,' said Zilanov extending a swarthy hand. 'Sit down.' Martin sat down. Zilanov again contemplated the half-filled sheet of paper upon his desk, picked up his pen, imparted to it a hovering flicker directly above the paper before transforming the flicker into the rapid glide of writing, then simultaneously gave the pen its freedom and said, 'They should be back any moment now.'

Martin reached for a newspaper lying on a nearby table. It turned out to be a Russian *émigré* one, published in Paris.

'How's school?' asked Zilanov, without raising his eyes from the evenly running pen.

'Pretty good,' said Martin, putting down the paper. 'How long have they been out?' Zilanov did not answer: the pen was going at full tilt. A few minutes later, though, he spoke again, still not looking at Martin. 'Idling away your time, I imagine. Only thing colleges care about here is *le sport*.'

Martin grinned. Zilanov rapidly thumped a blotter all over the lines he had written and said, 'Your mother keeps asking me for additional information, but I don't know anything more. I wrote her in the Crimea at the time, telling her everything I knew.' Martin cleared his throat.

'*Shto vï* (what's that)?' asked Zilanov, who had picked up that bit of bad Russian in Moscow.

'Nothing,' replied Martin.

'I'm referring to your father's death, of course,' said Zilanov, glancing with dull eyes at Martin. 'If you remember, it was I who notified you at the time.'

'Yes, yes, I know,' said Martin, nodding hurriedly. He always felt embarrassed when strangers – even with the best intentions – spoke to him about his father.

'Our last meeting is as clear in my mind as if it had happened today,' Zilanov went on. 'We chanced to meet on the street. I was already in hiding then. At first I did not want to go up to him. But Sergey Robertovich looked so appallingly sick. I remember, he was very concerned about what was happening to you and your mother in the Crimea. And a couple of days later I went to see him, and there they were carrying out the coffin.'

Martin kept nodding, searching agonizingly for a way to change the subject. Zilanov was telling him all this for the third time, and, on the whole, the narrative was a rather pale one. Zilanov turned over the sheet. His pen quivered and started again. To kill time Martin again reached for the newspaper, but just then the front-door lock clicked and from the entrance hall came the sound of voices, of shuffling feet, and Irina's awful cackling laugh.

Twenty

Martin went out to greet them, and, as generally happened when he encountered Sonia, he instantly had the sensation that he stood in relief against a dark background. The same thing had happened on her last visit to Cambridge (she had

come with her father, who had tormented him with questions about the age of various colleges and the number of
books in the Library, while she and Darwin kept quietly
laughing about something or other), and it came upon him
again now, that strange torpor. His light-blue necktie, the
sharp points of his soft collar, his double-breasted suit, all
seemed to be in order, and yet Martin had the impression,
under Sonia's impenetrable gaze, that he was dressed shab-
bily, that his hair was badly brushed, that he had shoulders
like a furniture mover's, and that the roundness of his face
was the shape of stupidity. No less repulsive were his big
knuckles, which had reddened and grown swollen of late,
what with his goalkeeping and his boxing lessons. The solid
sense of contentment somehow related to the strength in
his shoulders, the coolness of sleekly shaven cheeks, the
reliability of a recently filled tooth, all of it vanished instantly
in Sonia's presence. And what appeared particularly silly to
him was the way his eyebrows petered out: they were thick
only at their starting point and then, templeward, took on a
look of surprised sparseness.

Supper was served. Mrs Pavlov, a pudgy and dour lady who
resembled her sister (but smiled even more seldom than
she), kept a habitual and discreet eye on Irina, seeing to it
that her daughter ate decorously, without leaning on the
table too much and without licking her knife. Zilanov arrived
a moment later, rapidly and energetically inserted a corner

of his napkin under his collar and, half-rising in his chair, snatched from clear across the table a roll which he immediately sliced and buttered. His wife was reading a letter from Reval, and, as she read, saying to Martin, 'Help yourself.' On his left Irina fidgeted, scratched her armpit, and uttered sounds of endearment addressed to her cold mutton. On his right sat Sonia, and the way she had of taking salt with the tip of her knife, her short black hair with its harsh gloss, and the dimple on her pale cheek ineffably irritated him. After supper there came a telephone call from Darwin, who suggested they go dancing. Sonia played coy for a while, then agreed. Martin went to change and was already pulling on his silk socks, when Sonia told him through the door that she was tired and would not go after all. Half an hour later Darwin arrived, very gay, very big and elegant, his top hat cocked, with tickets to a very expensive ball in his pocket. Martin told him that Sonia had wilted and gone to bed, whereupon Darwin drank a cup of tepid tea, gave an almost natural yawn, and said that in this world everything was for the best. Martin knew that he had traveled to London for the sole purpose of seeing Sonia, and when Darwin, in his unneeded top hat and opera cloak, went off whistling down the empty dark street, Martin felt very hurt for him. He softly closed the front door and went upstairs to his bedroom. Sonia slipped out into the passage to meet him, wearing a kimono and looking very short in heelless bedroom slippers.

'Is he gone?' she asked.

'Really rotten of you,' Martin commented under his breath without stopping.

'You could have stopped him,' she said after him, adding quickly, 'I know what – I'll go down and ring him up and go dancing, that's what I'll do.'

Without answering, Martin slammed his door, angrily brushed his teeth, yanked open his bed as if he wanted to throw somebody out of it, and, dispatching the light with a murderous twist of his fingers, pulled the covers over his head. But a few minutes later the thickness of the blanket did not prevent him from hearing Sonia's steps hurrying up the passage and her door shutting – was it possible that she had actually been downstairs and telephoned? He listened attentively, and, after a new period of silence, there were her footsteps again, only now they had a different, lighter, almost ethereal sound. Martin could not restrain himself. He stepped out into the corridor and caught sight of Sonia hopping downstairs in a flamingo-colored frock, a fluffy fan in one hand and something bright encircling her black hair. She had left her door open and the light on. In her room there remained a cloudlet of powder, like the smoke following a shot; a stocking, killed outright, lay under a chair; and the motley innards of the wardrobe had spilled onto the carpet.

Instead of being glad for his friend, Martin felt very hurt. All was still, except for the heavy snores that came from the master bedroom. 'God damn her,' he muttered, and for a while debated with himself whether he too should join them at the ball – after all, there were three tickets. He saw himself dashing up the sumptuous stairs, wearing his pumps with flat bows, his dinner jacket and silk shirt with the frilled front (as sported by the dandies that year). The flame of music shot from the open doors. The resilient, tender caress of a girl's soft leg, which keeps giving way and yet pressing against you, the fragrant hair by your very lips, a cheek that leaves its powder on your silk lapel – all these immemorial and tender banalities stirred Martin deeply. He enjoyed dancing with a fair stranger, enjoyed the vacuous, chaste talk, through which you listen closely to that bewitching, vague something going on inside you and inside her, which will last a couple of bars more and then, finding no resolution, will vanish forever and be utterly forgotten. But while the bond of bodies is still unbroken, the outlines of a potential love affair begin to form, and the rough draft already comprises everything: the sudden silence between two people in some dimly lit room; the man carefully placing with trembling fingers on the edge of an ashtray the just-lit but impedient cigarette; the woman's eyes slowly closing as in a filmed scene; and the rapt darkness, and in it a point of light, a glossy limousine traveling fast through the rainy night, and suddenly, a white terrace and the dazzling ripple of the sea, and Martin softly saying to the girl he has carried off, 'Your name – what's your name?' Leafy shadows play on her luminous dress. She gets up, she goes away. The rapacious croupier rakes in Martin's last chips, and he has nothing left but to thrust his hands into the empty pockets of his dinner jacket and descend slowly into the casino garden and, then, sign on as a longshoreman – and there she is again, aboard someone else's yacht, sparkling, laughing, flinging coins into the water.

'Funny thing,' said Darwin one night, as he and Martin came out of a small Cambridge cinema, 'it's all unquestion-ably poor, vulgar, and rather implausible, and yet there is something exciting about all that flying foam, the *femme fatale* on the yacht, the ruined and ragged he-man swallowing his tears.'

'It's nice to travel,' said Martin. 'I'd like to travel a lot.'

This fragment of conversation, surviving by chance from one April night, came back to Martin when, at the beginning of summer vacation, already in Switzerland, he received a letter from Darwin in Tenerife. Tenerife – God, what a lovely, emerald word! It was morning. Marie, with dis-astrously deteriorated looks and an oddly bloated appearance, was kneeling in a corner, wringing out a floor rag into a pail. Large white clouds glided above the mountains, catching on the peaks, and from time to time some smoky filaments would descend the slopes, on which the light changed con-tinuously with the ebb and flow of the sun. Martin went out into the garden, where Uncle Henry, wearing a monstrous straw hat, was talking with the village curé. When the curé, a small man with glasses, which he kept adjusting with the thumb and little finger of his left hand, made a low bow and, with a rustle of his black cassock, walked off by the shiny white wall and climbed into his cabriolet hitched to a fat, pinkish-white horse all speckled with mustard, Martin said, 'It's wonderful here, and I adore this region, but, perhaps, just for a few weeks, I would like to take a trip somewhere – the Canary Islands, for instance.'

'What folly, what folly,' answered Uncle Henry with fright, and his mustache bristled slightly: 'Your mother, who waited for you so anxiously, who is so happy that you are staying with her until October – and suddenly you leave …'

'We could all go together,' said Martin.

'*Quelle folie*,' Uncle Henry repeated. 'Later, when you finish your studies, I'll have no objection. I have always believed that a young man should see the world. Remember that your mother is only now recovering from the shocks she suffered. No, no, no.'

Martin shrugged and, with his hands in the pockets of his shorts, wandered off along the trail that led to the waterfall. He knew his mother was waiting for him there by the larch-shaded grotto: that was the agreement. She would go out walking very early and, not wanting to wake Martin, would leave him a note: 'By the grotto at ten' or 'Near the spring on the road to Ste Claire.' However, even though he knew she was waiting, Martin suddenly changed direction, left the trail and started upward across the heather.

Twenty-One

The slope became steeper and steeper, the sun was scorching, flies kept trying to get at his lips and eyes. Upon reaching a circular birch grove, he rested, smoked a cigarette, pulled up his sports stockings tighter, and resumed the ascent, munching on a birch leaf. The heather was crunchy and slippery. Now and then he caught his foot in the low thornbushes. At the top of the incline gleamed an amassment of rocks, between which ran a crevice. It fanned out toward him, and was filled with fine debris that came into motion as soon as he stepped upon it. This way could not serve to reach the peak, so Martin began to climb straight up the face of the rocks. Occasionally some root or moss patch at which he clutched detached itself from the stone, and feverishly he would seek a support with his foot, or else it was his foothold that gave, and he would be left hanging by his hands and have to pull himself painfully up. The peak was almost within reach when he suddenly slipped and started to slither down, clutching at shrublets of rough flowers; he lost his grip, felt a burning pain as his knee scraped against the rock, attempted to embrace the steepness that was gliding up and past him – and abruptly salvation bumped against his soles.

He found himself on a cornice; to the right it narrowed and merged with the cliff, but to the left it could be seen going on for a few yards before turning a corner – what then happened to it remained unknown. His ledge recalled the stage setting of nightmares. He stood, pressing closely to the rock against which he had bruised his chest on the way down, and dared not unglue himself from it. With an effort, glancing over his shoulder, he saw under his heels a prodigious precipice, a sun-illumined abyss with, in its depths, several outdistanced firs running in panic after the descending forest, and still further down the steep meadows and the tiny, ivory white hotel. 'So that's what its message was,' thought Martin with a superstitious shiver. 'I'll fall, I'll perish, that's what it's watching for. That – that –' It was equally terrifying to look down the precipice or up the vertical cliff above him. A width of bookshelf underfoot and a knobby spot in the rock wall to which his fingers clung was all that Martin retained of the solid world to which he was used.

He experienced faintness, dizziness, sickening fear, yet at the same time he observed himself from the outside, noting with odd lucidity his open-collared flannel shirt, his clumsy clinging position on the ledge, the thistle ball that had attached itself to his stocking and the entirely black butterfly that fluttered by with enviable casualness like a quiet little devil and began to rise along the rock face; and though there was no one around to make showing off worthwhile, Martin began to whistle; then he vowed to himself that he would pay no attention to the invitation of the abyss and began to displace his feet slowly, as he moved to the left. Ah, if only one could see what the cornice did after it turned that corner! The rock wall seemed to push against his breast, crowding him toward the precipice, whose impatient breath he felt on his back. His nails dug into the stone, the stone was hot, the tufts of flowers were of an intense blue, a lizard traced a quick incomplete figure eight and froze again, flies tickled his face. Every now and then he had to stop, and he heard himself complaining to himself – I cannot any more, I cannot – and when he caught himself doing that, he began to produce with his lips a rudimentary tune, a fox-trot or the 'Marseillaise,' then moistened his lips and, again complaining, resumed his sidewise progress. There remained only a yard or so to the turn when something began to spill from under his shoe sole; he could not help turning his head, and in the sunny void the white spot of the hotel started to rotate slowly. Martin closed his eyes and stopped short, but then he controlled his nausea and began to move again. At the turn he said rapidly, 'Please, I beg you, please,' and his request was immediately granted: beyond the turn the shelf widened, became a platform, and beyond was the already familiar scree and the heather-covered slope.

There he caught his breath. His entire body ached and vibrated. His nails had become dark red as if he had been picking strawberries; the knee he had barked was smarting. The danger that he had just experienced seemed to him far more real than the one into which he had blundered in the Crimea. Now he felt proud of himself, but this pride suddenly lost all its flavor when Martin asked himself if he could again perform, this time deliberately, what he had performed accidentally. In a few days he gave in, climbed again up the heather-grown steeps, but when he reached the platform from where the cornice started, he could not make himself step on it. This angered him, he tried to incite himself, he taunted his own cowardice, imagined Darwin looking at him with a mocking smile – stood there for a while, then shrugged and turned back, doing his best to ignore the ruffian who was raging within him. Again and again, to the very end of vacation, that rowdy made irruptions and would riot so offensively that finally Martin decided not to walk up that mountain any more to avoid being tormented by the sight of the narrow shelf which he dared not tread.

In October he returned to England in a stinging mood of self-depreciation. Straight from the station he went to see the Zilanovs. The housemaid who opened the door was new, and this was unpleasant, making it seem he had come to a strange house. Sonia, dressed all in black, stood in the middle of the living room smoothing her temples, then proffered her hand, in a straight sharp gesture as was her wont. With amazement Martin realized that not once during the summer had he thought of her, not once had he written, but that nonetheless it would have been worthwhile to travel a long way, if only for the sake of that embarrassment that he now felt as he looked at her pale sullen face. 'You probably have not heard of our grief,' said Sonia and in an oddly cross tone related that the week before, on the same day, they had received information that Nelly had died in childbirth in Brindisi, and her husband had been killed in the Crimea. 'Ah, then he left Yudenich to join Wrangel,' said Martin lamely, and with exceptional clarity visualized that husband of Nelly's whom he had seen but once, and Nelly herself who at the time had seemed to him dull and insipid, and now had gone and died in Brindisi. 'Mother is in a terrible state,' said Sonia leafing through a book that lay abandoned on the sofa. 'And father's been traveling in secret to God knows what places, possibly as far as Kiev,' she added after a while and, separating several pages with a thumb, allowed them to mill rapidly. Martin seated himself in an armchair rubbing his hands. Sonia slapped the book closed and said raising her face: 'Darwin has been perfect, simply perfect. He was a tremendous help to us. So touching, and not one wrong word. Are you staying for the night?' 'Actually,' said Martin, 'I could go up to

Cambridge tonight. It would surely bother you to put me up, and so forth.' 'No, what nonsense,' said Sonia and sighed. The sound of the dinner gong reached them from downstairs, and this clashed with the atmosphere of mourning that pervaded the house. Martin went to wash his hands. As he entered the lavatory he collided with Zilanov who did not make it a custom to lock the door. He glanced at Martin out of lusterless eyes while unhurriedly buttoning his fly. 'Accept my deepest sympathy,' muttered Martin and stupidly clicked his heels. Zilanov lowered his lids in sign of gratitude and shook hands with Martin. The fact that all this occurred on the threshold of the lavatory underlined the absurdity of the handclasp and the ready-made words. Zilanov slowly walked off, his thighs twitching as if he were shaking down something between them. Martin's nose, as its owner noticed in the mirror, was wrinkled in anguish. 'After all I did have to say something,' he muttered through his teeth.

Dinner proceeded in silence if one discounted the old-fashioned slurp with which Zilanov ate his soup. Irina and her mother were at an out-of-town sanitarium, and Mrs Zilanov did not come down, so that they dined just the three of them. The telephone rang, and Zilanov marched to his study chewing on the way. 'I know you don't like mutton,' Sonia said softly, and Martin silently smiled a slightly muted smile. 'Iogolevich will drop in,' said Zilanov resuming his place at the table. 'He has just returned from St Petersburg. Pass me the

mustard. He says he crossed the border wrapped in a shroud.'
'Less conspicuous on snow,' said Martin a moment later to
keep up the conversation, but no conversation ensued.

Twenty-Two

Aleksandr Naumovich Iogolevich turned out to be a fat
bearded man in a knit gray waistcoat and shabby black suit,
with dandruff on his shoulders. The side-ears of his black
prunella boots stuck out, and the ankle ties of his underpants
glimmered through his sagging socks. The way he completely
ignored inanimate objects (such as the arm support of the
chair which he mechanically kept tapping with his hand, or
the thick book on which he sat down by mistake, then took
out from under him without a smile, and put aside without
glancing at it) pointed to a secret affinity with Zilanov. Nodding his large frizzly head, he only responded with a short
clucking of his tongue to the news of his friend's bereave-
ment; then quickly passing the palm of his hand down
his coarsely fashioned face, without any preliminaries,
launched into his story. It was obvious that the only thing
that filled his consciousness, the only thing that preoccupied
and affected him, was Russia's woe, and with trepidation

Martin pictured to himself what would happen were he to interrupt Iogolevich's stormy tense speech by telling the anecdote about the student and his girl cousin. Sonia sat at a distance, propping her elbows on her knees, and her face on her palms. Zilanov listened, one finger stretched along his nose, occasionally removing the finger to say: 'Excuse me, Aleksandr Naumovich, but, for instance, when you mention –' and Iogolevich would stop for an instant, blink, then resume his tale, with a constant remarkable motion of his rough, ceaselessly changing features – his shaggy brows, the nostrils of his pear-shaped nose, the folds of his bearded cheeks – nor did his hands with black hair on the phalanges rest for one second: they lifted something, tossed it upward, seized it again, strewed it in every direction, and all the while, hotly, in a rolling delivery, he spoke of executions, of famine, of St Petersburg turned into a desert, of the regime's malice, stupidity and vulgarity. He left after midnight and suddenly turning around on the threshold asked how much *kaloshi* (rubbers) cost in London. After the door had closed, Zilanov remained standing, lost in thought, then went upstairs to his wife. The doorbell rang three minutes later: Iogolevich had come back; it turned out that he did not know the way to the tube station. Martin offered to take him there and while striding at Iogolevich's side cast about in distress for a subject of conversation. 'Remind your father,' said Iogolevich abruptly, 'I quite forgot to tell him that Maksimov is impatient to receive the article on his impressions from visiting the Southern Volunteer Army. He will know what it's about. Just tell him. Maksimov has written to your father before.' 'Certainly,' answered Martin; was about to add something but checked himself.

He slowly returned to the house, imagining now Iogolevich crossing the border wrapped in a white sheet, then Zilanov with his briefcase at some demolished railroad station under the starry Ukrainian sky. All was silent in the house when he went up the stairs. He kept yawning while he undressed. He felt an odd, vague anguish. The lamp on the bedside table burned bright, the wide bed looked white and soft, his dressing gown of lustrous blue silk had been taken out of his bag by the maid and was slung invitingly over the armchair. He noticed with a shock of vexation that he had forgotten to bring up from the living room a book he had set his heart on there, and had been looking forward to reading in bed. He pulled on his dressing gown and walked down to the second floor. The book was a dilapidated volume of Chekhov's stories. He found it – for some reason it was lying on the floor – and returned to his bedroom. But the heartache did not dissipate, although Martin was one of those people for whom a good book before sleep is something to look forward to all day. Such a person, upon happening to recall, amidst routine occupations, that on his bedside table a book is waiting for him, in perfect safety, feels a surge of inexpressible happiness. Martin began to read, choosing the story he knew, loved, could read through one hundred times in a row: 'The Lady with the Little Dog.' Ah, how nicely she lost that lorgnette in the crowd on the pier at Yalta! And here, without any apparent reason, he realized what it was that disturbed him so. Only a year before, in this room, Nelly had slept, and now she was dead.

'What nonsense,' muttered Martin, and tried to resume his reading, but this proved impossible. He recalled those nights of long ago when he waited for the ghost of his father to make a scratching sound in a corner. Martin's heart started to beat fast; the bed became hot and uncomfortable. He imagined how he himself would be dying some day, and felt as if the ceiling were coming down on him slowly and inexorably. Something began to drum rapidly in the darker part of the room, and his heart missed a beat. But it was merely water that had been spilled on the washstand and was now dripping onto the linoleum. Yet how strange: if ghosts exist, then all is well for it proves that souls *can* move after death – why then is it so frightening? 'How shall I be dying myself?' thought Martin and began to pass mentally in review several varieties of death. He saw himself placed against a wall, standing there with as much air in his lungs as he could inhale, waiting for the volley of rifle shots and recollecting with wild despair this present minute, this bright room, the soft night, unconcern, safety. Then there were illnesses, dreadful illnesses rending one's entrails. Or it might be a railway accident. Or, simply, the serene slowing down of old age, death in one's sleep. Or else, a dark wood and pursuit. 'Nonsense,' thought Martin. 'I have plenty of time in reserve. Besides, every year represents a whole epoch. Why worry? Yet perhaps Nelly is here, and is seeing me now? Perhaps – now, this instant – she will give me a sign?' He looked at his watch, it was close to two. The tension was becoming unbearable. That silence seemed to be waiting: the distant hoot of an automobile horn would have been rapture. The level of silence kept rising, and all at once poured over the brim: someone on tiptoe was coming barefoot along the passage.

'Are you asleep?' came the whispered question through the door, and for an instant a constriction in his throat prevented Martin from replying. She slipped in, she softly shifted from tiptoe to heel. She wore yellow pajamas, her black hair was rumpled. Thus she remained standing for a moment or two blinking through matted lashes. Martin, sitting up in bed, grinned foolishly. 'Sleep is utterly out of the question,' said Sonia in an odd voice. 'I'm jumpy. I'm scared. And on top of it, those horrors he talked about!' 'Why are you barefoot, Sonia? Want my slippers?' She shook her head, pouting pensively, then tossed her hair and cast a vague glance at Martin's bed. '*Allez hop*,' said Martin tapping the blanket at the foot of the bed. She climbed onto the bed, first kneeled upon it, then moved about slowly, and finally curled up on the blanket in the corner formed by footboard and wall. Martin pulled out the pillow from under his head to place it behind her back. '*Spasibo* (thanks),' she said quite soundlessly: the outline of the word could only be guessed from the movement of her plump pale lips. 'Are you comfortable?' asked Martin nervously, pulling up his knees so as not to be in her way, but presently he bent forward again, and, taking his dressing gown from the adjacent chair, covered her bare feet with it. 'Give me a cigarette,' she asked after a minute of silence. A waft of delicate warmth emanated from her; a thin chainlet of gold surrounded her adorable neck. She inhaled, slitting her eyes, and handed the cigarette to Martin. 'Too strong,' she said sadly. 'What did you do this summer?' inquired Martin struggling to subdue a dark something that was quite mad and unthinkable and that even induced a febrile chill. 'Nothing in particular. We went to Brighton.' She sighed and added, 'I flew in a hydroplane.' 'And I very nearly got killed,' said Martin. 'Yes, yes, very nearly. High up in the mountains. Rock climbing. Lost my hold. Saved by a miracle.' Sonia smiled dimly and said, 'You know, Martin, she always maintained that the most important thing in life was always to do one's duty and think of nothing else. It's a very deep thought, isn't it?' 'Yes, possibly,' Martin replied, shoving the unfinished cigarette into the ashtray with an uncertain hand. 'Possibly. But sometimes a bit boring.' 'Oh, no, not at all – You don't understand, she didn't mean work or job, but a kind of – well, the kind of thing which has an inner importance.' She paused, and Martin saw her shiver in her light little pajamas. 'You are cold,' he said. 'Yes, I think I am. And *that* was the duty to be performed, but some – I, for instance – do not have any such thing inside.' 'Sonia,' said Martin, 'maybe you'd like –?' He turned back a corner of the blanket, and she rose to a kneeling position and moved slowly in his direction. 'And it seems to me,' she continued as she crawled under the bedclothes, which Martin, hearing nothing of what she was saying, awkwardly pulled over her and himself, 'It seems to me that lots of people do not know this, and because they don't –' With a deep intake of breath Martin embraced her and attached his lips to her cheek. Sonia seized him by the wrist, and forthwith rolled out of the bed. 'Good God,' she said, 'Good God!' Her dark eyes glistened with tears, and within an instant her whole face was wet, with bright long streaks creeping down her cheeks. 'Oh please, please don't – I merely – oh I don't know, oh Sonia –' Martin kept muttering, not daring to touch her, losing his head at the thought that she might start screaming and arouse the entire household. 'How couldn't you see,' she said plaintively, 'how couldn't you see that this was the way I used to come to Nelly, and we talked and talked till dawn.' She turned away and left the room, crying. Martin sat in a chaos of bedclothes with a helplessly ingratiating expression on his face. She closed the door behind her, but reopened it, and introduced her head: 'Idiot,' she said in a perfectly calm, businesslike manner, whereupon the patter of her bare feet receded along the passage.

For some time Martin kept staring at the white door. Then he put out the light and attempted to sleep. This appeared to be hopeless. He reflected that at daybreak he must dress, get packed, and noiselessly leave the house to go straight to the station; unfortunately he fell asleep amidst those meditations and woke up only at a quarter past nine. 'Maybe it was all a dream?' he said to himself with some hope, but at once shook his head and with a pang of excruciating shame wondered how he would meet Sonia again after this. He had an unfortunate morning: when he rushed in to take his bath, there, at the washstand, was Zilanov, his short legs in black trousers set wide apart, his torso in a thick flannel undershirt bent forward, dousing his face over the basin, rubbing cheeks and forehead until the skin squeaked, snorting under the spouting faucet, pressing each nostril in turn, fiercely relieving his nose, and expectorating. 'Come in, come in, I'm through,' he exclaimed and, blinded by water, dripping, and holding his arms in the semblance of short wings, he dashed to his bedroom where he preferred to keep his towel.

Then, a little later, as Martin was on his way downstairs to the dining room to drink his cup of hemlock, he ran into Mrs Zilanov: her face, livid and swollen, looked awful, and he felt dreadfully embarrassed, not daring to utter stock words of compassion, but not knowing any others. In acknowledgment of his silence she put her arms about him, kissed him on the forehead – and, with a hopeless wave of her hand, walked away, to the bottom of the corridor, where her husband mentioned to her something about a passport with a totally unexpected tender break in his voice of which he had seemed wholly incapable. Sonia met Martin in the dining room, and the first thing she said to him was, 'I forgive you, because you are Swiss, and "cretin" is a Swiss word, jot that down.' Martin had planned to explain that he had had no wicked intentions, which on the whole was the truth, that all he had wanted to do was to lie close to her and keep kissing her cheek – but Sonia looked so cross and cheerless in her black dress that he thought it best to say nothing. 'Papa is leaving today for Brindisi,' she said, 'thank goodness they did give him a visa at last.' She contemplated with disapproval the poorly contained greed with which Martin, who always felt ravenous in the morning, was devouring his fried eggs. Martin told himself there was no point in hanging around, the day promised to be topsy-turvy, the seeing-off ritual and all the rest. 'Darwin has telephoned,' added Sonia.

Twenty-Three

Darwin made his appearance with comedy precision —
immediately in the wake of Sonia's remark, as if he had been
waiting in the wings. The seaside sun had given him a roast-
beef complexion and he wore a marvelous pale-gray suit.
Sonia's greeting struck Martin as a little too languorous.
Martin himself was grasped, hit on the shoulder, hit in the
ribs, and asked repeatedly why he had not phoned. Indeed,
the usually indolent Darwin displayed that day unprecedented energy. At Liverpool Street station he took a stranger's
trunk from the porter to carry it balanced on his nape. In
the Pullman, midway between London and Cambridge, after
a glance at his wristwatch, he called the conductor, handed
him a banknote, and solemnly pulled the emergency cord.
The train groaned agonizingly and came to a stop, while
Darwin smugly explained to everybody at large that he
was born exactly twenty-four years ago. A day later, one of
the livelier newspapers had a note about it conspicuously
headlined: 'YOUNG AUTHOR STOPS TRAIN ON BIRTHDAY.'
Meanwhile Darwin had been summoned by his tutor whom
he was now trying to hypnotize with a detailed report on

the leech commerce, what were the better sorts and how they were bred.

The same damp greeted Martin in his bedroom; there was the same interchime of towers, and in the same old way Vadim would tumble in with a sample of the same rhymed Russian alphabet consisting of couplets, the first verse containing a didactic item of general interest ('Armenians like to fish and hunt' or 'Balloons are never made of brick') and the second, equally didactic, beginning with the same letter, but quite unrelated to the first line and considerably more improper.

Archibald Moon, however, although in a sense the same, seemed to be different: Martin could not manage to recapture the old enchantment. Moon told him that during the summer he had completed as many as sixteen new pages of his history of Russia, fully sixteen pages; he explained that he was able to accomplish so much because he devoted to work every hour of the long summer day, and as he said it he made with his fingers a gesture representing the ripple and plasticity of every phrase that he had nursed to life; in that gesture Martin seemed to discern something extremely depraved, and to listen to Moon's rich speech was like chewing thick elastic Turkish Delight powdered with confectioner's sugar. For the first time Martin felt personally offended by Moon's treating Russia as an inanimate article of luxury. When he confided this to Darwin, Darwin laughed and nodded, and said that Moon was like that because of his addiction to uranism. This called for closer attention, and after one occasion when Moon without any excuse stroked Martin's hair with trembling fingers, Martin stopped dropping in, and would noiselessly climb out of his window and down a rainpipe into the lane whenever there came that yearnful, lonesome knock on the door of his room. He nevertheless continued to attend Moon's lectures, but now in studying Russian literature he endeavored to efface from his hearing Moon's intonations, which kept pursuing him, especially in the rhythm of verse. He ended by switching to another teacher, grand old Professor Stephens, whose interpretation of Pushkin and Tolstoy was as honest as it was ponderous, and who spoke Russian in gasps and barks with the frequent addition of Serbian and Polish. Still it took time to shake off Archibald Moon for good. He would recall with involuntary admiration the artistry of Moon's discourse, but the moment after would perceive as a vivid reality the picture of Moon carrying away to his rooms a sarcophagus with Russia's mummy. In the end Martin did get entirely rid of Moon, while appropriating this and that element, but converting it into his own property, and then, at last, the voices of the Russian muses began to sound in complete purity. Moon would occasionally be seen in the street in the company of a beautiful chubby youth with abundant blond hair who impersonated girls in the university productions of

Shakespeare's plays, whereat Moon would melt with tender emotion in an orchestra seat, and together with other amateurs try to shush Darwin, who, sprawling in feigned rapture, exploded with clownish applause at the wrong moments.

But Martin had some unsettled accounts with Darwin, too. It happened sometimes that Darwin went to London alone, and Martin spent Saturday night, till daybreak, till a total exhaustion of coal, sitting in the sepulchral draft of the fireplace and persistently, savagely, as if pressing upon an aching tooth, imagining Sonia and Darwin in a dark automobile. Once, when unable to stand it any longer, he set off for London, to attend a dance to which he had not been invited, and paced the halls under the impression that he looked very pale and stern, but then happened to catch in a mirror the reflection of his pink round face with a bump on the forehead – the result of his diving for the ball under rushing feet the day before. Presently, they arrived: Sonia costumed as a gypsy girl, seemingly having forgotten that not quite four months had elapsed since her sister's death; and Darwin dressed as an Englishman out of a Continental novel: a large-checked suit, a tropical helmet with a bandana to protect the nape from the Pompeiian sun, a Baedeker under his arm, and carroty sidewhiskers. There was music, there was *serpentin*, there was a snowstorm of confetti, and for one intoxicating moment Martin felt he was taking part in a subtle drama of masks. The music stopped. Ignoring

Darwin's obvious desire to be alone with Sonia, Martin climbed into the same taxicab with them. In a chance beam of light that penetrated the dark car he thought he noticed Darwin and Sonia holding hands and tried wretchedly to convince himself that it had only been a trick of shimmer and shadow. Even more depressing were the occasions when Sonia came to Cambridge: Martin felt unwanted, imagined they kept trying to shed him. His second summer in Switzerland was marked by his beating one of the best Swiss tennis players – but what did Sonia care about his triumphs in tennis, boxing, or soccer? Sometimes Martin visualized in a picturesque daydream how he would return to Sonia from fighting in the Crimea, and the word 'cavalry' thundered by, the wind whistled, clods of black mud flew in one's face – attack, attack! – tac-a-tac of the horseshoes, anapaest of the gallop. But it was too late now, fighting in the Crimea had ceased long ago, long gone was the day Nelly's husband riding full speed at an enemy machine gun came nearer and nearer to it until he inadvertently swept across the invisible line into a region still tingling with echoes of earthly life, but where there are neither machine guns nor cavalry attacks. 'Always remiss, always remiss,' grumbled Martin at himself gloomily, and, with the piercing sense that something had been missed forever, kept again and again imagining the ribbon of St George, the light wound in the left shoulder (it had to be the left), and Sonia coming to meet him at Victoria station. He was irritated by his mother's tender smile, by the words she could not withhold: 'Now you see it was all for nothing, and you would have perished for nothing. Nelly's husband – that's a different matter, he was a real professional soldier, such people cannot exist without a war, and he died the way he wanted to die. But those thousands of youngsters mowed down –' However, in the presence of foreigners, she would hotly insist on the necessity of continued military action – especially now that all was over, and there was nothing there that could lure her son. In later years, when she remembered her relief and her calm, Mrs Edelweiss groaned aloud – oh yes, she could have preserved him, should have so easily dismissed her forebodings, been more observant, been always on the lookout – and who knows? it might have been better had he really joined the White Army, been wounded, caught the typhus, and, at this price, got rid once and for all of the attraction that danger has for young boys. But why harbor such thoughts, why give in to despair? More courage, more faith. People do get lost, and then come back. A rumor may circulate that someone has been seized at the border and shot as a spy, yet, all at once, there he is, alive, with his familiar laugh and deep voice, right there, in the entry hall. And if Henry again –

Twenty-Four

Not only his mother's fleeting smile of content had irritated Martin that second summer; there was something else besides, something far more unpleasant. Life at the chalet seemed to him strangely changed, as if moving on tiptoe, with bated breath. It was odd to hear Uncle Henry call Mrs Edelweiss not 'Sophie,' as before, but '*chère amie*'; and she, too, addressed him now and then as 'my dear.' A new softness, an increased welling of sentiment, showed in him; his voice had grown lower, his movements gentler; one's praise for the soup or the joint was now enough to veil his eyes with moisture. The cult around Martin's father's memory had acquired a tinge of unbearable mysticism; Mrs Edelweiss was more than ever conscious of her guilt before her late husband, while Uncle Henry seemed to be tracing for her a difficult but sure road of expiation when remarking how happy Serge's spirit must be to see her in his cousin's house; once he even produced a nail file and with agreeable melancholy began to pass it back and forth over his nails, but at this Mrs Edelweiss could not contain herself and emitted a hollow laugh, which unexpectedly became a fit of hysterics.

In his haste to help, Martin opened the kitchen faucet so briskly that the water splashed his white flannels.

Not infrequently did he observe his mother as she walked in the garden leaning wearily on Henry's arm, or as she fetched for Henry a bedtime cup of fragrant linden tea. It was all depressing, embarrassing, and strange. Just before his departure for Cambridge she obviously wanted to break the news to him, but she found it as embarrassing as he; she faltered and only said that she perhaps would soon write to him of an important event; and indeed, that winter, Martin received a letter, not from her but from his uncle, who on six pages informed him in a flowing hand in bombastic tear-jerking language that he was marrying Martin's mother – a very modest ceremony at the village church – and only upon reaching the postscriptum Martin realized that the wedding had already taken place and mentally thanked his mother for having scheduled this grim celebration to coincide with his absence. At the same time he kept asking himself how he would face her again, what they would talk about, and would he manage to forgive her the betrayal. For no matter how you approached it, it was, beyond any doubt, a betrayal of his father's memory. Furthermore, he was plagued by the thought that for stepfather he had Uncle Henry of the fluffy whiskers and limited wits. Martin arrived for Christmas, his mother could not stop hugging him and weeping, as if forgetting, to oblige Uncle Henry, her usual restraint; and there was simply nowhere to hide from the soft emotion in his stepfather's kindly eyes and from the solemnity of that little cough of his.

In general, during his last university year, Martin was made aware again and again of the presence of some malevolent force obstinately trying to convince him that life was not at all the easy happy thing he had imagined. Sonia's existence, the constant gratuitous attention it extorted from his soul, her visits that only tormented him, the derisive tone of the banter that had become established between them, all of it was extremely exhausting. That unrequited love did not prevent him, however, from running after every pretty girl, and tingling with bliss when, for instance, Rose, the goddess of the tearoom, consented to go with him for a motorcar drive. In that shop, much frequented by students, you could buy pastry of every imaginable color: bright-red with speckles of cream that made them look like deadly amanitas; purplish-blue, like violet-scented soap; and glossy-black, Negroid, with a white soul. One went on devouring cake after cake till one's innards got glued together, in the ever-present hope of at last discovering something really good. With a dusky flush on her velvety cheeks and a liquid gaze, clad in a black dress with a soubrette's little apron, Rose tripped rapidly back and forth through the room, nimbly evading collision with the other waitress navigating also at full speed. Martin immediately noticed Rose's thick-fingered

red hand not in the least embellished by the tiny star of a cheap ring, and decided wisely never again to look at her hands but to concentrate on her long eyelashes which she lowered so beautifully while writing out a check. One day, while drinking rich sweet chocolate, he passed her a note, and that same evening walked with her in the rain. On Saturday he hired the usual ramshackle limousine and spent the night with her at an ancient inn, some fifty kilometers from Cambridge. He felt somewhat taken aback, though flattered, when she said it was her first affair; she made love stormily, clumsily, rustically, and Martin, who had expected to find in her a frivolous and experienced siren, felt so disconcerted that he turned to Darwin for advice. 'You'll get kicked out of the university,' calmly said Darwin. 'Nonsense,' retorted Martin frowning. Yet when, three weeks later, Rose, as she put down a cup of chocolate before him, informed him in a quick whisper that she was pregnant, it seemed as if that meteorite which ordinarily lands somewhere in the Gobi desert had fallen straight upon him.

'Congratulations,' said Darwin; after which, not without artistry, he began to delineate the fate of a sinful girl with a babe in her belly. 'And *you* will be sent down. That's a fact.' 'No one will know, I shall straighten out everything,' stammered Martin. 'It's hopeless,' said Darwin.

Martin suddenly lost his temper and walked out, banging the door. He ran out into the lane, and nearly crashed under the impact of a large pillow that his friend had skillfully aimed at his head from the second-floor window. When Martin reached the corner and glanced back, he saw Darwin come out, pick up the pillow, shake it, and return to the house. 'Cruel brute,' muttered Martin and went straight to the tearoom. It was crowded. Bright-eyed, dusky Rose flitted from table to table, tripped along with a tray, or, tenderly moistening her pencil with the tip of her tongue, wrote out a check. He also wrote some lines on a leaf from his agenda, namely 'I want you to marry me. Martin Edelweiss.' He thrust the leaflet into her hideous hand; then he left, spent a couple of hours roaming about the town, returned home, lay down on the sofa, and remained lying until nightfall.

Twenty-Five

At nightfall Darwin dropped in, magnificently flung off his gown, sat down by the fire, and immediately began livening up the coals with the poker. Martin lay in silence, full of self-pity, again and again imagining himself coming out of the church with Rose, who was wearing white kid gloves, pulled on with difficulty. 'Sonia is coming alone tomorrow,' said Darwin unconcernedly. 'Her mother's got the flu, a bad case of flu.' Martin said nothing, but visualized with a stab of excitement tomorrow's soccer match. 'How are you going to play, though?' said Darwin. 'That, of course, is the question.' Martin remained silent. 'Badly, probably,' Darwin resumed. 'Goalkeeping needs presence of mind, and you're in one hell of a state. You know, I just had a chat with that woman.'

Silence. The tower chimes rang across the town.

'A poetic nature, inclined to fantasy,' Darwin went on a minute later. 'She's no more pregnant than, for instance, I am. Want to bet a fiver that I can twist this poker into a monogram?' (Martin lay like a dead man.) 'I interpret your silence as assent. Let's see.'

He grunted once, twice. 'No, can't do it today. The money's yours. I paid exactly five pounds for your stupid declaration. We're even, and everything's in order.'

Martin was silent, only his heart had begun beating violently.

'But,' said Darwin, 'just remember, if you ever set foot in that bad and expensive pastry shop again, you'll get kicked out of the university. That lass can be impregnated by a mere handshake, don't forget that.'

Darwin got up and stretched. 'You're not very talkative, chum. I must confess that you and your hetaera have somehow marred tomorrow for me – I mean the morrow one has in one's mind.'

He went out, quietly closing the door behind him, and Martin had three simultaneous thoughts: that he was terribly hungry, that you couldn't find another friend like that, and that tomorrow this friend would propose. At that moment he joyously and ardently wished that Sonia would accept, but the moment passed, and next morning, when he and Darwin met Sonia at the station, he felt the old familiar, dreary jealousy (his only, rather pathetic advantage over Darwin was his recent, wine-toasted transition to the intimate second-person singular, the Russian 'ty,' with Sonia; in England that form had died out with the bowmen; nonetheless Darwin had also drunk *auf Bruderschaft* with her, and had addressed her all evening with the archaic 'thou').

'Hello, flower,' she said casually to Martin, alluding to his botanical last name; then, at once turning away, she began telling Darwin things that might have interested Martin too.

'What's so attractive about her, after all?' he thought for the thousandth time. 'All right, she has those dimples, that pale complexion – that's not enough. Her eyes are so-so, gypsy-esque, and her teeth are uneven. And her lips are so thick, so glossy – if one could just stop them, shut them up with a kiss. And she thinks she looks English in that blue suit and those low-heeled shoes. Don't you people see she's just a short little thing?' Who these 'people' were Martin did not know; and they would have had a difficult time passing judgment, for, as soon as Martin achieved an attitude of indifference toward

Sonia, he would suddenly notice what a graceful back she had, how she tilted her head – and her slanted eyes ran across him with a swift chill, and the undercurrent of mirth in her speech bathed the base of each phrase, until, abruptly, her laughter burst into the open; and she would stress her words with a shake of her tightly furled umbrella, which she held not by its handle but by its body of silk. And, ambling despondently, now behind them, now alongside, on the cobbled pavement (it was impossible for three people to walk abreast on the sidewalk because of the resilient cushion of air surrounding Darwin's massive form, and because of Sonia's short, weaving steps) Martin reflected that, adding up all the random hours he had spent with her, here and in London, the total would be no more than a month and a half of constant companionship – and to think that he had first met her more than two years ago, and that now the third, and last, Cambridge winter was already on the wane, yet he really could not tell what sort of person she was, and whether or not she was in love with Darwin, and how she would react if Darwin were to tell her about yesterday's experience, and whether she had spoken to anyone about that night, that miserable, yet by now oddly ravishing and not in the least shameful night when, shivering, barefoot, in her skimpy yellow pajamas, she had been borne ashore by a wave of silence and gently deposited on his blanket.

They reached their destination. Sonia washed her hands in Darwin's bedroom. She took out her puff, blew on it, and powdered her face. The luncheon table was laid for five. Vadim had of course been invited, but Archibald Moon had long since disappeared from their circle of friends, and it was even a little strange to recall that he had once been considered a desirable guest. The fifth member of the party was a slender, snub-nosed, blond youth, not handsome but nicely built and somewhat eccentrically dressed. He had the fine, elongated hands with which popular novelists endow artistic individuals, yet he was neither poet nor painter, and the graceful, delicate fluttery something about him, along with his knowledge of French and Italian and slightly un-British but very elegant manners, was attributed at Cambridge to his father's Florentine origin. Teddy, kindly, ethereal Teddy, belonged to the Roman Church, liked climbing and skiing in the Alps, was a good oarsman, played the old royal game of court tennis, and, while he knew how to be very tender with women, carried chastity to a ridiculous extreme (a year later, however, he announced a certain change in a note to Martin from Paris: 'Yesterday,' he wrote. 'I got myself a wench, quite clean, and all that.' Underneath the studied vulgarity there was something sorrowful and nervous about that statement. Martin recalled his sudden fits of melancholy and self-castigation, his love for Leopardi and for snow, and how he had furiously smashed a perfectly innocent Etruscan vase upon receiving an insufficiently brilliant grade in an examination).

'What fun to stare when a great big bear' – and Sonia echoed Vadim, who had long since become chummy with her (but prudently omitted the punch line after 'tiny bitch') – '*vedyot za ruchku malen'kuyu suchku*,' while Teddy, who did not understand Russian, cocked his head to inquire, 'What does "*malenxus*" mean?'

Whereupon everybody laughed, and no one would explain, and he began addressing Sonia thus, 'Have some more peas, *malenxus*.'

'Jittery, jittery?' Vadim asked Martin.

'Don't be silly,' replied Martin. 'I didn't sleep well last night and that means muffing today. They have three international-class players, and we have only two.'

'Can't stand soccer,' declared Teddy. Darwin upheld him. Both were Etonians, and Eton had its own special ball game in place of soccer.

Twenty-Six

Martin was in fact jittery, and considerably so. He kept goal for Trinity; his team, after a keen struggle, had reached the finals, and that day was to meet St John's for the Cambridge University championship. Martin was proud that he, a foreigner, had made the first team, and, for his brilliant play, had qualified for the title of College Blue entitling him to wear a splendid light-blue blazer. He would now recollect with pleasant amazement his childhood days in Russia when, curled up in a soft hollow of the nursery night, and having abandoned himself to reveries that would imperceptibly bear him off into sleep, he would see himself as a crack foot-baller. It was enough for him to close his eyes and picture a soccer field or, say, the long, brown, diaphragm-joined cars of an express that he was driving himself, and his mind would gradually catch the rhythm, grow blissfully serene, be cleansed, as it were, and, sleek and oiled, slip into obliv-ion. Instead of a train, going full tilt (gliding through bright-yellow birch forests, then above foreign cities, across bridges that spanned streets, and on, southward, through tunnels which had their own sudden daybreak, and along the shore of a dazzling sea), it might be an airplane, a race car, a bobsleigh, taking a sharp turn in a whirl of flying snow, or else simply a forest path along which you run and run. As he reminisced, Martin noted a certain peculiarity about his life: the property that his reveries had of crystallizing and mutating into reality, as previously they had mutated into sleep. This seemed to him a guarantee that the new series of reveries he had recently evolved – about an illegal, clandes-tine expedition – would also grow solid and be filled with life, as his dreams about soccer matches had grown solid and incarnate, those dreams in which he used to luxuriate so lengthily, so artfully, when, afraid to reach the delicious essence too quickly, he would dwell in detail on the pre-game preparations – pulling on the stockings with the colored tops, putting on the black shorts, tying the laces of the robust boots.

He grunted and unbent. It was warm changing near his fireplace, and this helped in a way to dilute the tremor of his excitement. The celestial blazer buttoned snugly over the white V-necked sweater. How worn were his goalkeeper's gloves! There; he was ready. His clothes lay all around where he had discarded them. He gathered everything up and carried it into the bedroom. Compared with the warmth of the woolen sweater his bare-kneed legs felt wonderfully cool in their roomy, light shorts. 'Whew!' he said as he entered Darwin's room, 'you can't say I didn't change fast.'

'Let's go,' said Sonia, getting up from the sofa.

Teddy gave her a beseeching look. 'I beg a thousand pardons,' he implored, 'but, believe me, I can't come with you, I am expected elsewhere.'

He left. Vadim also left, promising to cycle over to the playing fields later.

'Maybe it really isn't so interesting after all,' said Sonia, addressing Darwin. 'Perhaps we might as well not go?'

'No, no, we'll go by all means,' said Darwin with a smile, giving Martin a squeeze on the shoulder. As the three of them set out along the street, Martin noticed that Sonia never looked at him once, and yet this was the first time he had appeared before her in soccer array.

'Let's walk a little faster,' he said, 'or else we may be late.'

'No great harm in that,' said Sonia, stopping in front of a shop window.

'All right, I'll go on ahead,' said Martin and, thumping firmly with the rubber cleats of his boots, took a short cut through an alley and strode off toward the pitch.

Quite a lot of spectators had turned out, owing partly to the fine day, with its pale-blue wintry sky and brisk air. Martin went on into the pavilion, where the other players had already gathered. Armstrong, the team captain, a lanky fellow with a clipped mustache, smiled shyly as he told Martin for the hundredth time that he ought to wear knee guards. A moment later all eleven players trotted single-file out of the pavilion, and Martin felt a beloved blend of impressions: the sharp smell of the damp turf, its resilience underfoot, thousands of people in the stands, the black bare spot in front of the goal, and the thud of the ball kicked around by the other team. The referee brought out and placed within the white circle of the field's hub a brand-new light-yellow ball. The players got into position and the whistle blew. At that instant Martin's nervousness vanished and, calmly leaning against the left upright, he glanced around in search of Darwin and Sonia. The action was taking place at the opposite end of the pitch, and he could revel in the cold air, in the mat green of the turf, in the chatter of the people standing just behind the goal net, and the glory of feeling that his boyhood dream had come true, that the red-haired chap over there, the St John's captain, who was receiving and passing the ball with such exquisite accuracy, had recently played against Scotland, and that there was somebody in the crowd for whom it was worth making a special effort. In childhood years sleep would overtake him just in those opening minutes of the game, for Martin would get so engrossed in the details of the preface that he never got to the main part of the text. Thus he would protract the delight, postponing to another, less sleepy night the game itself, bright and swift, with the pounding of feet getting closer and now he could hear the panting of the attack as the redhead broke loose − and there he came, his shock of hair bobbing, and then his fabled toe drove the ball whistling just above the ground toward the corner of the goal, but the custodian with a full-length dive succeeded in stopping that bolt, and now the ball was already in his hands and, eluding the nearest opponents, Martin sent it, with all the force of his thigh and calf, in a resounding punt that curved over the field to the roar of the stands.

During the short half-time interval the players sprawled on the ground, sucking on lemons, and when the teams changed goals, Martin, from his new position, tried again to make out Sonia and Darwin in the crowd. There was not much time for gawking, though, for the play immediately grew heated, and he constantly had to crouch on the alert. Several times, all doubled over, he caught cannonballs; several times he fisted high shots away; and thus he kept his goal virgin to the end of the game, smiling with joy when, a second before the final whistle, the opposing goalie fumbled the slippery ball, whereupon Armstrong promptly tapped it into the net.

Everything was over, the spectators flooded the field, and still he was unable to spot Sonia and Darwin. Somewhere beyond the grandstand, among the departing crowds, he noticed Vadim on his bike, waving cautiously and tooting with his lips. 'They decamped quite a while ago,' he said in answer to Martin's question, 'right after half-time, and, you know –' here followed some quip about Darwin which Martin, however, did not hear to the end, as at that moment Philpott, one of his teammates, squeezed by on a chugging red motor-cycle and offered him a lift. Martin got on behind and Philpott accelerated. 'Might as well not have managed to turn that last one over the bar,' thought Martin, wrinkling his face against the motley wind. He felt depressed and bitter, and when he had dismounted at the corner of his lane and was walking home, he ruminated with revulsion over the preceding day and Rose's craftiness, and felt even more hurt. 'They must be having tea somewhere,' he muttered, but just in case looked into Darwin's room. Sonia was reclining on the couch, and at the moment he entered, her hand went up in a clutching flick, trying to catch a clothes moth as it flew past.

'And Darwin?' asked Martin.

'Alive. Went out for some pastries,' she answered, malevolently following with her eyes the uncaught, whitish speck.

'Shame you didn't stay to the end,' said Martin, sinking into the abyss of an armchair. 'We won. One to nothing.'

'You ought to wash up,' she remarked. 'Just look at your knees. They're a sight! And you've tracked something black in here.'

'All right. Just let me recover my breath.' He breathed deeply several times and got up with a tired grunt.

'Wait a minute,' said Sonia. 'You've got to hear this, you'll die laughing. He just offered me his hand and heart. Of course, I knew it would happen — kept ripening and finally burst.' She stretched and glanced darkly at Martin, whose eyebrows had gone up. 'Intelligent expression you have,' she said, and, looking away, she continued, 'I simply don't understand what he expected. Very nice chap, etcetera, but a log, a log of real English oak. I'd die of boredom in a week. There it is, flying around again, that moth.'

Martin cleared his throat and said, 'I don't believe you. I know you said yes.'

'You're crazy!' shouted Sonia, sitting up and slapping the couch with both hands. 'How can you imagine such a thing?'

'Darwin is intelligent, perceptive, anything but a log,' Martin said in a strained voice.

She gave the couch another blow. 'But he isn't a real person – can't you see that, you idiot? This is getting downright insulting. He's not a person, but a dummy. Nothing inside except heaps of humor. That's just fine for going to a dance, but, in the long run, humor can get pretty exasperating.'

'He's a writer, connoisseurs are raving about his stories,' murmured Martin with an effort, and decided that now he had done his duty, had tried enough to convince her, and that there was a limit to noble behavior.

'Exactly, exactly – for connoisseurs only! Very charming, very well written, but all so superficial, so comfortable, so –'

Here Martin felt the rush of a radiant torrent that had burst through the locks, he remembered the tricky cross he had collected so nicely, remembered that the Rose business was settled, that there was a banquet at the club that evening, that he was healthy and strong, that tomorrow, the day after tomorrow, and for many, many days more life would go on, replete with all kinds of happiness. All this overwhelmed him in one dizzy instant, and he merrily seized Sonia in his arms together with the cushion she had clutched at, and started kissing her moist teeth, her eyes, her cold nose, and she struggled, and kicked, and her black, violet-scented hair kept getting in his mouth; at last, laughing loudly, he dropped her on the sofa. Here the door was pushed open.

At first a foot appeared, then, laden with goodies, Darwin entered. He tried to close the door with his foot but dropped a paper sack out of which tumbled meringues.

'Martin's been throwing cushions,' said Sonia in a plaintive, breathless voice. 'One to nothing is not so grand after all, why behave like a madman?'

Twenty-Seven

Next day both Martin and Darwin had an armpit temperature of 100.5 Fahr., aches and pains, sore throats, and a singing in the ears: all the symptoms of flu. Pleasant as it might be to think that the agent of contagion had probably been Sonia, both of them felt rotten, and Darwin, who steadfastly refused to stay in bed, looked, in his colorful dressing gown, like a heavyweight boxer, all red and disheveled after a long fight. Vadim, heroically disdaining contagion, brought medicines, while Martin, who had thrown a laprobe and his winter coat (neither of which did much to allay his chills) on top of his blanket, lay in bed with a scowl on his face, and, in every pattern, in every relationship between chance objects, spots, or shadows, saw human profiles – snoutish mugs, Bourbon noses, Negroid pouts: one wonders why fever

specializes so assiduously in drawing rather vulgar carica-
tures. He would doze off, and immediately be dancing the
fox-trot with a skeleton, which, as it danced, began coming
unscrewed and losing bones, and he had to snatch them up
and hold them in place, at least until the end of that dance;
or else he had to take an outrageous examination, quite different from the one Martin had really to take a few months
later, in May. In the dream test he was offered monstrous
problems with large iron X's wrapped in cotton wool, while
in the real one, in a spacious hall intersected by a dusty sun-
beam, philology students had to knock off three compositions
in one hour, and Martin, glancing now and then at the
wall clock, wrote in his large, round hand about Ivan the
Terrible's Gangmen, about Baratynski, about Peter the First's
reforms, about Loris-Melikov.

His life at Cambridge was nearing its end, and something
of a radiant apotheosis attended the final days; while awaiting examination results you could bask all afternoon in the
sun, lying on cushions as you floated languidly down the
Cam under the majestic auspices of the pink chestnut trees.
That spring Sonia moved with her family to Berlin, where
Zilanov had begun editing a Russian-language weekly, and
now Martin, supine under the softly progressing branches,
recalled his last trip to London. Darwin had not wanted to
come; he indolently asked to have regards transmitted to

Sonia, wiggled his fingers in the air, and plunged back in his book. When Martin arrived, the Zilanovs' house was in that dreary state of havoc that is so hateful to elderly, homey dogs – fat dachshunds, for instance. The maid and a tousled-haired youth with a cigarette behind his ear were carrying a trunk downstairs. A tearful Irina sat alone in the living room, biting her nails and thinking impenetrable thoughts. Some glass object fell and broke in one of the bedrooms, and the phone in the study rang in immediate response but nobody paid any attention to it. In the dining room a plate, covered by another, meekly waited, but what food it contained remained a mystery. Zilanov arrived from somewhere, wearing a black overcoat despite the warm weather, and sat down to write as coolly as if it were an ordinary day. A confirmed nomad, he evidently did not care in the least that in an hour it would be time to leave for the station, and that a crate of books, still to be nailed shut, stood in a corner; he just sat and wrote, in a current of air that stirred shreds of excelsior and the sheets of old newspapers. Sonia was standing in the middle of her room, her hands pressed to her temples, her moody gaze shuttling between a large package and a suitcase that was already full. Martin sat on the low windowledge smoking. Several times either her mother or her aunt came in, looked for something, failed to find it, and went out. 'Are you glad to be going to Berlin?' Martin gloomily asked, considering his cigarette, with its excrescence of ash that resembled lichened fir foliage with an ominous sunset showing through.

'I don't care,' said Sonia, gauging mentally whether the suitcase would shut.

'Sonia,' said Martin a minute later.

'What? What is it?' she muttered, coming out of her trance, and suddenly began fussing fast, planning to take the suitcase by surprise, with a sudden onslaught.

'Sonia,' said Martin, 'is it really true −' Her aunt came in, looked into a corner, and, replying negatively to somebody in the corridor, went out hurriedly without closing the door.

'Can it really be true,' said Martin, 'that we'll never see each other again?'

'That's for God to decide,' replied Sonia absently.

'Sonia,' Martin began again. She glanced at him with a grimace (or was it a smile?).

'You know,' she said, 'he sent back all my letters, all the photos, everything. Funny chap. He could have kept those letters. I spent half an hour ripping them up and flushing them down, and now the toilet's clogged.'

'You didn't behave well with him,' grimly said Martin. 'You can't build up a person's hopes and then turn him down.'

'You keep out,' cried Sonia with a little squeal in her voice. 'Hopes of what? How dare you talk about hopes? What vulgarity, what filth! And, in general, why don't you stop pestering me? Try to sit on this bag instead,' she added, one tone lower in pitch. Martin sat down on the lid and pressed hard.

'Won't shut,' he said hoarsely. 'And I don't know why you have to fly into a rage like that. I just wanted to say'

At that point something clicked reluctantly and, without giving the suitcase time to collect itself, Sonia turned the little key in its lock. 'Everything's fine now,' she said. 'Come over here, Martin. Let's have a heart-to-heart talk.'

Zilanov peeked into the room. 'Where's Mother?' he asked. 'Didn't I say to leave my desk alone? Now the ashtray has disappeared, it had two stamps in it.'

When he was gone, Martin took Sonia's hand in both of his, squeezed it between his palms, and heaved a melancholy sigh.

'You're a very sweet boy after all,' said Sonia. 'We'll write to each other, and maybe some time you'll come to Berlin, or perhaps some day we'll meet in Russia – won't that be fun?'

Martin kept shaking his head and felt the tears welling. Sonia snatched her hand away. 'Oh well, if you want to sulk,' she said crossly, 'do by all means, to your heart's content.'

'Ah, Sonia,' he uttered sorrowfully.

'Just exactly what is it you want from me?' she asked, narrowing her eyes. 'Please tell me, what is it you want from me?' Martin turned his head away and shrugged.

'Listen,' she said, 'it's time to go down, time to leave, and your moping only exasperates me. For goodness' sake, why can't we keep everything nice and simple?'

'You'll get married in Berlin,' Martin mumbled hopelessly. As in a farce the maid dashed in and took the suitcase. Mrs Zilanov, already hatted, appeared behind her.

'Time to go, time to go,' she said. 'You took everything in here? Didn't forget anything? This is dreadful,' she addressed Martin. 'We had planned on a leisurely departure tomorrow.'

She vanished, but for a while her voice in the passage went on explaining to somebody about her husband's urgent business, and Martin felt so piercingly, so ineffably saddened by all this commotion and disorder that he actually yearned to bundle Sonia off, to get rid of her as quickly as possible, and return to Cambridge and its lazy sunshine.

Sonia smiled, took him by the shoulder, and kissed him on the bridge of his nose. 'I don't know – maybe,' she whispered, and, quickly wriggling out of Martin's violent embrace, raised a warning finger. '*Tout beau*, doggy,' she said, and then made big eyes, for at that moment, from downstairs, came the sound of awful, impossible, house-shaking sobs. 'Come on, come on,' hurried Sonia. 'I can't understand why the poor child is so unhappy about moving away. Cut it out, damn it – let me go!'

At the bottom of the stairs Irina was tossing, howling, clutching at the banister. Her mother kept coaxing her softly,

'Ira, Irochka,' while Zilanov, using an oft-tested expedient, took out his handkerchief, quickly made a long-eared, fat knot, pulled the handkerchief over his hand, and maneuvered it in such a way as to make a little fellow in nightshirt and cap cozily getting into bed.

At the station she burst into tears again, only more quietly and hopelessly. Martin slipped her a box of candy that had actually been intended for Sonia. Zilanov had no sooner taken his seat than he opened a newspaper. Mrs Zilanov and Mrs Pavlov were counting suitcases with their eyes. With a clatter the doors began closing; the train moved. Sonia thrust her head out, leaning her elbows on the lowered window, and for a few instants Martin walked alongside the car; then he fell behind, and an already much diminished Sonia blew him a kiss, and Martin stumbled against some box on the platform.

'Well, there they go,' he sighed, and felt a certain relief. He made his way to the other station, bought the new issue of a humor magazine with a puppet, all nose, chin, and hump, on the cover, and, when he had extracted the last joke out of it, fixed his gaze on the gentle fields that were sliding past. 'My darling, my darling,' he repeated several times, and, gazing through a hot tear at the green scenery, he imagined how, after many adventures, he would arrive in Berlin, look up Sonia, and, like Othello, begin to tell a story of hairbreadth escapes, of most disastrous chances. 'No, it can't go on like this,' he said, rubbing his eyelid with a finger and tensing his upper lip. 'No, no. Less talk and more action.' Closing his eyes, and wedging himself comfortably into the corner, he started preparing for a dangerous expedition, studying an imaginary map. No one knew what he planned to do, Darwin alone might be informed – good-bye, good luck, the northbound train moves, and amidst these preparations he fell asleep, as he once used to fall asleep while putting on football apparel in his reveries. It was dark when he arrived in Cambridge. Darwin was still reading the same book, and yawned like a lion when Martin came in. And here Martin yielded to a little mischievous temptation, which he was subsequently to pay for. Counterfeiting a pensive smile, he stared at nothing, and Darwin, having unhurriedly completed his yawn, gave him a curious look.

'I am the happiest man in the world,' said Martin in a low voice full of feeling. 'Oh, if I could only tell you everything.'

In a sense, this was no lie, for when he had dozed off on the train, he had dreamt a dream grown out of something that Sonia had said. In the dream she pressed his head to her smooth shoulder and bent over him, tickling him with her lips, murmuring warm muffled words of tenderness, and now it was hard to separate fancy from fact.

'Well, I'm very happy for you,' said Darwin. A sudden embarrassment overcame Martin, and, whistling to himself, he went off to bed. A week later he received a postcard with a view of the Brandenburg Gate crossed by Sonia's spidery handwriting, which he spent a long time deciphering, trying in vain to read a hidden meaning into trivial words.

And now, gliding down the river beneath low-hanging boughs in bloom, Martin went back over his last meeting with her in London, analyzing it, testing it with different acids: a pleasant, but not very fruitful labor. It was a hot day; the sun penetrated his closed eyelids with a languorous strawberry crimson; he could hear the restrained plash of water and the gentle far-off music of floating phonographs. Presently he opened his eyes and, in a flood of sunlight, there was Darwin reclining on the cushions opposite, dressed as he in white flannel pants and open-necked shirt. The pole propelling their punt was wielded by Vadim. His cracked pumps glistened with drops of water and there was an intent expression on his sharp-featured face – he was fond of navigation, and now performed a sacred rite, as it were, skillfully, rhythmically manipulating the pole, pulling it out of the water with a methodical change of hold and bearing down on it anew. The punt glided between flowery banks; the transparent green water reflected now chestnut trees, now brambles in milk-white bloom; occasionally a petal would fall, and you could see its reflection hurrying up to meet it out of the watery depths, and then both would converge. Lazily, soundlessly – if one discounted the cooing of phonographs – other punts, or now and then a canoe, glided past. Martin noticed ahead an open bright-colored parasol which rotated this way and that, but nothing was visible of the girl twirling it except a hand, incongruously clad in a white glove. Her punt was manned by a young chap with glasses, poling very inexpertly, so that the boat followed a weaving course, and Vadim seethed with contempt, and did not know on which side to pass. At the very first bend it headed inexorably for the bank, the convex parasol showed in profile, and Martin recognized Rose.

'Look, how amusing,' he said, and Darwin, without moving the fat arms upon which his nape rested, turned his eyes in the direction of Martin's gaze.

'You shall not say hello to her,' he observed calmly.

Martin smiled, 'Oh yes, I certainly will.'

'If you do,' drawled Darwin, 'I'll knock your head off.'

There was a strange look in his eyes, and Martin felt uneasy; but for the very reason that Darwin's threat did not sound jocular and frightened him, Martin shouted as he floated past the punt entangled in the riverside shrubbery, 'Hello, hello, Rose!' And she smiled silently, her eyes sparkling and her parasol spinning, and in his exertions the bespectacled chap dropped his pole with a splash, and next moment they were concealed by the bend, and Martin again lay back and contemplated the sky.

After they had glided in silence for some minutes, Darwin greeted somebody in his turn. 'John!' he roared, 'paddle over here!'

John grinned and started backing water. This black-browed, crew-cut portly young man was a gifted mathematician who had recently won a prize for one of his papers. He sat low in his pirogue (Vadim's nomenclature), moving a shiny paddle close to the boat's side.

'I say, John,' announced Darwin, 'I've been challenged to a fight here, and I want you as second. We'll choose a quiet spot and land.'

'Righto,' answered John, without showing the least surprise, and, as he paddled alongside, began a lengthy account about a student who had recently acquired a seaplane, and promptly crashed it during an attempted take off from the narrow Cam. Martin reclined on his cushions, motionless. Here it was, the familiar tremor and weakness in the legs. Maybe Darwin was joking after all. What did he have to get so furious about?

Vadim, immersed in the mystique of navigation, had apparently heard nothing. Three or four bends later Darwin asked him to head for shore. Evening was already drawing near. The river was deserted at that point. Vadim aimed the punt at a little green tongue of land that projected from beneath a leafy canopy. They thumped gently to a stop.

Twenty-Eight

Darwin jumped ashore first and helped Vadim moor the boat. Martin stretched, got up unhurriedly, and also debarked.

'Began reading Chekhov yesterday,' John said to him, wriggling his eyebrows. 'Very grateful to you for the advice. Appealing, humane writer.'

'Oh, he certainly is,' said Martin, and quickly thought to himself, 'Is there really going to be a fight?'

'There,' said Darwin, drawing near. 'If we go through these bushes we'll come out in a meadow, and we'll be out of sight of the river.'

Only here did Vadim understand what was about to take place. 'Mamka will kill you,' he said to Martin in Russian.

'Nonsense,' replied Martin. 'I'm just as good a boxer as he is.'

'Forget about boxing,' Vadim whispered feverishly. 'Give him a good kick right away!' and he specified exactly where. He was rooting for Martin solely out of patriotism.

The little meadow, ringed by hazel trees, proved velvet-smooth. Darwin rolled up his sleeves, but, on second thought, rolled them back down and took off his shirt, exposing a massive pink torso with a muscular gloss at the shoulders and a path of golden hairs down the middle of his broad chest. He tightened his belt, and suddenly broke into a smile. It's all a joke, thought Martin joyously, but, just to be safe, he too removed his shirt. His skin was of a creamier shade, with numerous little birthmarks, common among Russians. Next to Darwin he seemed sparer, even though solidly built and broad-shouldered. He pulled his cross over his head, gathered the chain in his palm, and thrust this handful of trickling gold in his pocket. The evening sun flooded his back with warmth.

'How do you want it, with breathers?' asked John, sprawling comfortably on the grass. Darwin glanced questioningly at Martin, who stood with spread legs and folded arms.

'Makes no difference to me,' remarked Martin, while through his mind rushed the thought: 'No, it's the real thing – how ghastly –'

Vadim slouched around restlessly with his hands in his pockets, sniffling, smirking uneasily, and then sat down cross-legged beside John.

John took out his watch. 'Anyway, they oughtn't to have more than five minutes in all – agreed, Vadim?'

Vadim nodded in confusion.

'Well, you can begin,' said John.

Fists clenched, legs flexed, the two started dancing around one another. Martin still could not imagine himself hitting

Darwin in the face, in that large, clean-shaven face with the soft wrinkles around the mouth; however, when Darwin's left shot out and caught Martin on the jaw, everything changed: all anxiety vanished, he felt relaxed and radiant inside, and the ringing in his head, from the jolt it had received, sang of Sonia, over whom, in a sense, they were fighting this duel. Dodging another lunge, he punched Darwin's gentle face, ducked under Darwin's retaliating right, attempted an upper-cut, and received himself such a black, star-spangled blow in the eye that he staggered and only just managed to evade the most vicious of half-a-dozen swipes. He crouched, he feinted, and jabbed Darwin in the mouth so nicely that his knuckles felt the hardness of teeth through the wetness of lips, but at once was punished himself in the belly by running into what seemed the protruding end of an iron girder. They bounced away from each other and resumed circling. Darwin had a red trickle at the corner of his mouth. He spat twice and the fight went on. John, pensively puffing on his pipe, juxtaposed in his mind Darwin's experience and Martin's speed and decided that if he were to choose between these two heavyweights in the ring, he would be inclined to bet on the elder. Martin's left eye was already closed and swollen, and both combatants were glossy with sweat and smeared with blood. In the meantime Vadim had got all worked up, and was shouting excitedly in Russian; John shushed him. Bang! on the ear. Martin lost his balance, and, as he was tumbling, Darwin managed to hit him a second time, whereupon Martin sat down heavily on a pebble patch, hurting his coccyx, but instantly sprang up and returned to the fray. Despite the buzzing pain in his head, and the crimson fog in his eyes, Martin felt sure he was inflicting more injury on Darwin than Darwin on him, but John, a lover of pugilism, already saw clearly that Darwin was only now getting into his stride, and that in a few moments the younger of the two would be down for good. But Martin miraculously withstood a series of resonant hooks and even managed to slam the other again on the mouth. He was panting now, and not thinking too clearly, and what he saw before him was no longer called Darwin, and in fact had no human name at all, but had become simply a pink, slippery, rapidly moving mass that must be punched with every last bit of strength. He succeeded in planting yet another very solid and satisfying blow some-where – he did not see where – but immediately a multitude of fists pummeled him at length from all sides, wherever he turned; he stubbornly searched for a breach in this whirl-wind, found one, hammered at a continuum of squelchy pulp, suddenly felt that his own head was flying off, slipped, and remained hanging on Darwin in a humid clinch.

'Time!' came John's voice from remote space, and the fighters separated. Martin collapsed on the grass, and Dar-win, his bloodied mouth forming a grin, plumped down beside him, tenderly put his arm around Martin's shoulders, and both froze motionless, inclining their heads and breathing heavily.

'You ought to wash up,' said John, while Vadim approached cautiously and started examining their bruised faces.

'Can you stand?' Darwin asked solicitously. Martin nodded and, leaning on him, straightened up. They trudged toward the river, arms across each other's shoulders. John patted them on their clammy bare backs; Vadim went on ahead to look for a secluded cove. There, Darwin helped Martin give face and frame a good wash, then Martin did the same for him, and both kept asking each other in low, solicitous tones where it hurt and if the water did not sting.

Twenty-Nine

Dusk was deepening, the nightingales had begun bubbling, the dim meadows and the dark shrubs breathed dampness. The river mists engulfed John and his black canoe. Vadim, once again propelling the punt, a white, ghostlike figure in the gloom, wordlessly and with a somnambulically smooth motion immersed his spectral pole. Martin and Darwin lay side by side on the cushions, limp, languid, swollen, staring with their three good eyes at the sky, across which a dark branch passed every now and then. And that sky, and the branch, and the barely plashing water, and the figure of Vadim, mysteriously ennobled by his love of navigation, and the colored lights of the paper lanterns on the bows of passing punts, and the thought that in a few days Cambridge would end, that perhaps the three of them were gliding for the last time along the narrow, misty river – all this merged in Martin's mind into something wondrous and spellbinding, and the leaden pain in his head and the ache in his shoulders struck him as having an exalted, romantic quality, for thus wounded Tristram had floated alone with his harp.

One last bend, and there was the shore. The shore on which Martin landed was very fair, very bright, and full of variety. He knew, though, that for example Uncle Henry remained firmly convinced that these three years of aquatics in Cambridge had gone to waste, because Martin had indulged in a philological cruise, and not even a very distant one, instead of learning a useful profession. But Martin in all honesty did not understand why it was worse to be an expert in Russian letters than a transportation engineer or a merchant. Actually, Uncle Henry's menagerie – and everybody has one – housed, among other creatures, a little black beast, and that *bête noire* was to him the twentieth century. Now this amazed Martin, since in his opinion one could not even imagine a better century than the one in which he lived. No other epoch had had such brilliance, such daring, such projects. Everything that had glimmered in previous ages – the passion for exploration of unknown lands, the audacious experiments, the glorious exploits of disinterested curiosity, the scientists who went blind or were blown to bits, the heroic conspiracies, the struggle of one against many – now emerged with unprecedented force. The cool suicide of a man after his having lost millions on the stock market struck Martin's imagination as much as, for instance, the death of a Roman general falling on his sword. An automobile advertisement, brightly beckoning in a wild, picturesque gorge from an absolutely inaccessible spot on an alpine cliff thrilled him to tears. The complaisant and affectionate nature of very complicated and very simple machines, like the tractor or the linotype, for example, induced him to reflect that the good in mankind was so contagious that it infected metal. When, at an amazing height in the blue sky above the city, a mosquito-sized airplane emitted fluffy, milk-white letters a hundred times as big as it, repeating in divine dimensions the flourish of a firm's name, Martin was filled with a sense of marvel and awe. But Uncle Henry, as if throwing tidbits to his black beastie, spoke with horror and revulsion about the twilight of Europe, about post-war fatigue, about our practical age, about the invasion of inanimate machines; in his imagination there existed some diabolical connection between the fox-trot and skyscrapers on one side and women's fashions and cocktails on the other. Furthermore, Uncle Henry had the impression he lived in an age of terrible haste, and it was particularly funny when he chatted about this haste, on a summer day, at the edge of a mountain road, with the local priest, while the clouds sailed serenely and the abbé's old, pink horse, shaking off flies with a tinkle, blinking its white eyelashes, would lower its head in a movement full of ineffable charm and munch succulently on the roadside grass, with its skin twitching or a hoof shifting now and then, and, if the talk about the mad haste of our days, about the almighty dollar, about the Argentines who seduced all the girls of Switzerland, dragged on too long, and the last tender stalk among coarser ones had been eaten at a given spot, it would move ahead a little, accompanied by the creak of the gig's high wheels. And Martin could not take his eyes off the gentle equine lips and the blades of grass caught in the bit.

'Here, this young man, for example,' Uncle Henry would say, indicating Martin with his walking stick, 'he has finished college, one of the most expensive colleges in the world, and you ask him what he has learned, what he is prepared for. I absolutely don't know what he is going to do next. In my time young men became doctors, soldiers, notaries, while he is probably dreaming of being an aviator or a gigolo.'

Martin had no idea what exactly he served as an example of, but the abbé apparently understood Uncle Henry's paradoxes and smiled commiseratingly. Sometimes Martin was so irritated by talk of this kind that he was ready to say something rude to his uncle – who was also, alas, his stepfather – but would stop in time, for he had noticed the look that appeared on his mother's face whenever Henry waxed eloquent at dinner. That look contained a faint trace of friendly raillery, and a certain sadness, and a mute appeal to forgive the crank, and yet something else inexpressible but very wise. Martin would keep still, mentally answering Uncle Henry like this, for example: 'It's not true that I devoted my time to trifles at Cambridge. It's not true that I did not learn anything. Columbus, before trying to take hold of his east ear across his west shoulder, traveled to Iceland incognito to gather certain information, knowing that the sailors there were a canny and far-ranging breed. I, too, plan to explore a distant land.'

Thirty

His mother did not pester him with the tedious talk of which Uncle Henry was so fond; she did not inquire what occupation he would choose, feeling as she did that all this would somehow work out by itself. She was satisfied with the happiness at hand – of his being with her now, healthy, broad-shouldered, tanned; of his slamming away at tennis, speaking in a bass voice, shaving daily, and making young, bright-eyed Madame Guichart, a local merchant's wife, blush as red as a poppy. Sometimes she wondered when Russia would at last snap out of the evil dream, when the striped pole of the frontier gate would rise and everyone return and resume his former place, and, goodness, how the trees have grown, how the house has shrunk, what sorrow and joy, what a smell of earth! In the mornings she would wait for the postman just as avidly as during her son's years at Cambridge, and now, when a letter came for Martin (and it was not often), in an office envelope, addressed in a spidery hand and bearing a Berlin postmark, she felt the keenest joy and, snatching the letter, hurried to his room. Martin still lay in bed, very tousled, sucking on a cigarette with his hand at his chin. He saw in the mirror the sun-bright wound of the opening door, and that special expression on his mother's pink, freckled face: by the fold of her lips, tightly compressed but ready to spread into a smile, he could tell there was a letter.

'Nothing for you today,' Mrs Edelweiss would lightly say, holding one hand behind her back, but her son's impatient fingers were already reaching out, and, beaming, she would press the envelope to her chest, and both would laugh. Then, not wishing to spoil his enjoyment, she would go to the window, lean out on its sill, cupping her face in her hands, and gaze with a feeling of complete happiness at the mountains, and in particular at one distant, rosy peak that was visible only from this window. Martin, who had consumed the letter in one gulp, pretended to be considerably happier than he actually was, so that his mother imagined those letters from the little Zilanov girl to be full of tenderness, and would probably have felt sadly hurt if she ever got to read them. She remembered the Zilanov girl with strange clarity: a black-haired, pale little thing who was always sick with an inflamed throat or convalescing after one, her neck either bandaged or yellow from iodine. She remembered how she had once taken ten-year-old Martin to a Christmas party at the Zilanovs' St Petersburg flat, and little Sonia was wearing a lacy white dress with a broad silk sash around the hips. As for Martin, he did not remember this at all; there had been many Christmas parties, and they merged in his memory. Only one thing remained very vivid, for it had recurred every time: his mother saying it was time to go home, and thrusting her fingers inside the collar of his sailor suit from behind to see if he was not too sweaty after all the running, while he, with a huge gold-papered cracker, kept trying to wrench himself free, but his mother's grip was tenacious, and presently his overpants (which reached nearly to his armpits) were being pulled on, and on went his overshoes and fur coat, with its tight-closing hook at the throat and the hideously tickly Caucasian hood, and next minute there was the streetlamps' frosty rainbow running across the window of the close carriage. It thrilled Martin to note that the expression of his mother's eyes was the same now as then, that now, too, she touched his neck when he came home after tennis, and that she brought Sonia's letter with the same tenderness as she had once brought, in its long cardboard box, an air rifle ordered from England.

The rifle had turned out to be not quite as he had expected, not matching exactly its foredream, just as now the letters from Sonia were not the kind he would have liked. She wrote, as it were, in abrupt jerks, without a single mystery-breathing phrase, and he had to be content with such remarks as 'I often recall good old Cambridge,' or 'Best of everything, my dear little flower, give me your paw to shake.' She told him that she had an office job – typing and shorthand – that they were having a very difficult time with Irina – constant hysterics – that her father had not got anywhere with his Russian-language newspaper and was now setting up a publishing business – books by émigré writers – that there was never a penny in the house – which was rather sad – that they had many friends – which was lots of fun – that the streetcars in Berlin were green, and that Berliners played tennis in braces and starched collars. Martin's endurance lasted all through summer, fall, and winter; then, in mid-April 1923, on his twenty-first birthday, he announced to Uncle Henry that he was leaving for Berlin. The latter looked dour, and said with displeasure, 'To me, *mon ami*, that seems devoid of all sense. You will always have time to see Europe. In point of fact, I was going to take you and your mother to Italy next autumn. But you can't go on loafing forever. In short, I was going to suggest that you try your youthful powers in Geneva.' (Martin knew full well what was meant: several times already this dismal subject had crept stealthily forth; it concerned some commercial firm or other belonging to the Petit brothers, with whom Uncle Henry had business relations.) 'That you try *tes jeunes forces*,' Uncle Henry repeated. 'In this cruel age, in this very practical age, a young man must learn to earn his bread and elbow his way through life. You have a solid knowledge of the English language. Foreign correspondence in the world of affairs is a most interesting thing. As for Berlin – Your German has not much improved, has it? I can't see what you are going to do there.'

'Suppose I do nothing,' Martin said gloomily.

Uncle Henry looked at him with surprise. 'That's a bizarre answer. I don't know what your father would have thought of an answer like that. I think he would be as astonished as I am that a young man full of sap and health despises all work. Please understand,' he hastily added, noticing that Martin had reddened unpleasantly, 'I am not being stingy – *je ne suis pas mesquin*. I am rich enough, thank God, to provide for you – I make a duty and a joy of it – but it would be folly not to take a job. Europe is passing through an unbelievable crisis, and a man can lose a fortune in the twinkling of an eye. That's the way it is, and you can't do a thing about it.'

'I don't need your money,' Martin said softly and rudely. Uncle Henry pretended not to hear, but tears welled in his eyes.

'Don't you have any ambition at all? Don't you ever think about making a career? We Edelweisses always knew how to work. Your grandfather began as a poor tutor – teaching French *à des princes russes*. When he proposed to your grandmother her parents threw him out of the house. And back he comes a year later, the director of an export company, and then, obviously, all obstacles were swept away.'

'I don't need your money,' repeated Martin, even more softly. 'And as for Grandfather, that's nothing but a silly family legend, and you know it.'

'What's the matter with him, what's the matter with him?' Uncle Henry muttered in fright. 'What right do you have to offend me like this? What wrong have I done you? I, who have always –'

'The short of the matter is that I'm going to Berlin,' Martin interrupted, and left the room, trembling.

Thirty-One

That evening there was a reconciliation, embraces, nose-blowing, emotional throat-clearing – but Martin stood his ground. His mother, who sensed his longing to see Sonia, proved to be an ally, and smiled bravely as he got into the car.

Hardly had the house disappeared from view when Martin changed places with the chauffeur. Holding the wheel delicately, almost tenderly, as if it were something alive and precious, and watching the powerful car gobble up the road, he experienced nearly the same sensation as when, in childhood, seated on the floor with his feet resting on the piano pedals, he would hold the stool with its round, revolving seat between his legs and handle it like a steering wheel, taking splendid curves at full speed, pushing the pedal again and again (which made the piano hum), and slitting his eyes against the imaginary wind. Then, in the German express, where, between the corridor windows, hung small maps of regions the train did not pass through, Martin relished the journey, eating chocolate, smoking, poking his cigarette butt under the metal lid of the ashtray, filled with the remains of cigar. It was night by the time he neared Berlin. Looking from the train onto the wet lighted streets he relived his childhood impression of Berlin, whose fortunate inhabitants could enjoy daily, if they wished, the sight of trains with fabulous destinations, gliding across a black bridge over a humdrum thoroughfare; in this respect Berlin differed from St Petersburg, where railroad operations were concealed like a secret rite. A week later, though, when his eyes had got used to the city, Martin was already powerless to reconstruct that perspective from which its features had seemed familiar. It was as when you meet someone you have not seen for years: first you recognize his figure and voice; then you look more closely, and there, before your eyes, the transformation imperceptibly wrought by time is run through in quick display. Features alter, likeness deteriorates, and you have before you a stranger, looking smug after having devoured his own young and fragile double, whom it will henceforth be hard to picture, unless chance comes to the rescue. When Martin deliberately visited in Berlin that intersection, that square, which he had seen as a child, there was nothing that gave him the least shiver of excitement, but on the other hand, a chance whiff of coal or automobile exhaust, a certain special pale hue of the sky seen through a lace curtain, or the shudder of the windowpanes awakened by a passing truck, instantly brought back the essence of city, hotel, and drab morning, part of an image that Berlin had once impressed upon him. The toy shops on the once elegant

Friedrichstrasse had thinned out and lost their sparkle, and the locomotives in their windows looked smaller and shabbier. The pavement of this street had been torn up, and shirt-sleeved workmen were drilling, and digging deep smoky holes, so that you had to pick your way over planking, and sometimes even across loose sand. In the Panopticon of Waxworks on the Unter den Linden the man in a shroud, energetically climbing out of his grave, and the Iron Maiden, that instrument of strong and hard torture, had lost their ghoulish charm. Martin went to the Kurfürstendamm to look for that enormous roller-skating rink that he remembered so well, with its rumble of wheels, instructors in red uniforms, band shell, slightly salty mocha cake served in the encircling boxes, and the *pas de patineurs* that he used to dance to any kind of music, flexing now his right, now his left skate-shod leg (and what a spill he took once!), only to find a dozen years had been enough to abolish it completely. The Kurfürstendamm itself had changed too, maturing, growing longer, and somewhere – perhaps beneath a new building – lay the grave of a twenty-court tennis establishment, where Martin had been a couple of times with his mother, who would accompany her underhand service with a bright-voiced 'Play!' and whose skirt would rustle as she ran. Now, without even leaving the city limits, he could reach the Grunewald, where the Zilanovs lived, to learn from Sonia that it was pointless to go to Wertheim's for his shopping, and that it was by no means obligatory to visit the Wintergarten, under whose fabulous star-dusted black ceiling tight-corseted Prussian officers sat at lighted tables in the boxes, while on stage twelve bare-legged girls sang with brassy voices and undulated with linked arms from right to left and back again, kicking up twelve white legs, and little Martin had uttered a soft exclamation of surprise upon recognizing in them the demure, pretty English misses who, like him, went skating daily at the wooden rink.

But perhaps the most unexpected thing about this new, much expanded, post-war Berlin, so peaceful, rustic and bumbling, compared to the compact and elegant city of Martin's childhood, was the free-mannered, loud-voiced Russia that chattered everywhere, in the trams, in the shops, on street corners, on the balconies of apartment houses. Some ten years before, in one of his prophetic daydreams (and any person with a lot of imagination has prophetic daydreams occasionally – such is the statistics of daydreams), Martin, a schoolboy in the secure St Petersburg of 1913, imagined himself in years to come as an exile, and felt tears rising when, on the strange dim railway platform of his reverie, he unexpectedly encountered – whom? – a compatriot, sitting on a trunk, on a night of shiverings and delays, and what a marvelous talk they had! For the roles of these fellow exiles he simply chose Russians he had noticed during that earlier trip abroad: a family in Biarritz, complete with governess, tutor, clean-shaven valet, and brown dachshund; a fascinating fair-haired lady at the Kaiserhof in Berlin; or, in the corridor of the Nord-Express, an old gentleman in a black skullcap, whom Martin's father had identified, in a whisper, as 'the writer Boborykin.' Then, having selected for them appropriate costumes and speeches, he would dispatch them to meetings with himself in the remotest parts of the world. Today, in 1923, that chance fantasy (the consequence of Heaven knows what children's book) found full incarnation, marked even by some overplaying. When the fat, heavily made-up Russian lady in the tram hung with blatant dejection from her strap, and volleyed over her shoulder some resounding Russian to her companion, an old man with a gray mustache, 'Astounding, really astounding, how not one of these ill-bred foreigners offers his seat,' Martin jumped up and, with a radiant smile, repeating what he had rehearsed in his boyhood fantasies, exclaimed, '*Pozhaluysta!*' and, instantly growing pale from the experienced thrill, clutched the strap in his turn. The peaceable Germans whom the lady had called ill-bred were all tired, hungry working people, and the gray sandwiches they chewed in the streetcar, even if they did irritate Russians, were indispensable. For real dinners were expensive that year of monstrous inflation, and, when Martin changed a dollar note in the tram, instead of investing that dollar in real estate, the conductor's hands would shake with amazement and joy. Martin earned his American *valuta* in a special way, which made him very proud. True, the labor was arduous. Ever since May, when he had stumbled upon that job (thanks to Kindermann, a charming Russian-German, who for a couple of years already had been teaching tennis to whatever wealthy clients turned up), and until mid-October, when he left to spend the winter with his mother, and then again in the spring of 1924, Martin worked almost daily from early morning to sunset, holding five balls in his left hand (Kindermann managed to hold six) and sending them one by one across the net with an identical smooth stroke of his racket, while the tense, middle-aged pupil (male or female) on the other side of the net swung diligently and as often as not did not hit anything. At first Martin would get so tired, his right shoulder would ache and his feet burn so badly, that as soon as he had earned his five or six dollars he would go to bed. His hair grew lighter and his skin darker from the sun, so that he seemed a negative of himself. His landlady, a major's widow from whom he concealed his profession so as to seem more mysterious, supposed that the poor fellow – like many cultured people, alas – was obliged to work as a laborer, lugging rocks, for instance (hence the suntan), and was embarrassed about it, as would be any refined person. In the evening, with genteel sighs, she would treat him to sausage that her daughter sent from their Pomeranian estate. The lady was six feet tall, with a ruddy complexion, used cologne on Sundays and kept a parrot and a tortoise in her room. She considered Martin an ideal roomer: he was seldom at home, did not receive guests, and never used the bath (the latter was amply replaced by the shower at the tennis club and the lake in Grunewald). This bath was plastered with the landlady's hair on the inside, anonymous rags dried on a clothesline overhead, and an old, dusty, rusted bicycle leaned against the opposite wall. Moreover, it was no easy task getting there: one had to follow a long, dark corridor, with an extraordinary number of corners and piled full of all sorts of junk. Martin's room, on the other hand, was not bad at all, and had its amusing side. It contained such objects of luxury as an upright piano, locked tight from time immemorial, and a massive, complicated barometer that had stopped working a couple of years before the war, while on the green wall above the couch, like a constant, benevolent reminder, the same naked old chap armed with a trident rose out of his Böklinian waves as he did – although in a plainer frame – on the wall of the Zilanovs' parlor.

Thirty-Two

The first time Martin visited them and saw their cheap, dingy flat, consisting of four rooms and a kitchen, where a strange Sonia with a different hairdo sat on the table, swinging her legs in their darned-up stockings, sniffling, and peeling potatoes, Martin realized that he could expect nothing but sorrows from Sonia, and that his Berlin trip was pointless. Everything about her was unfamiliar: the bronze-colored sweater, the exposed ears, the stuffy voice – she was in the throes of a bad cold, and the skin was red around her nostrils; she would stop peeling to blow her nose, give a dejected grunt, and slice off a new spiral of brown skin with her knife. For supper they had buckwheat groats with margarine instead of butter. Irina came to table holding a kitten from which she was inseparable and greeted Martin with a joyous and dreadful laugh. Both mothers had aged during the past year and had grown to resemble each other even more. Only Zilanov was still his old self, and cut into the bread as mightily as ever.

'I hear' – crunch, creak – 'that Gruzinov is in Lausanne. Did you' – creak – 'happen to run into him? Great friend of mine and a remarkably strong-willed, determined person.'

Martin had not the faintest notion who Gruzinov was but did not ask any questions for fear of committing a blunder. After dinner Sonia washed the plates and he dried them, breaking one.

'It's an impossible situation,' she exclaimed, and elucidated, 'I mean not our finances but my nose, I can't breathe through it. The financial situation is also pretty bad for that matter.'

Then she accompanied him downstairs to unlock the front door; at the press of a button there was a cute click and the staircase lights flashed on, and Martin kept clearing his throat and could not manage a single word of the many he had prepared. Evenings of a quite different nature followed – a multitude of guests, dancing to records, dancing in a nearby café, the murk of the corner cinema. New people materialized around Martin on all sides, nebulae gave birth to worlds. Definite labels and features were found for the Russian substance scattered about Berlin, for all those elements of expatriation which so excited Martin, be it merely a snatch of routine conversation amid the shoving sidewalk crowd, a chameleon word (such as that russified plural with its wandering accent: *dóllary, dolláry, dollará*), or a squabbling couple's recitative, caught in passing ('And I'm telling you –' for female voice; 'Oh, have it your way –' for male voice); or, on a summer night, a man with his head thrown back clapping his hands under a lighted window and shouting a resonant name and patronymic that made the whole street vibrate and caused a taxi to emit a nervous squeal and shy to one side after nearly running over the vociferous visitor, who had by now backed to the center of the asphalt, the better to see if the person he needed would appear like Punch in the window. Through the Zilanovs Martin met people among whom he at first felt ignorant and alien. In a certain sense he experienced all over again what had embarrassed him when he first saw the Zilanovs in London. And now, when at the apartment of Stepan Bubnov the talk rolled on in great waves, full of allusions to modern authors, and knowledgeable Sonia cast at Martin a sidelong glance of ironic compassion, Martin blushed, faltered, was about to launch his own frail little contribution on the billows of other people's speeches, but feared it would capsize immediately, and so kept still. In compensation, shamed by the backwardness of his erudition, he devoted every hour of rain to reading, and very soon became familiar with that special smell, the smell of prison libraries, which emanated from Soviet literature.

Thirty-Three

The writer Bubnov (who used to point out with satisfaction how many distinguished Russian literary names of the twentieth century began with the letter B) was a bearish, balding man of thirty, with a huge forehead, deep-set eyes, and a square chin. He smoked a pipe, sucking in his cheeks deeply with every puff, wore an old black bow tie, and considered

Martin a fop and a foreigner. As to Martin, he was much taken with Bubnov's energetic, rotund delivery and with his quite justified fame. Bubnov, whose writing career had begun in exile, had already had three excellent novels brought out by a Russian émigré publisher in Berlin, and was now writing a fourth. Its hero was Christopher Columbus, or, to be more exact, a Muscovite scrivener who, after many escapades, had miraculously ended up as a sailor on one of Columbus's caravels. Bubnov knew no language other than Russian, so that when he had to go to the State Library for his research and Martin happened to be free, he willingly took him along. Martin's command of German being mediocre, he was glad when a text chanced to be in French, English, or, better still, Italian. True, he knew that language even less than German, but he particularly prized his scant knowledge, remembering how he used to read Dante with melancholy Teddy's assistance. Bubnov's flat was frequented by the émigré literary set – fictionists, journalists, pimply young poets; in Bubnov's opinion these were all people of middling talent, and he reigned over them justly, hearing out, with his hand over his eyes, yet another poem about nostalgia for the homeland or recollections of St Petersburg (with the Bronze Horseman inevitably present) and then saying, as he unscreened his beetling brows and kneaded his chin, 'Yes, that's good.' Then, focusing his pale-hazel eyes on some fixed point, he would repeat 'Good' with a less convinced intonation; and, once again changing the direction of his gaze, he would say, 'Not bad,' and then, 'Only, you know, you make Petersburg a little too portable.' And thus, gradually lowering his evaluation, he would reach the point where he muttered in hollow tones, with a sigh, 'That stuff is all wrong, all unnecessary,' and dejectedly shake his head; upon which, abruptly, with vivid enthusiasm he would thunder out a poem by Pushkin. Once, when a young poet took offense and objected, 'That's by Pushkin, and this is by me,' Bubnov thought for a moment and replied, 'Still, yours is worse.'

Then again, there would be occasions when some newcomer brought a really fine piece, whereupon Bubnov — especially if the piece were in prose — would grow strangely glum and remain out of sorts for several days. Bubnov's friendship with Martin, who never wrote anything (except letters to his mother and for this was dubbed by a wit 'our Madame de Sévigné'), remained sincere and free of misgivings. There was even a night when, relaxed and transparent after his third mug of Pilsener, Bubnov began talking dreamily (and this brought back a campfire in the Crimean mountains) about a girl whose soul was a song, whose dark eyes sang, whose skin was pale like precious porcelain. Then, with a fierce look, he added, 'Yes, that's trite, that's nauseous, ugh! Despise me if you like, I may lack all talent, but I'm in love with her. Her name is like a church dome, like the swish of doves' wings. I see radiant light in her name, that special light, the "kana-inum" of the ancient Khadir sages. A light from there, from the East. Ah, that's a great mystery, an awesome mystery –' Lowering his voice to a demented whisper, he added, 'A woman's charm is a terrible thing – you understand me, terrible. And her poor little slippers are worn down at the heel, yes, worn down –'

Martin felt uncomfortable and nodded in silence. In Bubnov's company he always had a strange feeling, as if it were all a dream, and somehow he did not have complete faith either in him or in the Khadir elders. Sonia's other acquaintances, for example jolly, bright Kallistratov, a former officer now in the 'automobile transport business,' or the pleasant, fair-skinned and buxom Veretennikov girl, who played the guitar and sang 'There's a Volgan high cliff' in a rich contralto, or young Iogolevich, an intelligent, viperish, taciturn youth in horn-rimmed glasses who had read Proust and Joyce, were far less complicated than Bubnov. Mixed in with these friends of Sonia's were the elderly acquaintances of her parents, all respectable, politically active, pure-hearted people, fully deserving a future obituary of a hundred limpid lines. But when, one July day, old Iogolevich heavily fell prone on the sidewalk, dead of heart failure, and the émigré papers carried a great deal of stuff about the 'irreplaceable loss' and the 'true toiler,' and Mihail Platonovich Zilanov, improperly hatless, with his briefcase under his arm, walked in the vanguard of the funeral procession among the roses and the black marble of Jewish graves, Martin had the impression that the obituary writer's words 'he burned with love for Russia' or 'he always held high his pen' somehow debased the deceased inasmuch as those same words would have been equally applicable both to Zilanov and to the venerable necrologist himself. Most of all Martin felt sorry for the originality of the deceased, who was truly irreplaceable – his gestures, his beard, his sculpturesque wrinkles, the sudden shy smile, the jacket button that hung by a thread, and his way of licking a stamp with his entire tongue before sticking it on the envelope and banging it with his fist. In a certain sense this was all of greater value than the social merits for which there existed such easy little clichés, and with an odd shift of thought Martin swore to himself that he himself would never join a political party or attend a meeting, that he would never be the personage who is 'given the floor' or who 'adjourns the proceedings,' while reveling in the joys of civic virtue. And often Martin would marvel at his inability to mention his long-treasured secret plans to Zilanov or to Zilanov's friends or to any of those industrious, upstanding Russians, so full of disinterested love for their country.

Thirty-Four

But Sonia, ah, Sonia – From his night-time thoughts about
the glorious and dark expedition, from his literary chats
with Bubnov, from his daily labors at the tennis club, he
would return to her again and again and hold a match over
the gas stove for her, whereupon, with a loud gush, the blue
flame would extend all its claws. To talk to her of love was
useless, but once, while walking her home from the café,
where they had imbibed Swedish punch through straws to
the wail of a Rumanian violin, he was overwhelmed with
such soft passion, because of the warm night and because in
every doorway there stood a motionless couple, so infectious
was their gaiety and whispering, and sudden silences, and
the crepuscular undulation of lilacs in villa gardens, and the
fantastic shadows with which the light of a streetlamp ani-
mated the scaffolding of a house in the process of renovation,
that he forgot his usual reserve, his usual fear that Sonia
would make fun of him, and, by some miracle, began to
speak – of what? – of Horace. Yes, Horace had lived in Rome,
and Rome, despite a good number of marble edifices, looked

like a sprawling village, and there you could see people chasing after a mad dog, and hogs splashing in the mud with their black piglets, and construction was going on all over the place: carpenters hammered away; a wagon carrying Ligurian marble or an enormous pine would clatter past. But toward evening the racket would cease, just as Berlin grew silent at twilight, after which came the rattle of iron chains from shops being shut for the night, quite like the rattling of the Berlin shops' shutters at closing time, and Horace strolled off to the Field of Mars, debile but paunchy, with a bald head and big ears, clad in a sloppy toga, and listen to the tender whispers under the porticoes, to the enchanting laughter in dark nooks.

'You're such a dear,' Sonia said all at once, 'that I have to kiss you – wait, let's go over there.'

Near a park gate, under the overflow of dark foliage, Martin pulled Sonia to him, and, so as not to lose the least part of that moment, he did not close his eyes as he slowly kissed her cool, soft lips, watching the while a reflection of pale light on her cheek, and the quivering of her lowered eyelids: they rose for an instant, revealing a moist, blind glistening, and shut again; little shivers shook her, her lips parted under his, but breaking the spell her hand pushed his face aside, and her teeth were chattering, and in a half-whisper she implored him to stop.

'And what if I'm in love with somebody else?' asked Sonia with unexpected vivacity when they were once again strolling along the street.

'That would be awful,' said Martin. He sensed there had been a moment when he could have taken a firm hold of Sonia, but now she had flipped away again.

'Remove your arm,' she remarked, 'I can't walk like that – you behave like a Sunday shop clerk,' and his last hope, the blissful sensation of her warm upper arm under the palm of his hand, vanished also.

'At least he has talent,' she said, 'and you, you're nothing, just a traveling playboy.'

'Talent? Whom are you talking about?'

She did not answer and kept silent all the way home. She did, however, kiss him again on the doorstep, throwing her bare arm around his neck, and her expression was serious and her gaze downcast as she locked the door from the inside. He watched through the door pane: there she goes, up the stairs, caressing the banister, and now the stair bend conceals her – and that is her light going out.

'She did the same to Darwin,' thought Martin, and he felt a tremendous urge to see his old friend; Darwin, however, was far away in America, on an assignment for a London newspaper. Next day all trace of romance had vanished, as if it had never been, and Sonia went with friends to the country, to Peacock Island, for a swim and a picnic, and Martin didn't even know about it. That evening, a minute before closing time, he had bought a large crimson-ribboned plush dog and was approaching her house with the thing under his arm when he met the whole returning party on the street; Sonia had Kallistratov's jacket over her shoulders, and between him and her there flashed repeatedly a chance jest, whose meaning nobody bothered to explain to Martin.

He wrote her a letter, and stayed away for several days. She replied a week or so later with a color postcard showing a pretty boy bending over the back of a green bench on which sat a pretty girl, admiring a bouquet of roses, with a German rhyme in gilt letters at the bottom: 'Let a true heart leave unsaid what is told by roses red.' On the reverse Sonia had scribbled: 'Aren't they sweet? That's real courtship for you. Look, I need your assistance, three strings have snapped on my racket.' And not a word about the letter! However, during one of his next visits she said, 'I think it's ridiculous that you can't skip a day or two now and then. Surely, Kindermann will replace you.'

'He has his own lessons,' replied Martin hesitantly, but he did speak to Kindermann, and so, one marvelous, impeccably cloudless morning, Martin and Sonia were off for the lacustrine, reedy, piny outskirts of the city, and Martin heroically kept his promise not to make 'marmalade' eyes, as she put it, and did not attempt to kiss her. Something they discussed that day happened to lead to a series of quite special exchanges between them. With the intent of striking Sonia's imagination, Martin vaguely alluded to his having joined a secret group of anti-Bolshevist conspirators that organized reconnaissance operations. It was perfectly true that such a group did exist; in fact, a common friend of theirs, one Lieutenant Melkikh, had twice crossed the border on dangerous missions; it was also true that Martin kept looking for an opportunity to make friends with him (once he had even invited him to dinner) and always regretted that while in Switzerland he had not met the mysterious Gruzinov, whom Zilanov had mentioned, and who, according to information Martin had gathered, emerged as a man of great adventures, a terrorist, a very special spy, and the master-mind of recent peasant revolts against the Soviet rule.

'It never occurred to me,' said Sonia, 'that you thought about things like that. Only, you know, if you really have joined that organization, it's very naive to start blabbing about it right away.'

'Oh, I was only joking,' said Martin, and slit his eyes enigmatically so as to make Sonia believe he had deliberately turned it into a joke. She, however, did not catch that nuance; stretched out on the dry, needle-strewn ground, beneath the pines whose trunks the sun blotched with color, she put her bare arms behind her head, exposing her lovely armpits which she had recently started to shave and which were now shaded as if with a pencil, and said it was a strange thing, but she too had often thought about it – about there being a land where ordinary mortals were not admitted.

'What shall we call that land?' asked Martin, suddenly recollecting his games with Lida on the Crimean fairy-tale shore.

'Some northern name,' answered Sonia. 'Look at that squirrel.' The squirrel, playing hide-and-seek, jerkily climbed a tree trunk and vanished amidst the foliage.

'Zoorland, for example,' said Martin. 'A Norman mariner mentions it.'

'Yes, of course – Zoorland,' Sonia concurred, and he grinned broadly, somewhat astounded by her unexpectedly revealed capacity for daydreaming.

'May I remove an ant?' he asked parenthetically.

'Depends where.'

'Stocking.'

'Scram, chum' (addressing the ant). She brushed it off and continued, as if reciting, 'Winters are cold there, and monster icicles hang from the eaves, a whole system of them, like organ pipes. Then they melt and everything gets very watery, and there are sootlike specks on the thawing snow. Oh, I can tell you everything about it. For instance, they've just passed a law that all inhabitants must shave their heads, so that now the most important, most influential people are the barbers.'

'Equality of heads,' said Martin.

'Yes. And of course the bald ones are best off. And you know –'

'Bubnov would have a grand time there,' Martin interjected facetiously.

For some reason Sonia took offense and dried up. Yet from that day on she occasionally condescended to play Zoorland with him, and Martin was tormented by the thought that she might be making sophisticated fun of him and that any moment she might cause him to take a false step, prodding him toward the boundary beyond which phantasmata become tasteless – and the dreamwalker is jolted into seeing the roof edge from which he is dangling, his own hiked-up nightshirt, the crowd, looking up from the sidewalk, the firemen's helmets. But even if this was a form of derision on Sonia's part, no matter, he enjoyed the opportunity to let himself go in her presence. They studied Zoorlandian customs and laws. The region was rocky and windy, and the wind was recognized as a positive force since by championing equality in not tolerating towers and tall trees, it only subserved the public aspirations of atmospheric strata that kept diligent watch over the uniformity of the temperature. And, naturally, pure arts, pure science were outlawed, lest the honest dunces be hurt to see the scholar's brooding brow and offensively thick books. Shaven-headed, wearing brown cassocks, the happy Zoorlanders warmed themselves by bonfires as the strings of burning violins snapped with loud reports, and discussed plans to level the land by blowing up mountains that stuck up too presumptuously. Sometimes during the general conversation – at table, for instance – Sonia would suddenly turn to him and quickly whisper, 'Have you heard, there's a new law forbidding caterpillars to pupate,' or 'I forgot to tell you, Savior-and-Mauler' (the sobriquet of one of the chieftains) 'has ordered physicians to stop casting around and to treat all illnesses in exactly the same way.'

Thirty-Five

When he returned for the winter to Switzerland, Martin looked forward to an entertaining correspondence, but Sonia made no mention of Zoorland in her infrequent letters. In one of them, however, she asked him to give her father's regards to Gruzinov. It turned out that Gruzinov was staying at the Majestic, the hotel that had had such an odd attraction for Martin. But when he skied down to it, he found that Gruzinov had left and would be away for some time. He transmitted Zilanov's regards to Gruzinov's wife, a young-looking, brightly dressed lady in her forties, with blue-black hair and a cautious smile that attempted to conceal protruding front teeth always smeared with lipstick. Martin had never seen such exquisite hands as hers. They were small and soft, and adorned with glowing rings. But though everybody considered her attractive, and admired her grace and melodious, caressive voice, Martin's senses remained unstirred; in fact it irked him to think that, maybe, she was trying to charm him. His suspicions were unfounded. Mrs Gruzinov was as indifferent to him as to the tall big-nosed Englishman with gray bristly hair on his narrow head and a striped scarf around his neck who took her sleigh-riding.

'My husband won't be back before July,' she said, and began questioning Martin about the Zilanovs. 'Yes, yes. I do pity her mother' (Martin had mentioned Irina). 'You know, don't you, how it all started?' Martin knew. During the civil war, in Southern Russia, Irina, then a quiet, plump, normal though melancholy girl of fourteen, was on a train with her mother: they had had to be content with a bench in a freight car crammed with all sorts of riffraff, and during the long journey two rowdies, ignoring the protests of some of their pals, palpated, pinched, and tickled the child, saying monstrous obscenities to her. Mrs Pavlov, wearing the smile of helpless horror, and doing her best to protect her, kept repeating, 'Never mind, Irochka, never mind – oh please leave the child alone, you should be ashamed of yourselves – never mind, Irochka –' then, on the next train, nearer to Moscow, with similar cries and mutterings, she again cradled her daughter's head when other roughs, deserters or the like ejected her corpulent husband by squeezing him through the window with the train going full speed. Yes, he was very fat, and he laughed hysterically, having got stuck halfway through, but finally, with a unanimous heave-ho they succeeded, he disappeared from sight, and there only remained the blind snow driving past the empty window. Miraculously he rejoined his family at some little railway station buried in snow; and, miraculously, too, Irina survived a severe typhoid infection; but she lost the power of speech, and it was only a year later in London that she learned to produce mooing sounds with different intonations and to pronounce 'ma-ma' with tolerable clarity.

Martin, who somehow had never paid much attention to Irina, having soon become used to her mental deficiency, now experienced a strange shock as Mrs Gruzinov added, 'That's how they have in their home a permanent living symbol.' The night of Zoorland seemed to him even darker, its wildwood deeper, and Martin already knew that nothing and nobody could prevent him from penetrating, as a free pilgrim, into those woods, where plump children are tortured in the dark, and a smell of burning and of putrefaction permeates the air. When he returned in the spring to Berlin and to Sonia, he could have almost believed (so crowded with adventures had been his winter-night fantasies) that he had already concluded that solitary and courageous expedition, and now was going to talk and talk about his adventures. As he entered her room, he said (being anxious to express it before the familiar frustrating effect of her lusterless eyes had reasserted itself): 'Like this, like this, I shall return some day, and then, ah, then –' 'There'll never be anything,' she exclaimed in the tones of Pushkin's Naïna ('Hero, I still do not love thee!'). She was even paler than usual, her office work was very fatiguing; at home she wore an old black velvet dress with a narrow leather belt around the hips and backless slippers with frayed pompons. Often after supper she would put on her raincoat and leave, and Martin, after strolling aimlessly from room to room for a time, would leave too and walk slowly to the streetcar stop, hands deep in trouser pockets; at the opposite end of Berlin he would whistle tenderly under the window of a cabaret dancer whom he had met at the tennis club. She flitted out onto the balcony, froze for an instant at its parapet, disappeared, flitted out again and tossed him the house key wrapped in paper. In her bedroom Martin drank green crème de menthe and kissed her naked golden-brown back, and, tossing her head, she would tightly contract her shoulder blades. He liked to watch her as she rapidly paced the room setting close together her muscular sun-tanned legs and furiously reviling always the same theatrical agent; he liked her bizarre little

face with its orange-tinted incarnadine, unnaturally thin eyebrows, and smoothly brushed-back hair; and he vainly tried
not to think of Sonia. One night in May he emitted his soft
whistle with a special trill, but instead of his mistress, an
elderly man in braces came out onto the balcony and Martin
sighed and walked away. He went back by tram to the
Zilanovs' street and started to walk back and forth between
two lamps. Sonia returned past midnight, alone, and while
she rummaged in her handbag in search of her keys, Martin
approached and asked timidly where she had been. 'Won't
you ever leave me alone?' cried Sonia and without waiting
for an answer turned her key with a double crunch, and the
heavy door swung open, stopped for a moment, banged shut.
Then came a time when Martin began to imagine that not
only Sonia, but all their common acquaintances, were avoid-
ing him, that he was unwanted, that no one cared for him.
He dropped in on Bubnov, and the latter stared at him in an
odd way, excused himself, and continued to write. At last –
feeling that after a little more of this he would turn into
Sonia's shadow and to the end of his life continue to haunt
Berlin's sidewalks, wasting on a futile passion the important
and solemn thing that was ripening in him – Martin decided
to have done with Berlin in order to think over in purifying
solitude the plan of the expedition. In mid-May 1924, with
the ticket for Strasbourg already in his wallet, he went to take
leave of Sonia, and, of course, did not find her at home.

Amidst the twilight of the room, all in white, sat Irina, seeming to float in the dusk like a ghostly turtle. She did not take her eye off him. He wrote on an envelope, 'Polar night decreed in Zoorland,' put it on the pillow in Sonia's room, got into the waiting taxicab, and, wearing neither overcoat nor hat, with only one bag, left for the station.

Thirty-Six

As soon as the train began to move, Martin revived, regained his gaiety, began to enjoy the excitement of traveling – something that he considered to be a kind of indispensable training. When he transferred to a French train going south by way of Lyon, it seemed to him that he was definitely free of Sonia's nebulous spells. Beyond Lyon, the southern night gradually spread overhead; the pale rectangles of the reflected coach windows sped along the black bank; in the dirty, insufferably stuffy second-class compartment, Martin's only companion was a middle-aged Frenchman. The man discarded his coat and in one downward run of his fingers undid all the buttons of his waistcoat; pulled off his cuffs as if screwing off his wrists, and carefully placed the two starched cylinders in the baggage net. He perched on the edge of the seat and swaying – the train was going fast – with lifted chin, he unfastened his collar and tie; and since the tie was of the ready-made variety that unhooked in the back, one again had the impression that here was a man taking himself apart and about to remove his head. The front skin of his neck was as flabby as a turkey's; he moved his head right and left with relief, then bent over and, grunting, changed from boots to bedroom slippers. With his shirt opened on his curly chest he now looked like a hearty enough fellow who had had one too many: for those fellow travelers in a night coach, with their shiny pale faces and glazed eyes, always appear to be drunk with the carriage's swaying and heat. From a hamper he produced a bottle of red wine and a large orange; first he took a swallow from the bottle, smacked his lips, forcefully pressed home the squeaking cork, then began to strip the orange with his thumb after biting open the skin on its pate. At this moment his eyes met those of Martin who had just put down his Tauchnitz on his knee in preparation for a yawn, and the Frenchman spoke. 'We're already in Provence,' he said jovially, one shaggy eyebrow pointing toward the window, in whose mirror-black glass his dim double was peeling an orange too.

'*Oui, on sent le sud*,' answered Martin.

'You an Englishman?' queried the other tearing in two his peeled gray-tufted orange.

'Correct,' answered Martin. 'How did you guess?'

The Frenchman, chewing juicily, shrugged one shoulder: 'It was not very hard,' he said, swallowed, and, after a look of inspection, pointed a hairy finger at the Tauchnitz. Martin smiled indulgently. 'And I'm from Lyon,' the Frenchman continued. 'I'm in the wine business. I have to travel a lot but I like to be moving about. One gets to see new places, new people – the world, quoi. I have a wife and a small daughter,' he added, wiping with a bit of newspaper the tips of his spread-out fingers. Then, contemplating Martin again, his battered bag and wrinkled trousers, and concluding that a British milord would hardly be traveling second class, he observed with an anticipatory nod: 'You're a traveler?' Martin understood that this was a mere abbreviation for 'commercial traveler.'

'Yes, I am indeed a traveler,' he answered, diligently imitating a British accent, 'but in a wider sense of the word. I am traveling very far.'

'But you are in the commerce?'

Martin shook his head.

'Then you're doing it for pleasure?'

'If you like,' said Martin.

The Frenchman ruminated in silence; presently he asked, 'At the moment, you're going to Marseille, aren't you?'

'Yes, probably to Marseille. Not all my preparations are completed, yet.'

The Frenchman nodded but was visibly puzzled.

'In such cases,' Martin went on, 'preparations must be made with the greatest care. I spent close to a year in Berlin where I had hoped to obtain some essential information, and you can't imagine –'

'My nephew is an engineer,' the Frenchman hopefully interposed.

'Oh no, I am not concerned with technology, that was not why I visited Germany. But, as I was saying: you can't imagine how difficult it is to ferret out that sort of information. The fact is I'm planning to explore a certain remote, almost inaccessible region. It has been reached by a few adventurers, but how to find them, how to make them talk? What do I have? Only a map,' and Martin pointed to his valise, which indeed contained, besides his silk shirts and collapsible tub, a map on a scale of a vershok to a verst, acquired in Berlin at the former Military Headquarters. There followed a silence. The train clattered and swayed.

'I always affirm,' the Frenchman said, 'that our colonies have a great future. Naturally, yours do too, and you have so many of them. One of my friends spent ten years in the tropics and he says he would gladly go back. He told me once how he saw monkeys using a fallen tree trunk to cross a river, each holding the tail of the one in front – it was devilishly drôle – holding tails! holding tails!'

'Colonies are something else again,' said Martin. 'I'm not planning to go to our colonies. My trail will take me through perilous places, and – who knows – I may not be able to return.'

'Is that a scientific expedition or something?' asked the Frenchman squashing a yawn with his back teeth.

'Partly. But – how shall I put it? – science, knowledge – all that is not the main point. The main point, the main purpose is – No, I really don't know how to explain.'

'I know, I know,' said the Frenchman wearily. 'You, *les Anglais*, are fond of wagers, of records' (his '*records*' sounded like a drowsy growl). 'Who wants a bare rock in the sky? Or – good Lord, how sleepy one gets on a train! – or icebergs or whatever one calls them – or, indeed, the North Pole? Or those marshes where one perishes from malaria?'

'Yes, you may have put your finger on it. And yet even that, even *le sport*, is not all. There are besides – how shall I say? – glory, love, tenderness for the soil, a thousand rather mysterious feelings.'

The Frenchman gaped and then, moving forward, lightly slapped Martin on the knee. 'One is mocking me, eh?' he commented good-naturedly. 'Oh no, not at all!' 'Come,' he said leaning back in his corner. 'You are too young to roam the Saharas. With your permission, I'll now put out the light and take a nap.'

Thirty-Seven

Darkness. Almost at once the Frenchman began to snore. 'Yes, he did believe I was English. *Ong sahng le soude.* Like this I shall travel north, exactly like this, in a coach that one cannot stop – and after that, after that –' He began to follow a forest path, the path unwound, kept unwinding, but sleep did not come to meet him. Martin opened his eyes. Good idea to lower the window. A mild night flooded his face and straining his eyes Martin leaned out, but invisible dust flew into his eyes, speed blinded him; he drew back his head. A cough resounded in the darkened compartment. 'No, no. Be so kind,' said a cross voice. 'I have no desire to sleep under the stars. Close it, close it.' 'Close it yourself,' said Martin. He stepped out into the lighted corridor and walked past the compartments where one could guess the jumbled presence of slumbering, helpless, half-undressed bodies, wheezes and sighs, mouths opened fish-fashion, a sinking head jerking up again, a soft foot right next to a stranger's nose. Making his way from one vestibule to another across the grind of connecting plates, Martin passed through two third-class coaches. The sliding doors of some of the compartments stood open; in one of them gray-blue soldiers were noisily playing cards. Farther on, in the corridor of a sleeping car, Martin stopped at a half-lowered window, and recalled, with exceptional clarity, his childhood journey through Southern France: that *strapontin* seat by the window, that cloth loop which permitted him to drive the train, that lovely melody in three languages – especially: *pericoloso*. He reflected what a strange, strange life had fallen to his lot, it seemed as if he had never left a fast train, had merely wandered from car to car – and one was occupied by young Englishmen, among whom was Darwin in the act of solemnly taking hold of the emergency cord; in the other were Alla and her husband; or else the Crimean crowd; or snoring Uncle Henry; or the Zilanovs, her father with his eternal newspaper, and Sonia, her velvet-dark eyes staring through the window. 'And then I'll continue on foot, on foot,' muttered Martin excitedly – a forest, a winding path – what huge trees! Here, in this sleeping car, his childhood must have traveled, must have shivered, as it undid the button of the leathern blind; and if one followed the blue corridor a little farther, one would get to the dining car where his parents had supper, and there would be on the table the same mock-up of chocolate bar in a violet wrapping, and over the door a helical ventilator would shimmer in a garden of ads. At that moment, in response to his recollections, Martin saw through the window what he had seen as a child – a necklace of lights, far away, among dark hills. Someone seemed to pour them from one hand into the other, and pocket them. While he looked, the train began to slow down, and Martin told himself that if it stopped, he would get off and go in search of those lights. A station platform drifted into sight, then the moonlike disk of a clock, and the train came to a halt exhaling a sigh. Martin dashed back to his coach, twice burst into the snoring dark of a wrong compartment, found the right one, snapped on the light, and the Frenchman half-rose from his seat rubbing his eyes with his fists. Martin jerked down his valise, and snatched up his Tauchnitz. In his haste he failed to notice that the train had begun to move again, and therefore very nearly fell when he jumped down onto the gliding platform. A long row of windows passed by, and were gone. Nothing remained except empty rails with the glitter of coal dust between them.

Still panting, Martin traversed the platform. A porter who was pushing a luggage cart with a big box labeled 'Fragile' said to him gaily, with the metallic accent peculiar to Provence: 'You woke up at the right moment, Monsieur.' 'Tell me,' Martin inquired, 'what's in that box?' The porter looked at it as if he had only just noticed its presence, and read out the address: 'Museum of Natural Science.' 'Ah yes, a collection of insects, no doubt,' said Martin, and walked toward the little group of tables at the entrance of the dimly lit buffet.

The air was velvety and warm; around a milky white arc light swirled pale midges and one ample dark moth with hoary margins. A six-foot poster adorned the wall: it was an attempt on the part of the War Department to picture for the benefit of young men the allurements of military service: in the foreground, a valiant French soldier; in the back, a date palm, a dromedary, and a burnoosed Arab; and in the corner, two opulent forms in charshafs.

The platform was deserted. A little way down stood some cages with sleeping hens. On the farther side of the rails one could make out a tangle of black bushes. The air smelled of coal, juniper, and urine. A dusky old woman looked out of the *buvette*, and Martin asked for an *apéritif* whose delightful name he had seen advertised. A workman in blue sat down at the next table and fell asleep with his head on his arm.

'There is something I would like to know,' said Martin to the woman. 'Just before the train stopped, I saw lights in the distance.' 'Where? Was it there?' she asked pointing in the direction from which the train had arrived. Martin nodded. 'That could only have been Molignac,' she said. 'Yes, Molignac. A small village.' Martin paid and walked with his bag toward the exit. A dark square, plane trees, a row of ghostly houses and a narrow street. He had already turned into it when he realized he had forgotten to look at the station sign, and now did not know the name of the town where he chanced to be. It thrilled him pleasantly. Who knows –

perhaps, by some caprice of space, he was already beyond the Zoorland border, in the uncertain night, and presently would be challenged.

Thirty-Eight

When he woke up next morning, Martin could not at once reconstruct the previous day; and the reason why he woke up was that flies were tickling his face. A remarkably soft bed; an ascetic washstand, and, beside it, a toilet utensil in the shape of a violin; hot blue light was breathing through a chink in the window curtain. It was a long time since he had had such a good night of sleep, a long time since he had been so hungry. He drew the curtain aside and saw before him a dazzling white wall. Farther off to the left there were shops with striped awnings, a piebald dog sat on the pavement scratching behind its ear with its hind paw, and a streamlet of glittering water ran along the curb.

The sound of the bell button he pressed resounded through the entire two-story inn and, stomping boldly, there arrived a bright-eyed dirty maid. He ordered a lot of bread, a lot of butter, a lot of coffee, and when she had brought it all, asked her how he could get to Molignac. She proved to be talkative and inquisitive. Martin mentioned casually that he was German, had been sent here by a museum to collect insects; at this she glanced pensively at the wall where there were some suspicious-looking reddish-brown dots. Gradually it transpired that in a month, and maybe even before, a bus line would be established between the town and Molignac. 'It means, one has to walk?' asked Martin. 'Fifteen kilometers,' exclaimed the maid with horror. 'What an idea! And in this heat!'

He left his things at the inn and, having bought a map of the region at the tobacconist's whose sign was a tricolor pipe protruding over the door, started to stride down the sunny side of the street, and immediately noticed that his open shirt collar and absence of headgear were attracting general attention. The town seemed drawn in bright chalks and was sharply divided into light and shadow; it boasted numerous pastry shops. Presently the crowded houses dropped away, and the paved road between its double row of huge plane trees with flesh-colored patterns on their green trunks went flowing past vineyards. The rare people he met, such as stone breakers, schoolchildren, and country wives in black straw hats, ate him up with their eyes. It occurred to Martin to try out something that might prove useful in the future. He proceeded to advance with the utmost stealth, crossing ditches and hiding behind brambles whenever he glimpsed in the distance a cart drawn by a donkey in black blinders or a dusty ramshackle motor van. After a couple of kilo-meters he abandoned the road altogether and began to work his way parallel to it along the hillside where he was screened by the oak scrub, the glossy myrtles, the nettle trees. The sun blazed fiercely, cicadas trilled, the hot spicy smells made him dizzy and for a minute he lay in the shade wiping his sticky neck with his handkerchief. A glance at the map showed him that at the fifth kilometer the road made a loop, and that to rejoin it one might cut across yonder hill, all yellow with flowering broom. When he came down on the other side, the white snake of the road did reappear, and as he walked on parallel to it through the fragrant undergrowth, he rejoiced at his capacity to find his bearings.

Suddenly he heard the cool sound of running water. No better music could exist in the world! A brook quivered on flat stones in a tunnel formed by the foliage. Martin got down on his knees, quenched his thirst, and heaved a deep sigh. He lit a cigarette. In the brilliant air the match burned with an invisible flame and from its sulfur a sweetish taste spread to his tongue. Thus, sitting on a rock and listening to the brook's gurgling, Martin enjoyed his fill of viatic free-dom from all concerns: he was a wanderer, alone and lost in a marvelous world, completely indifferent toward him, in which butterflies danced, lizards darted, and leaves glistened – the same way as they glisten in a Russian or African wood.

It was long past midday when Martin reached Molignac. So this was where they sparkled at night, the lights which had beckoned to him ever since his childhood! Silence, a burning heat. Through the knotty streamlets of water that ran by the narrow sidewalk shone its varicolored bed made of broken crockery. On the cobblestones timid, dreadfully emaciated white dogs were napping. In the middle of a small square stood a monument: a female personage, with wings, raising a banner.

First of all Martin visited the post office, a cool, darkish and drowsy place. There he wrote his mother a postcard, to the accompaniment of the piercing complaint of a housefly, one of whose legs had got stuck in the glue of the treacle-colored flypaper affixed to a windowledge. That postcard was the first of a new little batch of letters which Mrs Edelweiss stored in her chest of drawers: the penultimate batch.

Thirty-Nine

He told the woman who ran the only Molignac inn that he was Swiss (which was confirmed by his passport) and gave her to understand that he had long been roving the world, working at odd jobs here and there. The same information he conveyed to her brother, a farmer, purple with wine and sanguineness, by whom, in consequence of the rover's complete destitution, he was hired as day laborer. It was thus the third time in a couple of days that Martin changed his nationality, testing the credulity of strangers and learning to live incognito. The fact of his having been born in a remote northern land had long since acquired a shade of enchanting mystery. A carefree visitor from a distant shore, he strolled through the bazaars of the infidels, and everything was entertaining and colorful, but no matter where he might go, nothing could weaken in him the wonderful sense of being different and elect. Such words, such notions and images, as those that Russia had engendered did not exist in other countries, and it often happened that he would lapse into incoherence, or start to laugh nervously when vainly trying to explain to a foreigner the various meanings of some special term, say, *poshlost'*. He felt flattered by the infatuation of the English with Chekhov, by that of the Germans with Dostoevski. Once, in Cambridge, he discovered in a sixty-year-old issue of the local review a poem coolly signed: A. Jameson. It began:

I walk along the road alone.
My stony path spreads far,
Still is the night and cold the stone,
And star talks unto star.

and was a shameless paraphrase of Lermontov's greatest lyrical poem. A strange pensiveness would pervade him when, at times, from the depths of a Berlin courtyard would rise the sound of a hurdy-gurdy which was not aware that the tune it had borrowed had once touched the hearts of sentimental drunks in Russian taverns. Music! Martin regretted that an inner sentinel forbade to his vocal cords the sounds that lived in his ears. Still, when his fellow workers, young Italians, sang loudly, among the branches of Provence cherry trees, Martin would start his own song – hoarsely, boldly, and phenomenonally out of tune – and that song would echo the nights when at picnics in the Crimea the baritone Zaryanski, drowned out by the choir, sang about the 'seven-stringed companion,' or the 'little goblet.'

Far below him the lucerne rippled in the wind, from above the glowing blue pressed upon him, silver-veined leaves rustled close to his cheek, and the oilcloth-lined basket suspended from a bough gradually acquired weight as it got filled with the glossy-black fruit Martin pulled off by its taut stems. After the cherries had been harvested came sun-steeped apricots, and precious peaches which had to be tenderly cradled in one's palm lest they get bruised. There also were other kinds of labor. Naked to the waist, his back already the hue of terra cotta, Martin, to humor the young maize, loosened and heaped up the soil, grubbed out with the sharp corner of his hoe the wily and stubborn speargrass, or for hours on end stood bending over the shoots of infant trees, apple and pear, clicking his pruning shears. He especially enjoyed conducting the water from the reservoir in the yard to the nurseries, where the mattocked furrows joined with one another and with the hollows dug around the stems. As the water spread all over the young plantation, it picked its way like a live thing; here it would stop, there run on, extending bright tentacles, and Martin, grimacing occasionally from the strings of tiny thistleheads, sloshed up to his ankles in fat purple mud, driving in forcefully an iron shield for a barrier or, on the contrary, helping a streamlet to break through; the hollowed earth would fill with bubbling brown water and, feeling in it with a spade, he mercifully softened the soil, until something gave delightfully, and the percolating water sank away, washing the roots. He felt happy he knew how to satisfy a plant's thirst, happy that chance had helped him to find work that could serve to try out both his shrewdness and his endurance. Together with the other laborers he lodged in a shed, drank, as they did, one and a half liters of wine a day, and found satisfaction in looking like them – except for the little blond beard that he had quietly let grow.

In the evening, before turning in, he would walk over to the cork woods beyond the farm, and smoke and muse. Overhead the nightingales whistled in short rich phrases, from the pond came the rubbery croaking of frogs. The air was tender and dullish, not quite twilight yet, but no longer day, and the terraced olives and the mythographic hills in the distance, and that pine standing separate on a rock – the whole landscape was reliefless and a little swoony under an evenly fading sky which oppressed and lulled one, and made one long for the vivifying stars to appear. Night fell, lights trembled on the silhouetted hills, the windows of the farmhouse lit up; and when far, far away, in the unknown gloom, a tiny rattling train would pass by broken into small fiery segments, and vanish, Martin told himself with deep satisfaction that from there, from that train, the farm and Molignac looked like a handful of jewels. He was glad to have heeded the call of those lights, to have uncovered their lovely quiet essence. One Sunday night, in Molignac, he noticed a small white house, at the foot of steep vineyards; a crooked old post said: 'FOR SALE.' And, indeed, would it not be better to dismiss the perilous, daredevil project, to renounce the desire to peer into the merciless Zoorland night, and to get settled with a young wife right here, on this wedge of fertile soil waiting for an industrious master? Yes, he had to decide: time was running out, the dark autumn night he had marked for slipping across the border was nearing, and he now felt rested, refreshed, sure of being able to get away with any kind of impersonation, of never losing his presence of mind, of adjusting whenever and wherever it might be to the kind of life that circumstances demanded.

Testing fate, he wrote to Sonia. The answer came quickly and, after reading it, Martin sighed with relief. 'Stop tormenting me,' wrote Sonia. 'Enough, for Christ's sake. I will never marry you. Moreover, I loathe vineyards, the heat, snakes, and, especially, garlic. Cross me out, do me that favor, darling.'

The same day he left for town on the brand-new bus, shaved off his beard, fetched his valise from the inn, and walked over to the station. There, at the same table, his head on his arm, slept the same workman. The lamps were being lit, bats skimmered by, the greenish sky was fading. *Proshchay, proshchay* (adieu, adieu) sounded in Martin's ears with the refrain of a Russian song as he looked at the tousled junipers on the other side of the already vibrating rails, at the signal lights, at the black outline of a man pushing the black outline of a luggage cart.

The night express pounded into the station; a minute later it started again and Martin experienced a momentary urge to jump out and return to the happy, fairy-tale farm. But the station had already ceased to exist. He stood looking through the window, waiting for the appearance of his beloved lights, to bid them good-bye. Here they came, far away, spilled jewels in the blackness, unbelievably lovely – 'Tell me,' Martin asked the conductor, 'Those lights there – that's Molignac, isn't it?' 'What lights?' the man asked glancing at the window, but at this moment everything was shut out by the

217

sudden rise of a dark bank. 'In any case, it's not Molignac,' said the conductor. 'Molignac can't be seen from the rail-road.'

At the kiosk of the Lausanne station Martin bought the Sunday issue of a Russian *émigré* paper published in Berlin. He could hardly believe his eyes when he found in the lower half of the second page a feuilleton entitled: 'ZOORLAND.' It was signed 'S. Bubnov,' and turned out to be a short story in that author's admirable style 'with a touch of the fantastic,' as critics like to put it. In it Martin recognized with disgust and embarrassment (as if he were witnessing some dread-fully obscene act) much of what he and Sonia used to think up – now oddly illuminated by the imagination of an intruder. 'How treacherous she is, after all,' Martin reflected and in a surge of acute and hopeless jealousy recalled having once observed Bubnov and her walking arm in arm down a dark street; and how he had tried to believe what she told him on the following day – that she had gone to the movies with the Veretennikov girl.

It was drizzling, and only the lower half of the mountains could be made out, when, wedged among hampers and cor-pulent females, he reached by public charabanc the village situated at ten minutes' walk from his uncle's villa. Mrs Edel-weiss knew that her son was about to arrive. For three days she had been expecting a wire, and had looked forward to the excitement of driving down to the station to meet him.

She was in the living room doing some embroidery when there came from the garden her son's deep young voice and the soft husky laughter which was typical of his demeanor when he came back after a long separation. He was walking beside flushed Marie, who was trying to relieve him of his valise while he shifted it from one hand to the other and back again as he walked. His face was copper-dark, the color of his eyes seemed to have paled by contrast, and he smelled wonderfully of stale tobacco, wet woolen jacket, and train. 'You've come for a long, long time now,' she kept repeating in a happy barking voice. 'Generally speaking, yes,' Martin answered sedately. 'I'll just have to go to Berlin on business in about a fortnight, then I'll return.' 'Oh, forget about business, it can wait!' she cried – and Uncle Henry, who had been resting in his room after lunch, woke up, listened, quickly put on his shoes, and came down.

'The prodigal son,' he said entering. 'Delighted to see you again.' Martin touched his cheek with his own, and both simultaneously kissed the void, as was their wont on such occasions. 'I hope – for some time?' the uncle asked, without taking his eyes off Martin; still staring, he groped for the back of a chair and sat down with knees apart. 'Generally speaking, yes,' answered Martin while he devoured some ham. 'I'll just have to go to Berlin in about a fortnight, but I'll return.' 'You won't,' said Mrs Edelweiss laughing, 'I know you. Come, tell us how it all was. Can it be that you actually plowed, and made hay, and milked the cows?' 'Milking is fun,' said Martin and spreading two fingers showed how one does it (milking was precisely the one thing he never did at Molignac – that was the job of his namesake, Martin Roc – and it was not clear why he began his story with a spurious detail when there was so much else, authentic, to tell).

Next morning, as Martin glanced at the mountains, he thought again, to the same sobbing tune, 'Adieu, adieu,' but at once scolded himself for unworthy faintheartedness. At that moment his mother came in with a letter, and from the threshold said cheerfully, before her son would have time to assume mistakenly that it was from Sonia, 'I think it's Darwin's hand. I forgot to give it to you last night.' After reading the very first lines Martin began to chuckle quietly. Darwin wrote that he was about to marry a splendid English girl he had met at a hotel in Niagara Falls; that he was traveling around a great deal; and that in a week's time he would be in Berlin. 'Do invite him here,' Mrs Edelweiss said quickly. 'What could be simpler?' 'No, no, I tell you I have to go to Berlin. It all fits in perfectly.'

'Martin,' she began but hesitated and stopped. 'What's the matter?' he asked gaily. 'How is it working out? – Oh, you know what I mean – Maybe you're already engaged?' Martin slit his eyes, laughed, but did not answer. 'I shall be very fond of her,' whispered Mrs Edelweiss piously. 'Let's go for a walk. Such glorious weather,' said Martin, pretending to be deliberately changing the subject. 'You go,' she replied. 'Like a fool, I invited, precisely today, the old Drouet couple. They would die of a heart attack if one tried to phone them.'

In the garden Uncle Henry was adjusting a ladder against the trunk of an apple tree; then, with the greatest care, he climbed up to the third rung. By the draw well, arms akimbo, stood Marie looking away, forgetful of the pail which overran with gleaming water. She had gained much weight these last years, but at that instant, with the sun playing on her dress, on her neck, left uncovered by her twisted, tightly bunched-up braids, she reminded him of his fleeting infatuation. She suddenly turned her face toward him. It was a fat and expressionless face.

Forty

As he walked with springy steps through the mountainside fir forest whose blackness was broken from place to place by the radiance of a slender birch tree, he anticipated with rapture a similar sun-pierced thicket on a far Northern plain with spiderwebs spread on the sunbeams, and with damp hollows choked with willow herb, and, beyond, the luminous open spaces, the empty autumnal fields, and the squat little white church on a hillock tending as it were the isbas that looked on the point of wandering away; and, encircling the hillock, there would be the bright bend of a river brimming with enmeshed reflections. He was almost surprised when he glimpsed an alpine slope through the conifers.

This reminded him that before he left he had an account with his conscience to settle. Unhurriedly, purposefully, he ascended the slope and reached the broken gray rocks. He climbed up the stony steepness and found himself on the same little platform from which the familiar cornice started to round the sheer cliff. Without hesitation, obeying an inner command that could not be disregarded, he began to sidle along the narrow shelf. When it tapered to an end he looked down over his shoulder and saw, under his very heels, the sunny precipice and at the bottom of it the porcelain hotel. 'There,' said Martin to the little white thing, 'lump it!' and, fighting dizziness, began to move the way he had come. He stopped again, however, and, checking his self-control, attempted to extract his cigarette case from his hip pocket and light up. There came a moment when without holding onto the cliff he merely leant his chest against it, and felt the abyss behind him strain and pull at his calves and shoulders. He did not light that cigarette only because he dropped the matchbox. The absolute noiselessness of its fall was awesome, and when he resumed his progress along the cornice the feeling persisted that the matchbox was still plunging through space. Upon safely reaching the platform, Martin grunted with joy, and in the same purposeful way, with a stern sense of duty fulfilled, climbed down scree and heather, found the right path and descended toward the Majestic – to see what it would have to say. By the tennis court in the garden Mrs Gruzinov sat on a bench next to a white-trousered man. Martin hoped she would not notice him. He was loath to dissipate so soon the treasure he had brought down from the mountain-top. 'Hello, Martin,' she cried, and Martin grinned and went up to her. 'Yurochka, this is the son of Dr Edelweiss,' said Mrs Gruzinov to her companion. The latter half-rose and without removing his straw hat drew back his elbow, took good aim, and shooting his palm out, vigorously shook hands with Martin. 'Gruzinov,' he said softly, as if imparting a secret.

'Have you come for long, Martin?' asked Mrs Gruzinov with a smile, and hastened to lower her downy upper lip over her front teeth tinted with pink.

'Generally speaking, yes. I must take a quick business trip to Berlin, and then I shall be back.'

'Martin Sergeevich?' Gruzinov inquired, and after Martin had answered in the affirmative, dropped his eyes and once more repeated to himself Martin's patronymic.

'Well, you certainly have –?' said Mrs Gruzinov, and her beautiful hands outlined the shape of a vase in the air.

'No wonder,' Martin replied, 'I worked on a farm in the south of France. Life is so peaceful there that one cannot help gaining weight.'

Gruzinov pressed his finger and thumb to the corners of his mouth, a gesture which leant a somewhat peasant-woman expression to his substantial-looking, clean-featured face with a complexion so creamy as to suggest making toffee out of his cheeks.

'I've got it,' he said. 'The person's name is Kruglov, he married a Turkish woman.' ('Come, sit down,' interjected Mrs Gruzinov, and in two moves of her soft, generously perfumed body she made room for Martin.) 'He happens to have a small zamindary in the south of France,' Gruzinov explained, 'and I believe he makes a living by supplying the city with jasmin. Have you also been staying in the odorofacient region?' Martin told him the name of the nearest town. 'That's it,' chimed in Gruzinov. 'That's not far from where he dwells. Or maybe it isn't. Are you attending the university in Berlin?'

'No, I finished Cambridge.'

'Very interesting,' said Gruzinov weightily. 'They still have some Roman aqueducts there,' he continued, turning to his wife. 'Imagine, my dear, those Romans, so far from home, establishing themselves in a foreign land, and doing it, mind you, really well, comfortably, in patrician style.'

Martin had not met with any particular aqueducts in Cambridge, yet he found it necessary to nod. In the presence of
remarkable people, people with an extraordinary past, he
always felt a pleasant excitement, and now was trying to settle how to derive the most from this new acquaintance. It
turned out, however, that Yuri Gruzinov was not one to be
easily put into that euphoric state of mind in which a man
scrambles out of his own self, as out of a burrow, and sun-
bathes in the buff. Yuri Gruzinov refused to scramble out.
He was perfectly benevolent, and at the same time impenetrable; was ready to converse on any subject — natural
phenomena or human affairs — but there would always be
something about his talk that suddenly compelled his interlocutor to wonder if his leg was not being atrociously pulled
by that appetizingly smooth, compact, dapper gentleman,
whose icy eyes seemed somehow to be absent from the conversation. In the past, when Martin heard people tell of
Gruzinov's passion for danger, of his illegal crossings of the
most perilous border in the world and of the mysterious
rebellions he was said to spark in Zoorland, Martin imagined him as a man of powerful, aquiline aspect. But now,
watching Gruzinov separate with a little plop the two parts
of his spectacle case and hook on reading glasses of the
plain, granny sort that might have suited the nose of an
elderly carpenter with a yardstick folded in his blouse

pocket – Martin realized that Gruzinov could not have looked different. His simplicity grading into a certain flaccidity of demeanor, the old-fashioned stylishness of his clothes (that striped flannel waistcoat for instance), his obscure jokes, his circumstantiality – all this formed a solid cocoon which Martin could not manage to tear. However, the fact of having met him almost on the eve of attempting a secret exploit struck Martin as a portent of its success. And Martin had been doubly lucky: for had he returned to Switzerland but one month later, Gruzinov would not have been there: he would already have been in Bessarabia.

Forty-One

The walks they took: to the Waterfall; to Ste Claire; to the Grotto where once a hermit had lived. And back. September 1924 was especially fair. There might be a wet fog in the morning but by noon the world would delicately scintillate in the sun, the tree trunks would be glossed, blue puddles would shine on the road, and the sun-warmed mountains would be discarding their misty raiment. Mrs Edelweiss walked in front with Mrs Gruzinov; Gruzinov and Martin followed. Gruzinov strode along with pleasure, leaning firmly on his homemade stick and resenting it if anyone stopped to admire the view: he maintained that views destroyed the rhythm of the ramble. It happened once that a sheepdog dashed out of a farmyard and stood, growling, in their path. Mrs Gruzinov said 'I'm scared' and hid behind her husband's back, and Martin took his mother's cane out of her hand, while she tried to pacify the dog by emitting in its direction sounds used in Russia to urge on the horses. Alone Gruzinov did the right thing: he pretended to pick up a stone from the road, and the dog at once jumped away. A trifle, of course, but Martin cherished that kind of trifle. On another occasion, thinking that Martin had trouble walking without a stick up a very steep path, Gruzinov produced a jack-knife from his pocket, selected a suitable sapling, and, wielding the knife with great precision, skillfully and silently manufactured a walking stick for him. It was smooth and white, still living, still cool to the touch. Another trifle, but somehow that stick seemed to smell of Russia. Mrs Edelweiss found Gruzinov delightful and once told her husband at lunch that he simply must make friends with the man, that Gruzinov had become a legendary figure among émigrés.

'No doubt, no doubt,' Uncle Henry replied pouring vinegar over his salad, 'but he is an adventurer, and does not quite belong to our set. But, of course, invite him if you want.'

Martin regretted that he would not hear Gruzinov engage Uncle Henry in a conversation about the despotism of machines and the materialism of our age. After lunch Martin followed Uncle Henry into his study and said, 'I am leaving on Tuesday for Berlin. May I have a word with you?' 'What makes you gad about like that?' asked Uncle Henry with displeasure, and added, rolling his eyes and shaking his head, 'Your mother will be extremely upset – you know it yourself.' 'I am obliged to go,' Martin continued. 'I have a matter to settle.' 'An affair of the heart?' Uncle Henry was curious to know. Martin shook his head without smiling. 'What then?' muttered Uncle Henry examining the tip of a toothpick he had been using for some time to conduct excavations. 'Well, it's about money,' said Martin firmly enough. 'I want to ask you for a loan. You know that I earn well in the summer. I shall repay you then.' 'How much?' asked Uncle Henry, his face assuming a pleased expression, and moisture filming his eyes. He loved to show Martin his generosity. 'Five hundred francs.' Uncle Henry's eyebrows rose. 'Ah, a gambling debt, isn't it?' 'If you are disinclined –' began Martin looking with hatred at the way Uncle Henry sucked his toothpick. Uncle Henry took fright immediately. 'I have a rule,' he said in a conciliatory tone of voice. 'One should never expect frankness from a young man. I was young myself, and I know how rash a youth can be. It is only natural. But games of chance should be – Wait, wait, where are you going? I'll give you, I'll give you what you want, only too happy. And as to repaying –' 'Exactly five hundred then,' said Martin. 'And I shall be leaving on Tuesday.'

The door opened slightly. 'May I come in?' asked Mrs Edelweiss in a thin voice. 'What kind of secrets are you having together?' she continued a little archly, shifting her gaze from son to husband. 'Why can't I be told?' 'It's still the same subject – those Brothers Petit,' answered Martin. 'By the way, he is leaving on Tuesday,' said Uncle Henry and put the toothpick in his waistcoat pocket. 'What, so soon?' she said plaintively. 'Yes, so soon, so soon, so soon,' her son replied with unwonted irritation, and walked out of the room. 'He'll go crazy without a job,' observed Uncle Henry, commenting on the noise of the slammed door.

Forty-Two

When Martin entered the hotel garden whose sight bored him now, he found Gruzinov by the tennis court, on which a rather lively game was in progress between two young men. 'Look at them – skipping like two goats,' Gruzinov said. 'We used to have a blacksmith in Kostroma who was marvelous at tag-bat, he could belt a ball over the belfry or beyond the river – just like that. If we had him here, he would beat these lads hollow.' 'Tennis rules are different,' Martin remarked. 'He would have given it to them – rules or no rules,' Gruzinov retorted calmly. A silence. The knock of tennis balls. Martin slitted his eyes. 'The blond one has a rather classy drive.' 'You're a funny boy,' said Gruzinov and patted him on the shoulder. At that moment his wife appeared, gracefully swinging her hips. She noticed two English girls whom she knew and proceeded to navigate in their direction. 'Yuri Timofeich,' Martin said, 'I would like to consult you about something highly important and confidential.' 'Be glad to oblige. I'm as mute as a grave.' Martin looked around and hesitated. 'Let's go to my room,' suggested Gruzinov.

The hotel room was cluttered with objects, darkish, and imbued with Mrs Gruzinov's perfume. Gruzinov threw open the window – for one instant he resembled a large dark bird spread against a golden background, then sunlight invaded the floor in one stride, stopping short at the door which Martin had noiselessly closed behind him. 'The room is a mess, I'm afraid, hope you don't mind,' said Gruzinov with a sidelong glance at the double bed disarranged by the midday siesta. 'Take that armchair, my friend. These little apples are sweet as sugar. Help yourself.' 'Actually, I wanted to talk to you about the following matter: I have a pal who plans to cross illegally from Latvia to Russia –' 'Take this one, with the blush,' interposed Gruzinov. 'I keep thinking,' continued Martin, 'can he make it or not. Let us suppose he has thoroughly studied a topographic map, but that is not sufficient, there are sure to be frontier guards, intelligence agents, spies, all over. I wanted to ask you – well – for some pointers.' Gruzinov, his elbow propped on the table, was eating an apple, turning it around, taking a crunching bite out of it, now here now there, then turning it again to select a new point of attack. 'And why should your pal want to go roaming there?' he inquired with a rapid glance at Martin. 'I don't know, he keeps it a secret. I believe he wants to visit some relatives in Ostrov or Pskov.' 'What kind of passport?' asked Gruzinov. 'Foreign passport, he is a foreign citizen, Lithuanian or something.' 'Then what's the matter – do they refuse to give him a visa?' 'That I don't know. I believe he does not *want* to have any visa, he means to do it his own way. Or maybe, indeed, they do not give him permission to enter.' Gruzinov finished his apple and said, 'I keep looking for that special taste which our "antonovka" apples have. Sometimes I think: there, I've found it, but then I smack it more carefully, and no, the tang is not the same. Visas are a complicated business, generally speaking. Did I ever tell you how my brother-in-law outsmarted the American quota?' 'I thought you might want to give some kind of advice,' said Martin lamely. 'An odd thought! Surely your pal knows it all better.' 'And yet I'm a little worried about him,' Martin said softly.

He reflected with sadness that the conversation was turning out to be very different from what he had imagined, and that Gruzinov would never tell him how he had crossed the border so many times. 'And no wonder you do worry,' said Gruzinov, 'especially if he is a novice. However, one can always find a guide there.' 'Oh no, that would be dangerous!' exclaimed Martin, 'One might run into a traitor.' 'Naturally, one has to be cautious,' Gruzinov agreed, rubbing one eye and studying Martin through fat pale fingers. 'And, of course,' he added in a dullish voice, 'it's very important to know the locality.'

Here Martin quickly produced a rolled-up map. He knew it by heart, had often amused himself by copying it from memory – but for the moment he had to conceal his knowledge. 'You see, I have even provided myself with a chart,' he said breezily. 'For some reason it seems to me that Nick will cross here, for instance, or else here.' 'Ah, so his name is Nicolas,' said Gruzinov. 'I'll note it, I'll note it. This is a fine map. Wait a bit' – (the spectacle case was produced, the glasses gleamed). 'Let's see, what scale is this? Oh, good. Here's Carnagore, here's Torturovka, right on the border. I had a chum – also Nick by a strange coincidence – who once waded across this river here and went that way there; and another time he started from here and then all the way through the wood – it's a very dense wood, called Rogozhin, and then, if one turns north-east –'

Gruzinov's speech became lively and he talked faster and faster, prodding the map with the point of a safety pin which he had unbent, and in one minute he had traced half-a-dozen itineraries, and continued to spill out the names of villages, and to conjure up invisible footpaths; and the more animatedly he spoke, the clearer Martin could see that Gruzinov was making fun of him. From the garden two feminine voices called Gruzinov's name with the first syllable accented instead of the second. He looked out. The two English girls wanted him to come and have ice cream (he was popular with young ladies, for whose benefit he assumed the character of an easygoing simpleton). 'How they like to bother me,' Gruzinov said, 'I never eat ice cream, anyway.' It seemed to Martin for an instant that sometime somewhere the same words had been spoken (as in Blok's play *Incognita*), and that then as now he was perplexed by something, was trying to explain something. 'Now here's my advice,' said Gruzinov, dexterously rolling up the map and handing it back to Martin. 'Tell Nicky to stay at home and find something constructive to do. A nice fellow, I'm sure, and it would be a pity if he lost his way.' 'He knows everything better than I do,' replied Martin vengefully.

They went down into the garden. Martin forced himself to keep smiling and felt hatred for Gruzinov, his cold eyes, his smooth impenetrable forehead. One thing, however, gladdened him: the talk had taken place, was now in the past;

true, he had been treated like a schoolboy – never mind, to hell with Gruzzy, Martin's conscience was now clear, he could now pack his things and leave in peace.

Forty-Three

On the day of departure he woke up very early as he used to on Christmas morn in his childhood. Observing an English custom, his mother would have stolen into the nursery in the middle of the night to hang a stocking stuffed with presents at the foot of his bed. For the sake of complete credibility she would put on a cotton-wool beard and her husband's bashlyk. If Martin had happened not to be sleeping, he would have seen St Nicholas with his own eyes. Then, in the morning, with lamps switched on and glowing a dull yellow under the gloomy gaze of the wintry St Petersburg dawn (that brown sky over the dark house across the street, those façades, those cornices traced in white by the snow), Martin would palpate his mother's long crackling stocking tightly packed to its top with little parcels that could be distinguished through its silk; with bated breath he would thrust in his hand and begin pulling out and unwrapping tiny toy animals, and diminutive *bonbonnières* which represented only an introduction to the full-size present – an engine with carriages and tin rails (of which huge eights could be constructed) waiting for him in the drawing room. Today also a train was waiting for him; it would be leaving Lausanne toward evening to reach Berlin next morning by nine. Mrs Edelweiss felt quite sure that the only purpose of his trip was to see the Zilanov girl; she had noticed that no letters arrived for him from Berlin and was tormented by the thought that perhaps the Zilanov girl did not love Martin enough and would make a bad wife for him. She did her best to make his departure as cheerful as possible, concealing under a somewhat feverish animation her anxiety and sorrow. Uncle Henry, who suffered from a swollen cheek, remained morose and untalkative throughout dinner. Martin looked at the pepper caster Uncle Henry was reaching for, and it struck him that this was the last time he would see it. The pepper caster was in the shape of a fat manikin with perforations in his bald silver head. Quickly Martin transferred his gaze to his mother, taking in her slender pale-freckled hands, her delicate profile and the slightly raised eyebrow (as if she were amazed by the sight of the rich ragout), and again he told himself that this was the last time he would see those freckles, that eyebrow, that dish. Simultaneously all the furniture in the room, and the rainy view in the window, and the clock with its wooden dial over the sideboard, and the enlarged photographs of bewhiskered frock-coated

235

worthies in their black frames, everything in short seemed to break into tragic speech demanding attention before the impending separation. 'May I accompany you to Lausanne?' asked his mother. 'Oh, I know you don't care to be seen off,' she hastened to add as she saw Martin wrinkle his nose, 'but I would not go just for the sake of seeing you off, I would merely like to go for a ride, and besides I have to buy a few things.' Martin sighed. 'All right, I shan't go if you do not want me to,' said Mrs Edelweiss with exceptional gaiety. 'I stay behind when I'm not invited. But you are to wear your warm overcoat, on this I insist.'

Mother and son always spoke Russian between themselves, and this constantly irritated Uncle Henry, who knew only one word, *nichevo*, in which for some reason he perceived a symbol of Slav fatalism. That day he felt depressed, besides being bothered by the pain in his jaw, and now he sharply pushed back his chair, swept off the crumbs from his stomach with his napkin, and sucking on his tooth retired to his study. 'How old he is,' thought Martin watching his gray nape. 'Or is it the light – such gloomy weather.'

'Well, it's almost time for you to get ready,' remarked Mrs Edelweiss. 'The car has probably been brought up.' She looked out of the window. 'Yes, it has. Look, how amusing – nothing to be seen in the fog over there, as if there were no mountains at all. Amusing, isn't it?' 'I think I forgot my razor,' said Martin.

He went up to his room, packed his razor and slippers, and had trouble clicking shut the locks of his bag. In Riga or Rezhitsa he would buy plain coarse things – a cap, a short sheepskin coat, boots. Perhaps, a pistol? '*Proshchay, proshchay*' in rapid tempo sang out the bookcase crowned with the black figurine of a football player, which by some occult association of memories always made him think of Alla Chernosvitov.

In the roomy entrance hall downstairs stood Mrs Edelweiss, her hands thrust into the pockets of her raincoat, and hummed as was her wont in moments of stress. 'Hadn't you better stay at home?' she said as Martin came down. 'Really, why go away?' From the door on the right, with the antelope's head over it, came Uncle Henry, and looking at Martin from under his brows he asked, 'Are you sure you have enough money?' 'Quite enough,' answered Martin, 'thank you.' 'Good-bye,' said Uncle Henry. 'I am taking leave of you here because I avoid going out today. Had someone else ever had such a toothache, he would long ago have been in the madhouse.'

'Let's go,' said Mrs Edelweiss. 'I'm afraid you'll miss your train.'

Rain, wind. His mother's hair immediately became disarranged, and she kept smoothing it over her ears. 'Wait,' she said, just before reaching the garden wicket, at a spot near two firs between the trunks of which a hammock was hung in summer. 'Wait, I want to kiss you.' Martin put down his valise. 'Give her my greetings,' she whispered with a meaningful smile, and Martin nodded. Oh, to get going! This is unbearable.

The chauffeur obligingly opened the wicket for them. The car glistened with moisture, the rain made a tinkling sound against it. 'And please do write, if only once a week,' she said, and stepped back, and waved her hand smiling, and slushing along in the mud the black car vanished beyond the fir avenue.

Forty-Four

The night journey, in a Schnellzug sleeping car of a dark dirty-plum color, seemed to have no end: there were moments when Martin sank into sleep, then woke up with a start, then again found himself clattering down amusement-park slopes and again swung up, and caught through the dull knock of the wheels the snores of the lower-bunk passenger, a rhythmic wheeze that sounded like part of the train's motion.

Long before arrival, while everybody in the carriage was still asleep, Martin descended from his elevation, and taking

sponge, soap, towel, shaving kit, and collapsible tub proceeded to the lavatory. First of all he spread over its sickening
floor layered sheets of a London *Times* he had bought in
Lausanne; next he unfolded upon them his rather wobbly-
rimmed but still serviceable rubber tub; he took off his
pajamas and proceeded to coat with soap lather his muscular
sun-tanned body. There was not much space, the car rocked
violently, he was conscious of the transparent proximity of
the racing rails, and of the danger of coming inadvertently in
contact with filthy fixtures; but Martin could not manage
without his morning bath (in the sea, in a pond, in a shower,
or in this tub), which represented, he thought, a kind of
heroic defense: a defense against the obstinate attack of the
earth advancing by means of a film of insidious dust, as if it
could not wait to take possession of a man before his time.
No matter how poorly Martin might have slept, after bathing
he would be permeated with a beneficent vigor. At such times
the thought of death, the thought that sometime, maybe soon
(who could know?), he would be compelled to surrender and
go through what billions and trillions of humans had gone
through before him — this thought of an inevitable death
accessible to everyone troubled him but slightly. It gained
strength only toward evening, and with the coming of night
would sometimes swell to monstrous dimensions. The custom of performing executions at dawn seemed charitable to
Martin: may the Lord permit it to happen in the morning

when a man has control over himself – clears his throat, smiles, then stands straight, spreading his arms.

When he stepped out onto the platform of the Anhalter station, he inhaled with pleasure the cold, smoky morning air. Far away, in the direction from which the train had arrived, one could see through the opening of the iron-and-glass arch a pale-blue sky and a gleam of rails, and in comparison to this luminosity all was drab under the station vault. He walked past the dusky cars; past the huge hissing and sweating engine, and, having surrendered his ticket into the human hand of a control booth, descended the steps to the street. Out of attachment to the images of his childhood, he had decided to select as the starting point of his journey the Friedrich station, where, one remote day, his parents and he, after staying at the nearby Continental, had caught the Nord-Express. His valise was quite heavy, but Martin was in such an excited and restless state that he decided to walk. However, by the time he reached Potsdamerstrasse he began to feel ravenous, and upon estimating the remaining distance to the Friedrich Bahnhof, wisely took the bus. From the very start of that unusual day all his senses were on edge – it seemed to him that he was committing to memory the faces of all the passers-by, and that he absorbed with particular keenness colors, smells, and sounds. The automobile honkings that on rainy nights used to torture his hearing by their swinish moist tones now sounded somehow extra-mundane, melodious and doleful. As he sat in the bus he heard a ripple of Muscovite speech near him. It came from a couple, of Soviet rather than *émigré* aspect, and their two round-eyed little boys. The elder had settled close to the window, the younger kept pressing against his brother. 'A restaurant,' the bigger one said ecstatically. 'Look, a restaurant!' said the smaller one, pressing. 'I can see for myself,' snapped his brother. 'It's a restaurant,' said the smaller one with conviction. 'Shut up, idiot,' said his brother. 'It's not the Linden yet, is it?' the mother asked worriedly. 'It's still the Post Dammer,' said the father with authority. 'We've already passed the Post Dammer,' cried the boys, and there ensued a short argument. 'What an archway, that's class for you,' exulted the elder boy stabbing at the window with his finger. 'Don't yell like that,' remarked the father. 'What's that?' 'I said don't yell.' The boy looked hurt. 'In the first place I spoke softly, and did not yell at all.' 'Archway,' uttered the smaller boy with awe. The whole family became absorbed in the contemplation of the Brandenburg Gate. 'Historical site,' the bigger boy said. 'An ancient arch, yes,' confirmed the father. 'How shall we wriggle through?' the bigger boy wondered, fearing for the sides of the bus, 'it's a squeeze!' 'We did wriggle through,' the smaller boy whispered with relief. 'And now this is the Unter,' cried the mother, 'time to get off.'

'The Unter is such a long, long street,' said the bigger boy, 'I saw it on the map.' 'This is President Street,' said the smaller boy dreamily. 'Shut up, idiot! It's the Unter Linden.' Then, in chorus, 'Unter is long, long, long,' and a male solo voice, 'It's an endless journey.'

Here Martin got off. His childhood, he thought with strange anguish, his childish excitement had been similar, and yet utterly different. The juxtaposition lasted one instant: it sang by and subsided.

After checking his bag and buying a ticket for the evening train to Riga, he seated himself in the resonant station café where he was brought a regular sunburst of fried eggs. In the latest issue of an *émigré* weekly that he read as he ate he found a vicious review of Bubnov's latest book *Caravella*. Having appeased his hunger, he lit a cigarette and looked around. A young girl at the nearest table sat writing, and wiping her tears. She looked at him for an instant with dim wet eyes, pressing her pencil against her lips, and, having found the word she sought, scribbled again, holding her pencil the way children do: almost at the tip, with forefinger tensely bent. Black coat opened at neck, shabby rabbit-fur collar, amber beads, tender white neck, handkerchief crumpled in fist. He paid for his meal and, planning to follow her, began waiting for her to get up. But when she had finished writing, she leaned her elbows on the table and continued to sit there, looking up, with parted lips. She remained sitting for a long time while somewhere beyond the window-panes trains were leaving, and Martin, who had to get to the Latvian consulate before closing time, decided to give her just five minutes more, and go. The five minutes passed. 'All I would do would be to ask her to meet me for a drink in the afternoon – only that,' he pleaded mentally, imagining at the same time how he would allude to a distant perilous journey and how she would weep. Another minute passed. 'All right, forget it,' said Martin, and, throwing his raincoat over his shoulder in the English manner, made for the exit.

Forty-Five

The taxi sped with a susurrous sound; he admired the Tiergarten crowding around him, the lovely warm tints of its autumn foliage: 'O dismal period, visual enchantment –' Flowerless but still sumptuous chestnut trees looked at their own reflection in the canal. As he drove over the bridge Martin recognized Hercules' stone lion and noted that the recently repaired part of its tail still remained too white and would probably take a long time to acquire the seasoned tinge of the rest of the group – how much? ten, fifteen years? Why is it so difficult to imagine oneself at forty?

The basement floor of the Latvian consulate was alive with people. 'Knock-knock' went the rubber stamp. Within a few minutes the Swiss citizen Edelweiss had come out of there and walked over to a nearby gloomy mansion where he obtained the inexpensive Lithuanian transit visa.

Now he could seek out Darwin. His hotel faced the Zoological Gardens. 'Not in,' said the clerk. 'No, I don't know when he'll be back.'

'How tiresome,' thought Martin returning to the street. 'I should have given him a definite date – not merely "one of these days." A blunder. How tiresome!' He looked at his watch. Half past eleven. His passport was in order, his ticket was in his pocket. The day which had announced itself as crammed with activity all at once turned out to be empty. What next? Visit the zoo? Write mother a letter? No, that would come later.

But while he was meditating, muffled work went on in the depths of his consciousness. He resisted it, tried to ignore it, for he had firmly decided after the rejection of his desperate proposal never to see Sonia again. Alas – the air of Berlin was saturated with memories of her. Over there, at the zoo, they had stared together at the golden-red Chinese pheasant, at the fabulous nostrils of the hippopotamus, at the yellow dog dingo that could jump so high. 'She is at her office now,' reflected Martin, 'and I do have to call on the Zilanovs.'

The Kurfürstendamm began to drift by. Automobiles passed the streetcar, the streetcar passed the bicycles; then came the bridge, the smoke from the trains that ran far below, thousands of rails, the mysterious blue sky. Then a turn, and he was amidst the autumnal loveliness of Grune-wald.

Surprisingly, it was Sonia who let him in. She wore a black jumper, looked slightly disheveled, her slanted eyes appeared sleepy, there seemed to be unfamiliar dimples in her pale cheeks. 'Whom do I see,' she drawled making a very low bow, her arms dangling in front of her. 'Welcome, welcome,' she said unbending, and one black strand of hair fell in an arc on her temple. She threw it back with a flick of her index finger. 'Come this way,' she said and started walking along the passage slap-slapping softly with her bedroom slippers. 'I was afraid you might be at the office,' said Martin, trying not to look at the adorable back of her neck. 'Headache,' she said without turning and emitted a little grunt as she picked up in passing a mopping rag which she threw onto a trunk in the corridor. They entered the drawing room. 'Sit down and tell me all,' she said, dropping asprawl in an arm-chair, but at once she got up and sat down again with one leg under her.

The drawing room was its old self: the dark Böcklin on the wall, the worn plush of the furniture, some kind of indestructible pale-leaved plant in a pot, and that depressing chandelier in the shape of a tailed swimmer with the bosom and head of a Bavarian girl and deer horns growing out of all parts of her.

'Actually, I arrived only today,' said Martin lighting a cigarette. 'I intend to work here. That is, not here actually but in the neighborhood. It is a factory and, as a matter of fact, I shall work there as a simple workman.' 'Not really?' murmured Sonia and added, noticing his ash and questing gaze, 'Never mind, shed it on the floor.' 'Now there is this amusing circumstance,' Martin continued. 'You see, actually I don't want Mother to know that I'm a factory hand. So please, if she happens to write to your mother – sometimes, you know, she likes to find out if I'm all right in a roundabout way – well, then, do you see, she should be told, please, that I often come to see you. In reality, of course, I shall visit you very, very seldom, there will be no time for that.'

'You've lost your good looks,' said Sonia meditatively. 'And there's something coarse about your face – maybe it's the tan.'

'I've wandered all over southern France,' Martin said huskily, 'worked on farms, lived like a bum, and, on Sundays, got dressed up and went to Monte Carlo for a bit of good time. Fascinating thing, roulette! And you, what have you been doing? Is everybody all right?'

'The ancestors are all right,' said Sonia with a sigh, 'but Irina has become quite unmanageable. What a cross to bear!

And the financial situation is as gloomy as ever. Father says
we must move to Paris. Have you been in Paris?'

'Yes, for one day,' replied Martin negligently (that one day
spent in Paris, many years ago, on the way from Biarritz to
Berlin, children with hoops in the Tuileries Gardens, toy
sailboats on the pond, an old man feeding the sparrows, the
silvery filigree of the tower, Napoleon's tomb where the columns resembled wreathed *sucre d'orge*). 'Yes, just in passing.
Incidentally, have you heard the latest news – Darwin is here.'

Sonia smiled and blinked several times. 'Oh, do bring him!
You absolutely must, it would be such fun.'

'I have not seen him yet. He is here on business for *The
Morning News*. They sent him on a trip to America. But
the main thing is this: he has a fiancée back in England, and
he is getting married in the spring.'

'How marvelous!' said Sonia softly. 'Everything according
to pattern. I can imagine her so well: tall, eyes like saucers,
and her mother just like her, only leaner and ruddier. Poor
Darwin!'

'Nonsense, I'm sure she's very pretty and intelligent.'

'Well, what else can you tell me,' asked Sonia after a
silence. Martin shrugged. How rash of him to have used up
all at once his entire stock of conversational topics. It seemed
weirdly absurd to him that there was Sonia sitting in front
of him, and he dared not say anything of importance, dared
not allude to her last letter, dared not ask if she was going to

247

marry Bubnov – dared not say or do anything. He tried to see himself sitting there, in this same room, after his return: would he then, too, blurt out everything at once? And would Sonia lightly scratch her shin through the silk, as she did now, looking past him at things unknown to him? It occurred to him that he might have come at the wrong moment, that she might be expecting someone else, that she felt ill at ease with him. But he could not bring himself to leave, as he also could not think of anything amusing to say, and Sonia seemed to be deliberately trying to provoke him with her silence. In another moment he would lose control and spill it all – his expedition, and his love, and that inner-most, mysterious something, which bound together the expedition, the love, and Pushkin's ode to autumn.

The entrance door slammed, steps were heard, Zilanov entered the drawing room. 'Ah,' he said, 'delighted. How is your mother?' A little later Mrs Zilanov came in through another door and asked the same question. 'Won't you have lunch with us?' she said. They moved to the dining room. Irina, upon seeing Martin, froze still, then suddenly rushed over to him and started kissing him with wet lips. 'Ira, Iro-chka,' her mother kept repeating with a helpless smile. Dark meatballs were heaped on a large serving dish. Zilanov unfolded his napkin and stuck one corner behind his collar.

During the meal Martin showed Irina how to cross the second and third fingers so that you could touch a single small pellet of bread and feel two. For a long time she was unable to adjust her fingers properly, but when at last, with Martin's assistance, the pellet divided into two under her touch, Irina cooed with rapture. Just as a monkey seeing its reflection in a fragment of mirror looks to see if there is not another monkey underneath, so she, too, kept bending her head to check if there were not two crumbs under her fingers after all. When lunch was over and Sonia showed Martin to the telephone which was beyond the bend of a passage lined with boxes and trunks, Irina rushed after them with a moan, fearing that Martin might be leaving for good. After convincing herself that this was not so, she returned to the dining room to crawl under the table there in search of her bread pellet that had rolled out of sight. 'I want to call Darwin,' said Martin. 'I must look up the number of his hotel.' Sonia's face lit up, as she said, spluttering with excitement, 'Oh, let me, I'll do it, I'll talk to him, it will be fantastic. Come, I'll completely mystify him.' 'No, don't,' replied Martin, 'what's the use?' 'Then I'll only connect you. No harm in that, is there? What was the number?' She leaned over the telephone book he had opened, and he felt the warmth of her hair. On her cheek, just below the eye, was a little stray lash. Repeating the number rapidly in an undertone so as not to forget it, she seated herself on a trunk and picked up the receiver. 'You're only connecting us, mind you,' Martin remarked sternly. With painstaking clarity Sonia gave the number and waited, with shifting eyes, her heels tapping softly against the side of the trunk. Then she smiled, cuddling the receiver still closer to her ear, and Martin stretched out his hand, but Sonia pushed it aside with her shoulder and hunched over while asking for Darwin in a bright tone of voice. 'Give it me,' said Martin, 'this is not fair.' But Sonia gathered herself together even tighter. 'I'll cut you off,' threatened Martin. She made a sharp movement to protect the lever, and at the same moment her eyebrows went up. 'No, nothing, thank you,' she said and hung up. 'Not at home,' she told Martin, looking at him from below. 'You may rest assured, my dear, I shall not call him again. And you – you've remained the same boor that you were.' She slithered down from the trunk, groped, found her lost slipper with her toe, and went back to the dining room. The table was being cleared, Irina's mother was talking to her but she kept turning away. 'Shall I find you here later?' asked Zilanov. 'Well, I don't know. As a matter of fact, I should be going now.' 'I'll say good-bye to you just in case,' said Zilanov and retired to his room to work.

'Do not forget us,' said the two ladies simultaneously and each touched the other's black sleeve, with a smile that acknowledged the superstition. Martin bowed. Irina made a dash for him and clutched the lapels of his jacket with both hands. He felt embarrassed, tried cautiously to unclasp her fingers; but she held tight, and when Mrs Pavlov took hold of her shoulders from behind the poor creature broke out into loud sobs. Martin could hardly conceal his revulsion as he observed the dreadful expression of her face, the red rash on her forehead. With a sharp, if not rough movement, he tore loose from her hold. She was led away, her chesty howl retreated, and subsided at last. 'The same worries all the time,' said Sonia as she accompanied Martin to the hallway. Martin put on his raincoat – the raincoat was a complicated affair, and it took him some time to arrange the belt properly. 'Drop in sometime in the evening,' said Sonia as she watched his operation, her hands deep in the front pockets of her jumper. Gloomily Martin shook his head. 'We get together and dance,' Sonia said and with her legs close together, she shifted first her toes and then her heels, then again toes and again heels, in a slight sideways motion. 'Well,' said Martin slapping his pockets. 'I don't think I had any parcels.' 'Remember?' asked Sonia and began to whistle softly the tune of a London fox-trot. Martin cleared his throat. 'I don't like your hat,' she remarked. 'They don't wear them like that any more?' '*Proshchay*,' said Martin, and skillfully grabbing Sonia pushed his lips against her bared teeth, her cheek, the tender part behind her ear, then let her go (she backed away and almost fell), and quickly left, involuntarily slamming the door.

Forty-Six

He noticed that he was grinning and out of breath, and that his heart was beating fast. 'Well, that's that,' he said to himself, and began walking away with bold strides as if he were in a hurry. But there was no place to go. Darwin's absence confused his plans. As he went along the Kurfürstendamm, he kept noting with vague sadness Berlin's familiar features: the austere church at the crossroads, so lonely amidst pagan cinemas; the Tauentzienstrasse, where pedestrians inexplicably avoid the median boulevard, preferring to progress in a tight flow close to the display windows. The blind man, who sold sight and light, kept thrusting a box of matches into eternal darkness; there were stalls with heather and asters, stalls with bananas and apples; a person in a brown overcoat stood on the seat of an old convertible, holding out fanwise tablets of a nameless chocolate whose exquisite quality he eloquently described to a small crowd of loafers. Martin turned into a side street and entered a Russian bookshop where *émigré* and Soviet works lay next to foreign magazines. A corpulent gentleman with the face of a polite

reptile spread on the counter what he called *novinki*, 'novelties.'
Martin found nothing to his liking and bought a copy of
Punch. What next? That meal at the Zilanovs' had been
decidedly scant. He directed his steps toward the Pir Goroy
where he used to eat a year ago. From there he rang up Darwin's hotel. Darwin had not yet returned. '*Zwanzig pfennig,
pozhaluysta*,' said the thickly powdered lady behind the counter. '*Merci*.'

The proprietor was the painter Danilevski, whom Martin
had known at Adreiz, a short man wearing a stiff collar, with
a rosy infantile face and a blond wart under one eye. He
came up to Martin's table and asked shyly, 'Bo-borshch all
right?' (like many stammerers he was strangely attracted to
sounds that were the hardest to master). 'Yes, indeed,'
answered Martin, and as always felt heartrending tenderness
as he visualized Danilevski against the backdrop of the
Crimean night.

The latter sat down and watched with approval Martin
consuming his soup. 'Did I tell you that according to certain
information they've be-be-been living all these years at
Adreiz – remarkable!'

(Can it be that they were never disturbed in their manor?
reflected Martin. Can it be that everything has remained the
same – those little pears, for example, drying on the veranda
roof?)

'Mohicans,' murmured Danilevski pensively.

The room was emptyish. Small divans, a stove with a zig-zag pipe, newspapers on wooden holders.

'All this will be improved. I might paint the walls with bah! bah! babas, if only it were not so sad. Bo-bright dresses, but livid faces with eyes like horses. At least, that's the way it comes out in my sketches. Or else one could do clouds and below – and below – the fringe of a forest. We shall enlarge the premises, I asked a carpenter to come yesterday, but he never turned up.'

'Many customers?'

'Usually, yes. This is not the right time for dinner, so do not draw conclusions. The literary burrow-burrow brother-hood is well represented. Rakitin, for instance, the journalist, you know, the one that sports spats . . . And a few days ago, boo, a few days ago, boo, Sergey Bubnov, right here, smashed dishes, he's drinking heavily, disappointment in love, engagement babaroken.'

Danilevski sighed, his fingers drumming on the table; then he slowly got up and went into the kitchen. He re-appeared as Martin was taking his hat from the rack. 'There'll be shashlik tomorrow,' said Danilevski. 'We'll be expecting you.' Martin experienced a fleeting desire to say something very kind to that dear melancholy man with such a eupho-nious stutter; but what could one say?

Forty-Seven

He crossed the paved court with its noseless statue in the middle of a lawn on which grew a few thujas, pushed open a familiar door, walked up the stairs that reeked of cabbage and cats, and rang the bell. One of the lodgers, a young German, came out and said Bubnov was ill, but knocked in passing on the latter's door, and the writer's great voice, now hoarse and ill-humored, was heard to holler '*Herein!*'

Bubnov was sitting on the bed, clad in black trousers and an open shirt; his face was swollen and unshaven, his eyelids inflamed. Sheets of paper were strewn over the bed, the floor, and the table, on which stood a glass of turbid tea. It turned out that Bubnov was putting the finishing touches to a short story and at the same time attempting to compose in German an impressive letter to the gentlemen of the Finanzamt who were demanding he pay his taxes. He was not drunk but neither could one call him sober. His thirst had passed, but everything in him had been twisted out of shape and shaken loose by the hurricane; his thoughts wandered about looking for their old dwellings and finding only ruins. He showed no surprise at the appearance of Martin, whom he had not seen since spring, and at once started to upbraid a certain critic as if Martin were responsible for that critic's review. 'They're baiting me,' Bubnov kept repeating fiercely, and his face with the deep orbits looked rather ghastly. He had a tendency to assume that all disparaging reviews of his books were inspired by extraneous considerations, by envy, personal dislike, or the desire to avenge an offense. And listening to his disjointed survey of literary intrigue Martin found it amazing that anyone could take so much to heart another man's opinion, and he fought the temptation to tell Bubnov that his novella Zoorland was a failure, a pseudoartistic and worthless piece. But when Bubnov abruptly abandoned that topic and began to talk about his having been jilted, Martin cursed the wrongheaded curiosity that had brought him here. 'I will not name her, thou must not ask me,' said Bubnov who could switch to the Russian emotional second person singular with an actor's ease. 'Yet remember, I shall not be the last to perish because of her. God, how I loved her! How happy I was! It was the kind of tremendous feeling that makes one hear the thunder of angel wings. But she got frightened of my heavenly heights —'

Martin stayed on a little, felt a welling of intolerable heartache, and got up in silence. Sobbing, Bubnov accompanied him to the door. A few days later (when he was already in

Latvia) Martin discovered in an *émigré* newspaper another of Bubnov's 'novellas,' fresh from the oven. This time it was excellent, and in it the protagonist, a young German, wore the tie Martin had on that day, pale gray with pink stripes (the treasured relic of a Cambridge club), which Bubnov, though seemingly engrossed in his grief, had appropriated as would a deft thief who wipes his tears with one hand while removing a man's watch with the other.

Stopping at a stationer's Martin bought half-a-dozen post-cards and replenished his fountain pen; then he proceeded to Darwin's hotel where he resolved to wait to the very last moment of remaining time and go straight from there to the station. The late afternoon sky was a sunless cheerless blank. The sound of automobile horns now seemed muffled by the mist. An open van passed by drawn by a pair of scrawny horses; upon it enough furniture was heaped to furnish a house: a couch, a chest of drawers, a gilt-framed seascape, and a lot of other melancholy chattels. A woman in mourning crossed the damp-dappled asphalt; she was pushing a pram, and in it sat a blue-eyed attentive infant; on reaching the sidewalk she pushed down the handle forcing the pram to rear. A poodle ran past in pursuit of a black whippet; the latter stopped and looked back in fear, raising one bent front paw and quivering. 'What's the matter, for goodness' sake,' thought Martin. 'What's all this to me? I know I'm going to return. I must return.' He entered the vestibule of the hotel. Darwin still had not come back.

He found a comfortable armchair upholstered in leather, unscrewed the cap of his pen and began to write his mother. Space on the postcard was limited, his handwriting was large, so he did not manage to say much. 'Everything is all right,' he wrote, strongly pressing down on the pen. 'I stopped at the same old place, address your letters there. I hope Uncle's toothache is better. Have not yet seen Darwin. The Zilanovs send greetings. Shall not write for a week as I have absolutely nothing to say. Many kisses.' He reread all this twice and unaccountably felt sick at heart and a chill ran down his back. 'No nonsense, please,' Martin told himself, and, again pressing hard, wrote the Major's widow asking her to hold his mail for him. After posting the cards he returned to his chair, leaned back on it, and began to wait, glancing now and then at the clock. A quarter of an hour passed, then twenty minutes, then twenty-five. Two mulatto girls with unusually thin legs went up the stairs. All of a sudden he heard behind his back the powerful breathing he at once recognized. He jumped up, and Darwin, with throaty ejaculations, slapped him on the shoulder. 'You scoundrel,' mumbled Martin happily, 'you scoundrel, I've been looking for you since morning.'

Forty-Eight

Darwin had gained some weight, his hair looked thinner, he had grown a well-trimmed little mustache. Somehow both he and Martin felt embarrassed and could not find a subject of conversation; they kept poking each other, grinning and rumbling. 'What are you going to drink,' Darwin asked when they had entered his small but smart hotel room, 'whisky and soda? A cocktail? Or simply some tea?' 'No matter, no matter, anything you like,' answered Martin, taking up from the table a large photograph in an expensive frame. 'She,' said Darwin. Portrait of a young woman with a diadem. Those brows meeting above the bridge of the nose, those light eyes, that long graceful neck — everything about her looked very definitive and domineering. 'Her name's Evelyn, she sings rather well, I'm sure you'll become very good friends with her.' Darwin took the portrait and gave it a dreamy look before returning it to its place. 'Well,' he asked dropping onto the couch and immediately stretching out his legs, 'what's new? I see you still wear the C.C.C. tie.'

A waiter brought the cocktails. Without pleasure Martin took a sip of gin-laced vermouth and recounted in a couple of sentences how he had spent the last two years. It surprised him that as soon as he fell silent, Darwin began to talk about himself, circumstantially and self-complacently – something that never used to happen before. How strange it was to hear from those indolent, chaste lips a tale of success, of earnings, of splendid hopes for the future! It also transpired that now he no longer composed those charming trifles about leeches or sunsets, but wrote articles on political and financial subjects, and was particularly interested in the sepulchral-sounding 'moratoria,' whatever they were. When Martin, taking advantage of a sudden pause, reminded Darwin of the burning chariot, of Rose, of their fight, Darwin said indifferently, 'Yes, those were the times,' and to his horror Martin realized that Darwin's recollections had died, or were absent, and the only thing that remained was a discolored signboard.

'And what is Prince Vadim doing?' asked Darwin stifling a yawn.

'Vadim is in Brussels. Has a job there. And the Zilanovs are here. I often see Sonia. She still has not married.'

Darwin emitted a huge puff of smoke. 'Give her my greetings,' he said. 'But what about you? Pity you're sort of drifting. I'll introduce you to some important people tomorrow, I'm sure you'll like journalism.'

Martin coughed. Time had come to discuss the main matter, the matter he had so much wished to discuss with Darwin.

'Thanks,' he said, 'but that's impossible, I'll be leaving Berlin in an hour's time.'

Darwin raised himself slightly: 'Not really? Where are you going?'

'You'll see in a minute. I'm now going to tell you something no one else knows. For several years – yes, several years – but that's not essential –'

He faltered. Darwin sighed, and said, 'I've guessed everything. I'll act as best man.'

'Stop it, please. This is serious. I've been trying all day to get to you for the special purpose of talking it over. The fact is I'm planning to cross illegally into Russia from Latvia, just for twenty-four hours, yes, and then walk back again. Now here's where you come in: I'll give you four postcards, you'll send them to my mother, one every week – every Thursday let's say. I expect to be back within a shorter time, but I can't foretell how long it will take me to investigate things, to select the exact itinerary, and so forth. Of course I've already collected a lot of crucial information from a certain person. But I may get stuck, may not be able to wriggle out immediately. You understand, my mother must not know anything about it, must receive my postcards from Berlin regularly. I gave her my old address, it is all quite simple.'

Silence.

'Yes, of course, it is all quite simple,' said Darwin.

Silence again.

'Only I do not quite see what's the purpose of it.'

'Give it a little thought, and you will.'

'Some plot against the good old Soviets? Want to see someone? Deliver a secret message, rig up something? I confess that as a boy I rather fancied those gloomy bearded chaps who threw bombs at the troika of the ruthless governor.'

Morosely, Martin shook his head.

'And if you merely want to visit the land of your fathers – although your father was half-Swiss, wasn't he? – still, if you want to see it so badly, would it not be simpler to obtain a regular Soviet visa and cross the border by train? Don't want to? Perhaps, after the assassination in that Swiss café, you think you won't be given a visa? All right, I'll get you a British passport.'

'What you're imagining is all wrong,' said Martin, 'I expected you'd understand everything at once.'

Darwin folded an arm under his head. He could not make up his mind whether or not Martin was pulling his leg, and if not, what really prompted him to embark on that preposterous undertaking. For a while he puffed on his pipe, then said:

'If, finally, what you are after is just pure risk, there's no need to travel so far. Let us invent something unusual, something that can be executed right now, right here, without overstepping the windowsill. And then let's have a bite and go to a music hall.'

Martin remained silent, and his face looked sad.

'This is absurd,' reflected Darwin, 'absurd and rather peculiar. Stayed quietly in Cambridge while they had their civil war, and now craves a bullet in the head for spying. Is he trying to mystify me? What an idiotic conversation.'

Martin gave a start, looked at his watch, and got up.

'Look here, stop playing the fool,' said Darwin, smoke pouring profusely from his pipe. 'After all, this is scarcely polite. We have not seen each other since Cambridge. Either tell me all, intelligibly, or admit that you were joking, and we'll talk of other things.'

'I've told you all,' said Martin. 'All. And now I must go.'

He put on his raincoat, picked up his hat from the floor. Darwin, who lay calmly on the couch, yawned and turned his face to the wall. 'So long,' said Martin but Darwin did not respond. 'So long,' Martin repeated. 'Nonsense, it can't be true,' thought Darwin. He yawned again, and closed his eyes. 'He won't leave,' thought Darwin and sleepily pulled up one leg. For some time there endured an amusing silence. At last Darwin laughed softly and turned his head. But there was nobody in the room. It seemed impossible that Martin could have left so noiselessly. Perhaps he was hiding behind the furniture. Darwin remained lying a few minutes longer, then glanced warily around the already dimming room, put down his legs and straightened up. 'Enough of it, now. Come out,' he said as he heard a slight rustle from the baggage recess between the wardrobe and the door. Nobody came out. Darwin went over and glanced into the recess. Nobody. Only a sheet of wrapping paper left over from some purchase. Darwin turned on the light, stood frowning, then opened the door leading into the passage. The passage was long, well lighted, and empty. The evening breeze tried to shut the window. 'To hell with him,' said Darwin – and was lost in thought again. But suddenly he shook himself up and very deliberately started to change for dinner.

He felt uneasy, a feeling he seldom experienced lately. Not only had Martin's arrival excited him as a tender echo of their university days, but it had been in itself extraordinary, everything about Martin had been extraordinary – the roughish tan, the breathless voice, the bizarre dark utterances, and that new haughty look in his eyes. However, Darwin had recently had such a well-balanced kind of life, his heart had been beating so regularly (even when he proposed), his mind had so firmly concluded that after the troubles and thrills of youth he had now reached a smoothly paved road, that he could now hardly fail to subdue the disturbing impression made by Martin, and force himself to believe that the silly jester would reappear this very night. He had already donned his dinner jacket and was examining his powerful figure and large Roman-nosed face in the wardrobe glass, when the telephone rang on the night table. Either because the connection was bad or because he did not remember Martin's telephone tone, he identified it with difficulty: 'Reminding you of my request,' said the blurred deep voice. 'You'll get the batch within a few days, you'll send them off one by one. My train is about to leave. What? I said: my train – Yes, yes, train –'

The voice vanished. Darwin resoundingly put down the receiver and for a while kept scratching his cheek. Then he walked to the lift and rode down. There he asked for the timetable. Yes, correct. What the devil –

That night he did not go anywhere. He kept waiting for something, some sort of further development. When he sat down to write a letter to his fiancée he found nothing to write about. Several days passed. On Wednesday he received a fat envelope from Riga and found inside four picture postcards with Berlin views addressed to Mrs Edelweiss in Switzerland. On one of them, inserted in the Russian text, Darwin discovered a sentence in English: 'I often go to music halls with Darwin.' It gave him an eerie shock. On Thursday morning, with the dreadful feeling that he was taking part in some evil affair, he gingerly inserted the card with the earliest date into the blue mailbox next to the hotel entrance. A week passed; he posted the second card. After that he could not stand it any longer and traveled to Riga, where he visited the British consul, the Swiss consul, the General Registry, the police, but obtained no information whatever. Martin seemed to have dissolved in the air. Darwin returned to Berlin and reluctantly mailed the third postcard. On Friday, a huge man, obviously a foreigner, called at Zilanov's new publishing house (Russian calendars and political pamphlets); upon taking a closer look, Zilanov recognized in him the young Englishman who had courted his daughter in London. Speaking German (which Zilanov understood somewhat better than English) Darwin calmly related his conversation with Martin. 'But wait,' said Zilanov. 'There is something not logical here. He said to my daughter he would work in a factory near Berlin. You are sure he went away? What a strange history!' 'At first I thought he was joking,' said Darwin, 'but now I don't know what to think. If he has really —' 'What a crazy fellow,' exclaimed Zilanov. 'Who would have supposed! The young man produced an effect of good sense, of solidity. It's simply hard to believe, you know, looks like some kind of provocation. Gut. The first thing to do is to find if my daughter knows anything about this. Let's go to my quarters.'

When Sonia saw her father coming in with Darwin and noticed the odd, solemn expression of their faces, she thought for one hundredth part of an instant that Darwin had come to make, this time officially, an offer of marriage (such momentary nightmares are known to occur). 'Hello, hello, Sonia,' cried out Darwin with very artificial offhandedness. Zilanov, fixing his dull dark eyes on his daughter and 'preparing her,' begged her not to be frightened, and told her practically the whole story right there, in the hallway. Sonia turned white as a sheet and sank down on one of the vestibule chairs. 'But that's awful,' she said softly. After a little pause, she slapped her knees and repeated in a still smaller voice: 'That's awful.' 'Did he tell you anything? Do you have any information?' Zilanov kept asking her in Russian and German. Darwin stood rubbing his cheeks, trying not to look at Sonia. He felt the most appalling thing a man of his race and set can feel: the urge to break into tears. 'Of course, I know all about it,' said Sonia in a thin crescendo. Mrs Zilanov appeared in the background, and her husband signaled to her not to disturb them. 'Just what do you know? Come, out with it,' said Zilanov, and touched Sonia on the shoulder. She suddenly doubled over and began to sob loudly, burying her face in her hands. Then she unbent, emitted a great gasp as if she were choking, swallowed, and began to scream between sobs, 'They'll kill him, oh God, they'll kill him.' 'Control yourself,' said Zilanov. 'Don't scream. I demand that you explain quietly and clearly what it was that he told you. Olya' (addressing his wife), 'take this gentleman somewhere – Yes, to the drawing room, ach, never mind the electrician. Sonia, stop screaming! You'll frighten Irina. Stop, I demand it.'

He spent a long time comforting and questioning her. Darwin sat gravely in the drawing room. An electrician was also there, busy mending a socket and plug, looking up and down again as the light went on and off.

'The child is obviously right in demanding that immediate measures be taken,' said Zilanov when he and Darwin had regained the street. 'But what can one do? Besides, I don't think there is as much romance of adventure here as seems to her. She tends to see things that way. Very high-strung nature. I simply refuse to believe that a young man, pretty much removed from Russian political problems and more of a foreign cut I'd say, could prove capable of – well, of a high deed, if you like. Naturally, I shall get in touch with certain people, and I may have to go to Latvia, but the matter is fairly hopeless, if he has really tried to steal across the border. By the way, it is so strange, but I was the one, yes, I, who years ago informed Frau Edelweiss of the death of her first husband.'

A few more days passed. The only point to become clear was that one had to be patient and wait. Not Zilanov, but Darwin went to Switzerland to inform Mrs Edelweiss. In Lausanne everything looked gray, a fine rain was falling. Higher up in the mountains there was an odor of damp snow, and water dripped from the trees because of the sudden thaw that had followed the first frosts. The car he had hired brought him quickly to the village, skidded on a curve and overturned in the ditch. The only damage was the chauffeur's bruised arm. Darwin scrambled out, shook the wet snow off his overcoat and asked a villager how far it was to Henry Edelweiss's place. He was shown the shortest way – a footpath through a fir forest. Once out of the woods, he crossed a dirt road, went up an avenue, and saw the ornate greenish-brown house. The rubber soles of his sturdy shoes left patterned impressions on the dark soil in front of the wicket. These footprints slowly filled with muddy water, and a little later the wicket he had not closed properly creaked in a gust of damp wind and violently swung open. Then a titmouse alighted on it, uttered a *tsi-tsi-tsi* and an *incha-incha*, and flew over to the branch of a fir. Everything was very wet and dim. An hour elapsed. Darwin emerged from the brown depths of the melancholy garden, closed the wicket behind him (it promptly opened again), and started back along the path through the woods. There he paused to light his pipe. His ample camel-hair coat was unbuttoned, the ends of his striped scarf dangled at his chest. It was quiet in the woods, all one could hear was a faint gurgle: water was running somewhere under the wet gray snow. Darwin listened and for no perceptible reason shook his head. His pipe, which had gone out, emitted a helpless sucking sound. He said something under his breath, rubbed his cheek pensively, and walked on. The air was dingy, here and there tree roots traversed the trail, black fir needles now and then brushed against his shoulder, the dark path passed between the tree trunks in picturesque and mysterious windings.